Haunted Bookshop Mysteries by Alice Kimberly

THE GHOST AND MRS. MCCLURE
THE GHOST AND THE DEAD DEB
THE GHOST AND THE DEAD MAN'S LIBRARY

The Ghost
AND THE
Dead Man's Library

ALICE KIMBERLY

BERKLEY PRIME CRIME, NEW YORK

THE BERKLEY PUBLISHING GROUP
Published by the Penguin Group
Penguin Group (USA) Inc.
375 Hudson Street, New York, New York 10014, USA
Penguin Group (Canada), 90 Eglinton Avenue East, Suite 700, Toronto, Ontario M4P 2Y3, Canada
(a division of Pearson Penguin Canada Inc.)
Penguin Books Ltd., 80 Strand, London WC2R 0RL, England
Penguin Group Ireland, 25 St. Stephen's Green, Dublin 2, Ireland (a division of Penguin Books Ltd.)
Penguin Group (Australia), 250 Camberwell Road, Camberwell, Victoria 3124, Australia
(a division of Pearson Australia Group Pty. Ltd.)
Penguin Books India Pvt. Ltd., 11 Community Centre, Panchsheel Park, New Delhi—110 017, India
Penguin Group (NZ), Cnr. Airborne and Rosedale Roads, Albany, Auckland 1310, New Zealand
(a division of Pearson New Zealand Ltd.)
Penguin Books (South Africa) (Pty.) Ltd., 24 Sturdee Avenue, Rosebank, Johannesburg 2196,
South Africa

Penguin Books Ltd., Registered Offices: 80 Strand, London WC2R 0RL, England

This is a work of fiction. Names, characters, places, and incidents either are the product of the author's imagination or are used fictitiously, and any resemblance to actual persons, living or dead, business establishments, events, or locales is entirely coincidental.

THE GHOST AND THE DEAD MAN'S LIBRARY

A Berkley Prime Crime Book / published by arrangement with the author

PRINTING HISTORY
Berkley Prime Crime mass-market edition / September 2006

Copyright © 2006 by The Berkley Publishing Group.
Cover illustration by Catherine Deeter.
Cover design by Lesley Worrell.
Interior text design by Stacy Irwin.

ISBN: 0-425-21265-3

BERKLEY® PRIME CRIME
Berkley Prime Crime Books are published by The Berkley Publishing Group,
a division of Penguin Group (USA) Inc.,
375 Hudson Street, New York, New York 10014.
The name BERKLEY PRIME CRIME and the BERKLEY PRIME CRIME design are trademarks belonging to Penguin Group (USA) Inc.

PRINTED IN THE UNITED STATES OF AMERICA

10 9 8 7 6 5 4 3 2 1

ACKNOWLEDGMENTS

Sincerest thanks to Christine Zika, senior editor,
and John Talbot, literary agent,
for their "spirited" support!

Thanks also to Kimberly Lionetti
for the all-important start.

AUTHOR'S NOTE

Although real places and institutions are mentioned
in this book, they are used in the service of fiction.
No character in this book is based on any person, living or dead, and the world presented is completely
fictitious.

To Dad,
Antonio A. Alfonsi,
for being a good man in a bad world.

CONTENTS

Prologue   1

1. Descent into the Maelstrom   8

2. The Fall of the House of Chesley   22

3. Turnaround   34

4. Ratiocination   41

5. The Dreamer   49

6. Open for Business   62

7. The Accidentally Purloined Letter   72

8. Literary Treasure   79

9. School Daze   88

10.	Expert Opinion	95
11.	The Sleeper	108
12.	Remains of the Day	119
13.	Book-marked for Murder	127
14.	Quibble Me This	139
15.	Headline News	152
16.	Principally Speaking	161
17.	Assault and Battery	175
18.	Return to the Haunted House	189
19.	Dream in a Ditch	199
20.	Out of Order	215
21.	Fingered	227
22.	Male Drop	232
	Epilogue	244

What you need, young woman, is a trip around the Horn with a southeaster tearing the guts out of you and all hands on deck, with the sea coming over green for three nights and three days—then you'd sleep in sacking and be thankful.

—*The Ghost and Mrs. Muir* by R. A. Dick

(a.k.a. Josephine Aimée Campbell Leslie)

PROLOGUE

There was a sad fellow over on a barstool talking to
the bartender, who was polishing a glass and listening
with that plastic smile people wear when they are trying not to scream.

—Philip Marlowe in *The Long Goodbye*
by Raymond Chandler, 1949

New York City
October 18, 1946

BAXTER KERNS THE Third called Jack Shepard at noon
and invited him to dinner at six.

Jack left his cramped office early, ducked into his flat,
changed into his best double-breasted, checked the safety
on his gat, and headed into the chilly concrete night. He
would have taken a cab uptown, but he was close to

tapsville, so for a single silver buffalo, he jumped the Third Avenue el instead then hoofed it from Forty-Second.

The Madeleine was one of those private clubs in Midtown, near the hotel with the big, round table, where that literati crew used to drink and shoot their mouths off. The place reeked of money, like all the joints on University Club Row. Stone lions at the entrance, stone-faced doorman to match.

Inside Jack found the typical masculine décor: polished wainscoting and leather armchairs; oak side tables littered with finely carved pipes, neatly folded newspapers. Overseeing it all, a row of iron-haired gentlemen, rendered in dull oils, staring dully down at their living counterparts.

Jack didn't know what Baxter Kerns looked like, but that wasn't a problem. In a joint that served dinner with enough extra silverware to start your own hock shop, Jack was a dead giveaway. His lace-ups may have been polished, but they'd pounded far too much pavement. And although his suit was newly pressed, it was cheap goods among cliff-dwelling executives who didn't wear second-rate gear.

As for Kerns's glad rags, the custom-tailored Brooks Brothers' pinstripes and new patent leathers didn't change the fact that he was built like a street lamp, with an oblong head and a flagpole trunk. His features were well-chiseled beneath whiskey-colored hair, but his pale skin had a vaguely unhealthy undertone, which led Jack to believe the ruddy cheeks were less the result of a brisk walk in the autumn air than an indication he'd dipped his bill a few times already.

"I heard about you through Teddy Birmingham," said Kerns, holding out a hand.

Jack shook.

The man's skin was soft, but his grip firm. His age could have been anywhere from mid-thirties to early forties. The expression in his hazel-brown eyes appeared friendly but appraising at the same time, like a scavenging antiques agent sizing up whether a banged-up urn might prove lucrative on resale.

"I understand you helped old Ted out of a fix?"

"That's right."

Kerns stared, eyes candidly expectant, waiting for details. Jack Shepard let him wait.

"Well, Mr. Shepard? I should think you'd like a drink?"

Jack nodded, followed Kerns's loosey-goosey gait to the private club's dining room, a stoic, dimly lit arena with a vaulted ceiling and horn-headed beasts affixed to the walls. The setup was white linen and leaded crystal, fine wine and chilled salad forks. Jack let Kerns suggest the best of the menu, order the grape juice, and drive the streetcar.

Kerns's voice was quiet and even as he directed the conversation, like he was practiced at explaining complicated investments to society ladies. But for Jack, listening to a man with an overly smooth voice was like traveling a continuously flat landscape—it became tiresome fast.

Kerns gave his opinion on national and local politics, cultural events, and the postwar economy. He inquired about Jack's service, quizzing him about his job in army intelligence. Asked about his work before that as a flatfoot. Jack didn't especially enjoy talking about himself, but he gritted his teeth and answered every inquiry, knowing full well this wasn't a social engagement but a job interview.

It never ceased to amaze him how the upper classes did business. Aristocrats, real or aspiring, flinched at anything close to giving off the base, commonplace aroma of work. Even hiring and firing staff was suspect. Consequently, they were perpetually attempting to make business look like anything but.

Eventually, however, Kerns did get down to it.

". . . and, as I mentioned before, I'm a friend of Teddy Birmingham, and he recommended you, although for the life of me, I can't see why Teddy would need a private detective."

Jack let the repeated question-that-wasn't-a-question hang between them in the dim light of the fossilized club.

Men like Kerns used silence to great effect. Somewhere along the road, they'd learned what Jack already knew about the parturient pause: Weaker souls tended to feel terrorized by long silences in polite conversation. Pressured by the inferred censure in the paternal lift of the eyebrow, the slight downturn of the mouth, they almost always spilled their guts.

Jack wasn't a weaker soul.

He picked up his long-stemmed crystal goblet and sipped. The wine was good, full-bodied and sweet-smelling. It reminded him of Sally, a woman he'd known before the war. After two long minutes of Jack's breathing in perfumed memories, Kerns became the impatient party.

"You won't share your business with Teddy?" he pressed.

"No, Mr. Kerns," Jack replied, more than willing to give a straight answer to a straight question. "You won't find out from me. My discretion comes as part of the service."

Kerns shifted in his leather dinner chair. "Must I pay extra for your discretion, Mr. Shepard?"

"It's free of charge." Jack allowed a small smile. "Part of my per diem."

"Yes, so you quoted. Twenty dollars a day, plus expenses."

Kerns began to explain the specifics of the job. It seemed his sister, Dorothy, had gotten herself engaged to a savvy broker who'd claimed he'd made a real killing with prewar investments in steel manufacturing.

"His name is Vincent Tattershawe, or that's what he calls himself, anyway." Kerns frowned and shifted.

"Go on."

"He has pretensions to society, but I'm worried for my sister."

"I see." Jack pulled out a small notebook and jotted down Tattershawe's name.

"My sister has many virtues, but she's naïve about the ways of the world, and far too trusting. Without consulting me, she gave Mr. Tattershawe a considerable portion of her inheritance for him to invest."

"Why is that naïve? You said yourself that this Tattershawe is an up-and-comer with a nose for business."

"I'm not so sure he really does have the connections and background he recited to Dorothy. Nor can I be sure he actually made a lucrative investment in prewar steel. That's simply what he told her."

"So you'd like me to investigate this Vincent Tattershawe? Answer some of your questions?"

"I want you to locate the man."

"He's missing?"

"Shortly after Dorothy turned over her money to him, he vanished. I asked around a bit, and I'm troubled by what I've learned. I believe this man presented himself to my sister as something he is not. I understand he drinks a lot as well."

Jack raised an eyebrow. "We all drink a lot, don't we, Mr. Kerns?" During dinner, Baxter had consumed two Scotches, more than half their bottle of wine, and was now nursing a cognac. And Jack suspected the man had knocked back a few before Jack had even arrived.

"There's a difference between drinking"—Kerns lifted his snifter of liquid gold—"and being a drunk, Mr. Shepard."

"So you think Tattershawe either took off with the loot or fell back into a bottle?"

"Possibly both. My sister claims she convinced Vincent to give up drinking. But you and I both know that a man will tell a woman almost anything if he wants to . . . shall we say, grease the wheels?"

Jack sipped his wine. He didn't share Kerns's philosophy on dames. Lying to women was a boy's game; and he always figured any broad that required him to be something he wasn't, wasn't worth his time. But in Jack's experience, telling a disdainful Ivy Leaguer like Kerns that you knew something he didn't was like trying to crack a manhole cover with a soda straw. Jack saved his breath.

"I'll have to speak with your sister, Dorothy."

Kerns leaned forward, his relaxed posture tensing for the first time that evening.

"Listen, Mr. Shepard, I'm going to be perfectly blunt with you. I contacted you because my sister insisted a private investigator be hired. I don't like the idea myself. I stepped in because she had no idea how to proceed. I want you to find Mr. Tattershawe, but you are not to convey his location to my sister. Tell me and only me what you discover, so I can deal with him."

"*Deal* with him?"

In Jack's part of the civilized wilderness, "dealing" with someone usually meant helping them meet with an unfortunate accident.

"His theft of her money," Kerns clarified. "Dorothy has had a lot of heartache in her life. Her only serious suitor died in the war. Now she's forty, and far from a beauty. But she'd be better off staying a spinster than marrying a man like Tattershawe, who I believe would cause her harm. I wish to retrieve her money but not at the risk of reuniting her with the man who took it. Do you see what I'm trying to accomplish?"

Jack nodded.

"I'm trying to protect her. You understand wanting to protect someone you care about, don't you, Mr. Shepard?"

Kerns was still leaning forward, his hazel-brown eyes shining, intense. Clearly, he wanted Jack to understand that although he preferred to avoid the appearance of doing business, when it came to this, he meant it.

"I understand, Mr. Kerns."

Kerns downed an unfashionably large gulp of cognac, then finally leaned back, his tense limbs going slack again.

"I'm not a man who expresses gratitude often. But I do thank you for respecting my wishes."

Jack reassured his client that he understood the terms of the job. "For now, all I need to get started is your sister's address."

"Fifth Avenue, across from the park." Kerns reached into the breast pocket of his pinstripes. "Here's her calling card."

CHAPTER 1

Descent into the Maelstrom

The continuing popular appeal of Poe's works is owing
to their power to confirm once-real beliefs from which
most people have never entirely freed themselves . . .
that the dead in some form survive and return.

—Kenneth Silverman, *Edgar A. Poe:
Mournful and Never-ending Rememberance,* 1991

**Quindicott, Rhode Island
Today**

"HEY, MOM. DO you think they'll have a Halloween party
at school this year?"

Beneath his getting-too-long-again bangs, Spencer's
grass-green eyes looked up. I slapped a dollop of steaming
oatmeal into his bowl and mine, then set a fresh quart of

milk on the table. Yawning, I adjusted my black rectangular glasses and brushed aside a lock of my own copper hair.

Spence had my hair color, my late older brother's handsome features, and my late husband's eyes. But, although the light green hue and large, round shape were Calvin McClure's, the emotional expression inside them held little resemble to the man I'd married—and for that I was eternally grateful.

"Spencer," I said with all the sternness that I could muster after only four hours sleep. "You haven't seen a class since last June. I think you should worry about your education before you worry about Halloween parties."

"But Halloween's only two weeks away. That's a *fact*. The principal can't just ignore it."

My son, the budding trial lawyer.

Always precocious, Spencer's rhetorical skills had been initially influenced by the exclusive private school the McClure family had insisted he attend when we lived in Manhattan. He was in Quindicott's public school system now, of course. But his vocabulary and stubborn proclivities were lately a result of the crime shows and legal dramas he'd been watching on the Intrigue Channel.

This autumn he'd gotten a political education, too, thanks to City Councilwoman Marjorie Binder-Smith, locally known as the Municipal Zoning Witch for the charming taxes and regulations she continually attempted to slap onto Quindicott's businesses.

In her latest effort toward being "politically proactive," she'd insisted on soliciting outside bidders to compete for the contract to repair the severely damaged Quindicott Elementary School (an electrical fire in early June had completely wrecked the classrooms).

Typically, the town council would have hired Ronny Sutter, who'd been doing Quindicott's construction for decades. But hiring Ronny was what Marjorie termed "long-standing cronyism," and she insisted they search far and wide for outside bidders. The woman had swayed a majority of the council, many of whom were brand-new to their seats, and off they went, searching for bidders.

Because of the subsequent motions, consultations, and delays, too much of the town council's time was wasted accessing competing bids from contractors located in Providence, Warwick, Newport—even as far away as Brattleboro, Vermont. The project was delayed for six weeks. By the time the lowest bid was in and the builders went to work, the job was hopelessly behind schedule.

While Councilwoman Binder-Smith preened about the process at last being "impartial, unbiased, and fair," the rest of the town watched Labor Day come and go without the start of elementary school classes.

Now, finally, on the cusp of All Hallow's Eve, the children of Quindicott were heading off to their very first day of school. Needless to say, there would be no spring break this year. And I doubted a "snow day" would be called unless Quindicott was subjected to weather conditions bordering on Alaskan whiteout.

"Mom, can we go to the haunted house on Green Apple Road this weekend?"

I moved to the counter to fetch a squeeze bottle of clover honey. "I don't know, Spencer. It might be a little too intense for a ten-year-old."

A year ago, Spencer would probably have whined. Today he shot me a look that said I didn't know what I was talking about.

"Puh-leaze," he said. "You forget I watched *Silence of the Lambs* last month."

"You watched *half* of *Silence of the Lambs* before I caught you. That won't happen again, kiddo. The V chip has been activated and is in full force."

Spencer rolled his eyes. "How scary could a haunted house be? If it was too scary, people would be having heart attacks and stuff. Then people would sue, and there wouldn't be any haunted houses anymore. See my point?"

I saw his point. But the truth was, after last night, I'd had my fill of haunted houses. . . .

IT WAS A dark and stormy night.

No, really.

Just after my aunt and I set out for our drive, a nor'easter smashed against the New England coast. Rain came down in sheets, pelting the new wax job off my battered Saturn. Intermittent flashes lit up the indigo sky, burying the radio's weather report under bursts of static. And, after the lightening, of course, came the—

BOUMMMMMMM!

Sadie shuddered in the passenger seat. I glanced worriedly her way, my hands choking the life out of the steering wheel. We'd both agreed to take this trip to obtain a tasty commission. It was a "one-night-only" offer to claim a stash of rare books from a lifelong collector, and we didn't want to lose it.

New England winters were brutal. We were barely into fall and the energy bills were already murder. We needed the money. So we told ourselves we were being brave and responsible in defying the storm forecasts.

I began to reconsider that defiance.

Sadie saw me glancing her way. She gave me a little smile. "It's not a fit night out for man nor beast," she quipped, her bravado undercut by a nervous little laugh.

Apparently, it was also a night for clichés.

If you babes want to chin-dip for cornpone, piped up the masculine voice in my head, *just say, "It's raining cats and dogs," and be done with it.*

The spirit of Jack Shepard was nothing if not pithy. His gruff cynicism was also, *oddly*, a comfort to me in times of trouble. If Sadie had known about the ghost (which she didn't), she probably would have described him as the kind of friend who bucks you up when you need it the most.

"Offended by clichés, Jack?" I silently replied, his wise-crack momentarily averting my worries about the growing reduction of visibility in front of me. "I didn't know you were a literary critic."

Neither did I. Chalk it up to fifty years stuck in a hayseed library.

"Buy the Book is not a hayseed library, thank you very much. It's been a respected independent bookseller for years."

Of course, it had almost gone out of business in recent years, but I left that part out. Long ago, Sadie had taken over the shop from her father, but with her age, came the inability to manage alone, which had put the store in jeopardy. So, after Calvin took his flying leap out the bedroom window of our Manhattan high-rise, I leapt too (figuratively, anyway).

Defying the threats from my wealthy in-laws to cut me off financially, I'd left my publishing job and moved back to my Rhode Island hometown. I'd endured the enforcement of my in-laws' threats (Calvin's wealthy mother and sister did cut me off, although Spencer would still get his trust fund later in life). But Calvin's modest life insurance benefit was still mine, and I'd cashed it to relocate my life and go into business with Sadie.

We mortgaged Buy the Book for renovations, expansion, and inventory overhaul, and, for the most part, brought the nearly defunct store back to life. I was supremely proud of what we'd done thus far. Our little bookstore had led the way in resuscitating Cranberry, Quindicott's previously depressed main street.

"We have a smart, literate clientele from all over," I reminded Jack. "We have author chats and—"

Listen, baby, between your pulps, those glorified True Confessions *tomes, and the low-rent mooks and grifters you trot in for jawboning, I've heard every cliché in the book, going on times ten over.*

"They are not *mooks* and *grifters*. They are authors, reading their works."

Jack really was impossible with his complaints about the store. On the other hand, how thrilled would you be about a place where you'd had (as Jack put it) your lights put out and your ticket punched?

Jack Shepard was killed in our bookstore in 1949 while investigating the murder of an old army buddy. That's all I know. That's all, *apparently*, he knows. He claims his case files (hundreds of them), which I have on loan, contain notes on the investigation he'd been running at the time. But I have yet to locate them—and Jack refuses to help me out.

He says whoever killed him wasn't "playing," and he doesn't want me anywhere near that particular murder mystery. It hadn't stopped me from solving a few others, however, and, I have to admit, Jack had been a big help in that regard. But then, he had been a private detective.

In life, anyway.

A flash of lightning brought me back to the potentially deadly weather.

"It is an ugly night," Sadie murmured.

Clutched in her wrinkled, seventy-three-year-young hands was a frayed piece of paper containing the directions to our destination. The instructions had been faxed to her just two hours ago, right after the urgent phone call summoning us to Newport, which was between thirty to fifty minutes away from Quindicott, depending on the traffic and the—

BOUMMMMM!

"Jeez-Louise. I hate thunder."

"I am sorry about the storm, dear," my aunt said, as if she'd been the one who'd brought on the weather in the first place. "Mr. Chesley said it was important that we come tonight. *Urgent*, was the word he'd used."

Her voice was nearly lost under the constant swishing of the windshield wipers.

"Don't worry about the weather. It's not so bad," I fibbed, watching blasts of wind ripple the black water pooling on the roadway. "Anyway, we've practically arrived."

Sadie squinted at the directions in her hands. "You're right, Pen. The next turn is just ahead. But it's so dark you'd better slow down, or we might miss it."

With the autumn sunset around five o'clock, half past seven seemed black as midnight, and lights were plenty scarce along this remote section of the Atlantic coastline, which only magnified the gloom.

We swung off the main highway and onto a winding, two-lane blacktop. According to Peter Chesley's instructions, we were to follow this route until we reached Roderick Road.

On a sunny, dry day, this route might have been pleasant, even scenic. On a night like this, however, the eerie stretch seemed almost claustrophobic. Tall trees stripped of their leaves flanked our vehicle on either side like old, brown bones, rattling in the night.

On one narrow turn, the road swung onto the ledge of a high, narrow cliff. Jagged rocks swept down to the Atlantic's roiling black plane. Typically, I'd enjoy the rhythmic sound of the lapping waves. But tonight the nor'easter winds were whipping the surf into a seething froth, then crashing it over the ragged shoreline with a fulminating roar.

"It is so strange to think of Peter living out here," Sadie said with an eye on the desolate horizon. "When I knew him, he loved being in the middle of things, loved living in the bustle of Providence, loved teaching."

"What did he teach?"

"He was a professor of American history at Brown University."

I heard Jack groan. *Not another egghead. Maybe I'll just slip away now, before I croak from boredom.*

True to his promise, I felt Jack's presence recede. Where the spirit went, I don't know. At first, Jack's ghost appeared to be confined within the fieldstone walls of our bookstore. But last year I found a stray buffalo nickel in a cache of his yellowing private eye files. As bizarre and irrational as it sounded, as long as I had Jack's old nickel in my possession, his spirit traveled with me. (Sure, the ghost has tested my limits with his wisecracks, jibes, and off-color barbs, but his streetwise advice has gotten me out of some big, hairy jams, so I held tight to that coin. Frankly, I preferred running with the insurance.)

Of course, I'd already considered that Jack wasn't real at all, that the ghost was simply a figment of my imagination, some psychological split akin to the schizophrenia of John Nash, the famous Nobel Prize–winning mathematician.

Was Jack my alter ego? That small, buried nugget of id that had all the bravado I didn't? Maybe he was some composite of all the hard-boiled novels I'd read over the years; a subconscious realization of those *Black Mask* stories my late police officer dad and I had loved.

But even if that were true (and I doubted it was), it was just one more reason *not* to inform anyone of Jack's existence.

The McClure family owned a lot of land in this part of Rhode Island, and they wielded a lot of influence. They also blamed me for Calvin's suicide (having conveniently forgotten that they themselves had refused to acknowledge the severity of his depression). English boarding school for Spencer had been their idea of a "helpful" suggestion after Calvin died; after which, I'd told *them* to take a flying leap and then moved in with my aunt in Quindicott.

My former in-laws would be only too happy to find a reason to take Spencer away from me. So telling anyone (including and especially a therapist) that I, Penelope Thornton-McClure, was having regular conversations with Jack Shepard, the friendly PI ghost, wasn't something I'd be doing anytime soon.

The car radio was finally drowned out by static, so I switched the newscaster off and refocused on the task in front of us.

"Peter Chesley sounds like an impressive man," I said.

"Yes. Oh, yes . . . he was."

"How long have you known him? I don't remember you ever mentioning him before."

"I met Peter . . . let's see . . . going on thirty years ago now."

Sadie leaned back in the passenger seat—the first time since the thunder had started. Despite the tense storm around us, the thought of Peter Chesley appeared to relax her.

"He called to purchase a few titles in an estate library the store had taken on consignment. When he walked in to pick them up, that's when we first met. He loved the store and he became a regular customer after that . . . and a friend."

It sounded to me like he'd been more than "a friend," but I wasn't sure how to ask without prying.

"Of course, business was different in those days," my aunt went on. "You've set us up on the Internet now, but back when I was your age, we had buyers dropping by every week, folks from Newport, New Haven, Providence, even New York City. . . ."

She smiled at some memory. "Peter was one of the nicest. He never seemed to have much money, was forever scrimping to purchase rare books for his collection, but he was always well dressed in pressed slacks and a tweed jacket. I remember he had a glorious mop of thick golden hair and blue eyes, like Paul Newman . . ."

"Hmm." I smiled. "Can't wait to meet him."

Sadie laughed. "Oh, no, no, no, Pen. My description of the man is from my past memories. He must be close to eighty by now."

"Who cares?" I teased. "I'm a sucker for blue eyes."

"Ah . . . but what could you possibly have in common

with someone who was in their prime when FDR was president?"

I thought about Jack. "Actually, you might be surprised."

"Don't you go and start dating older men," Sadie warned. "You're too young for that . . . You're still young enough to give Spencer a little brother or sister, someday."

I snorted. "Considering the pool of available men in a little town like Quindicott, I probably have a statistically better chance of getting struck by—"

An electric flash lit the night sky, followed by an ominous boom.

" 'Nuf said," I concluded.

Aunt Sadie sighed. I could see she wasn't happy with my lack of confidence that I'd be finding some knight in shining armor around the next bend. But she didn't argue. The Thorntons always did have that in common—we were realists.

"So when was the last time you heard from Mr. Chesley? Before this morning's urgent summons, I mean. Did you two have a falling out?"

A shadow crossed Sadie's face. "Peter's marriage fell apart the same year my father passed away. At that time, we'd known each other only through the book selling, but, for a short time, we became much closer. I'd go to Providence and we'd . . . socialize . . . you understand, dear, don't you?"

"I understand."

"Peter helped me a great deal, and I believe I helped him . . . but it wasn't meant to be . . . we were different people, and after about a year, our relationship . . . well, it soured. Neither of us wanted to pursue anything permanent, but we parted friends. After that, Peter and I saw less of each other, but he remained a good customer, and he made a point of coming by the store at least once a month to see how I was, share a drink or some dinner. Like I said, he was always a good friend."

"But what happened to him?"

"One afternoon, around, oh . . . going on ten years ago now, Peter showed up at my shop in something of a state. He spoke about a crisis in his family. An emergency. He told me I wouldn't see him again for six months at least. But I never saw or heard from him again, until this morning, when he called out of the blue and told me he had some collectable books he wanted me to sell for him."

"He never contacted you before that?"

Sadie shook her head. "I did try calling him at his home in Providence, but his phone had been disconnected."

"What happened to him then?"

When he called today, Peter explained that he'd moved back to his boyhood home in Newport. That's where we're going now . . . Prospero House, his family's oceanfront estate. He apologized for losing touch, but he said after his return home all those years ago, he got busy with family affairs, became something of a recluse." Sadie sighed. "The truth is, dear, Peter could very easily . . . how do I put this? He could get lost in things."

"What do you mean 'get lost in things'?"

"He'd . . . obsess."

"You mean he'd become compulsive? Like OCD?"

"Yes, dear . . . I'm sure you've noticed that particular tendency in some of our more, shall we say, *enthusiastic* collectors."

"Now that you mention it . . ."

At least three regulars came to mind. They e-mailed or called like clockwork, looking for missing volumes in collections we'd never carried, signed editions we'd never advertised—just to be sure they hadn't missed an announcement on our Web site or listing in our catalog. But their searching was passionate and constant, almost ritualistic. I had engaged each of them in conversation at one time or another and discovered we were just one call on a long list of calls they made every day.

"If Peter found himself on the receiving end of a major

inheritance," Sadie continued, "any number of things related to it might have taken hold of him and pulled him in . . . consumed him."

"An estate in Newport is pretty impressive," I noted. "He must come from real money, then?"

"It was a surprise to me, I have to tell you. To think that Peter came from old Newport stock, that his family owned a mansion. He'd never mentioned it to me in all the years we'd been friends. The Peter Chesley I knew was so unassuming. And I would have never guessed he came from money. The man always seemed so frugal."

"So what kind of books did Mr. Chesley collect? Mysteries?"

"Oh, heavens no." Sadie waved her hand. "Peter's passion was history. The Revolutionary War—books by or about the Founding Fathers. I believe his great-great-great-grandfather was at Bunker Hill. He was crazy for anything dealing with that period."

"You moved books like that?"

Sadie shrugged. "I moved everything and anything, in my time. . . . Oh, look there!"

We both saw the next turn at the same moment. Roderick Road was downright schizophrenic. With twists and turns that seemed to leap out of the darkness, the road appeared to have been designed around the landscape. We circled a huge outcropping of pure New England granite, and what appeared in the gloom to be a tree at least two hundred years old, its protruding roots gnarled.

"You should feel good that Peter didn't forget you after all these years," I said.

Sadie nodded. "Yes, it's very nice of him to offer me first pick of the books he plans to sell. But for the life of me, I can't see why I couldn't come by tomorrow or Tuesday. Why we had to make this trip tonight of all nights."

I raised an eyebrow. If the man had obsessive-compulsive disorder, I figured that was reason enough—and it also gave me a clue why Sadie had walked away from the relationship all those years ago.

"There's the turn," Sadie said.

I saw the gateposts at the last possible second, and hit the brakes too suddenly—the tires immediately began hydroplaning across the wet asphalt. Careening out of control, the Saturn spun off the road, into the shoulder, the soft, wet mud finally stopping us with a teeth-rattling jolt.

The car stalled, cutting off the hissing heater and swishing windshield wipers along with the rumbling engine. The abrupt silence was followed by the *thump, thump, thump* of pelting rain hitting the roof, the hood, the trunk.

"Are . . . Are you okay?" My voice cracked from the tension.

Face pale, Sadie took a deep breath and nodded.

What are you trying to do, baby, pull a Dutch act? Jack piped up in my head. *If you wanted to off yourself, there's no reason to take your sweet little ol' auntie with you. And where did you learn to drive, anyway—the bumper cars at Coney Island?*

Sadie and I sat in silence for a moment, listening to the rain batter the metal. Then I shifted into neutral and turned the ignition key. The engine came to life. We both let out the breaths we'd been holding. I eased the car into reverse and slowly applied the gas. The tires skidded a little, but the sedan rolled back onto the pavement without incident.

Two tall granite gateposts flanked the driveway, bridged by a wrought-iron arch that spelled out the house's name in rusty, pitted letters. As I rolled through the open gate, lightning flared like a shattering bottle rocket, illuminating the sprawling mansion.

"Goodness!" Sadie exclaimed, getting a good look.

"Man alive," I murmured.

I felt a shiver—but not from the raw weather. We had arrived at Prospero House.

"Looks like the architect couldn't decide whether his client was the Addams Family or JP Morgan," I said.

The looming, four-story mansion was so grotesque it even gave my ghost the creeps.

Nice joint, this place you're going, Jack said. *It's got all the charm of Sing Sing.*

CHAPTER 2

The Fall of the House of Chesley

I was never kinder to the old man than during the whole week before I killed him.

—Edgar Allan Poe, "The Tell-Tale Heart," 1845

I SHIVERED AS I stepped out of the warm automobile. A gothic-style portico shielded the entrance to Prospero House from the brute force of the wind and rain, but the night air was downright frigid.

Side by side, Sadie and I climbed the three stone steps that led to the mansion's carved front doors. Flanking the entrance were two bronzed mermaids with long flowing hair and angelic faces, their scabrous tails encrusted by a green patina.

Before I located the doorbell, I heard the click of a bolt. Gradually, arthritically, one heavy door opened, its hinges moaning as if protesting the painful movement. Then a lashing burst of rain drummed the east wall of the portico, and a sudden bone-white flash revealed our host.

Tall but flimsy as a scarecrow, Peter Chesley's sallow flesh was the color of old parchment, his once-blue eyes milky and bloodshot. His hair, no longer thick and golden, was nearly gone, save for a bristle-brush of gray ringing his pasty scalp. His ashen cheeks appeared caved in, giving his face the look of a deflated soccer ball.

Swathed entirely in black, the man's soft velvet coat was natty and moth-eaten, with badly frayed sleeves. His threadbare pants hung too loosely over his thin hips, the cloth shiny with wear and stained with old food. The old man stood unsteadily on scuffed velvet slippers. The chipped and dented black cane he clutched in his gnarled left hand was more than an affectation.

This high-toned fruitcake's dirty with more than money, Jack groused. *He's got enough cabbage to own this palace, but he can't even clean up for his guests.*

"Take it easy, Jack," I silently replied. "He's old. And he doesn't look well."

Well, stand back, this geezer looks like he's going to peg out any second now.

At first glance, Chesley's gaze seemed almost fearful. But the man brightened with recognition when he saw my aunt.

"Sadie," he whispered.

The old man's rheumy eyes shined, and, for a moment, I could see a glimpse of that brilliant blue Sadie had mentioned from her memories.

Leading with his cane, Peter Chesley stumbled forward to greet us. Only then did I realize how frail he truly was. I felt my aunt stiffen when he confronted us, heard her catch her breath in surprise. But she quickly recovered from her initial shock. With a sincere smile Sadie Thornton stepped forward to take her old lover's thin arm.

"Peter, how good to see you again."

"Good to see you, too, my dear, dear, Sadie."

Chesley's voice was as wispy as his frame, his lungs barely providing enough air for his words to be heard over the howl of the storm.

"Let's get out of the cold. We can talk inside," Sadie said.

Deftly, she turned the man around and led us back into the house. I expected (and hoped for) light, warmth, hot tea—perhaps even a cozy fire roaring in a welcoming hearth. But my first sensations upon entering Prospero House were the pervasive smell of mildew, the oppressive feelings of cold and dampness. My surroundings more resembled a crumbling tenement than a century-old Newport mansion. Once stately, the house was literally disintegrating through age and neglect.

The interior entranceway was dominated by a grand staircase, which flowed down from a second-floor balcony in a gentle curve. The carpeted steps, obviously a deep burgundy at one time, had become a muddy brown, the cloth frayed and dotted with patches of mold.

The theme of the décor was obviously nautical. The bare stone walls were decorated with odd maritime knickknacks, including a harpoon, and massive oil paintings of tall ships from three centuries. On a heavy oak table, I noticed an antique brass ship bell. Next to it a glass display case brimmed with yachting cups and sailing trophies, their silvers and golds faded under countless layers of dust.

A drumming noise beat against our ears, a staccato thump like the beating of a heart. The sound came from a steel tub in the corner, placed there to catch large drops of water that plunged in a steady stream through a hole in the ceiling high above the stairs.

Peter Chesley noticed my stare. "The upper wings are sealed off. There's no one up there. It's quite uninhabitable." He said this in a conversational tone, but when his pale eyes glanced at the stairs, a shadow crossed his face. "I haven't been able to climb stairs for a year or more. Arthritis."

Hobbling with obvious pain, the man led us through a large door to the left of the stairway. "I've moved my bedroom down to the first floor," he remarked. "It's a small room off the kitchen, but it suits me just fine."

Despite his unkempt appearance and the dilapidated condition of his home, I was struck by Chesley's dignity, the air of shabby gentility he carefully maintained. Yet there was also a furtive nervousness about the man, which I found baffling. I suspected the tension might be caused by our presence—since it was fairly obvious Mr. Chesley didn't make a habit of entertaining guests.

We stepped through the archway with carved oak supports and found ourselves in the manor's library. Illuminated by the flicking fire in a massive stone hearth, the library was nearly the size of our display floor at Buy the Book. It boasted a vaulted ceiling with oak cross beams and a tall grandfather clock, which ticked loudly in one corner, its oddly shaped pendulum swinging in an arc behind cut leaded glass.

The sheer size of the manor's collection was impressive. Thousands of books lined the dark oak shelves. Along one shadowy wall near the clock, some portraits had been strategically hung—framed oils and old, posed photographs of men and women I assumed were Chesley ancestors.

This dump is duller than a gravesight, Jack complained in my head. *And I should know.*

"Take it easy, Jack."

I haven't seen a joint this wrecked since I was hired to make a drop at a run-down tenement for a blackmailed client.

"One of your cases?"

Yeah, baby, you can look it up.

"Why don't you tell me now? This place is creeping me out. Frankly, I could use the distraction."

Well, let's see now, how did that case start? . . . I got a visit from the vice president of a hat company. Short guy with a dopey face. Had a proclivity for two-toned shoes and carnations in his lapels. He was stepping out on his wife, who also happened to be the daughter of the company's owner.

"What a winner . . ."

Turns out Mr. VP had been doing the horizontal tango with a real piece of work. The floozie had secret photos taken of their hot dates, and she threatened to send the photos to his wife unless he cooperated.

"What did she—the floozie, I mean—want?"

In exchange for the incriminating photos and their negatives, Mr. Exec was supposed to pack five thousand dollars in small bills into a grocery bag and slap a few heads of lettuce on top—I gotta say, that piece of the puzzle did crack me up.

"What?"

Lettuce on lettuce.

"I don't get it."

What's not to get, baby? Lettuce is the lingo for money.

"Oh . . . yes, that's right, you've used that term before."

Jack sighed. *Try to keep up with me, doll, would you? So, anyway, Mr. VP is supposed to prepare this bag, then leave it in front of an apartment house door and knock three times. The door's supposed to open, the bag goes in, and if the money counts up okay, then an envelope with the photos is supposed to come sliding out right to him from under the same door.*

"Sounds straightforward."

Sure, but when the exec hears the address, he gets spooked and hires me to make the drop. So I dress in Mr. VP's tailored overcoat and matching fedora and take the bag of lettuce to the designated address.

"Where was it?"

Coney Island, Brooklyn. Guys like my VP client don't

cross the East River. Bridges and tunnels scare them worse than dwindling dividends.

"What happened, Jack? Did you exchange the money for the photos?"

Nope.

"You didn't get the photos."

No, baby, I got the photos, the negatives, and without giving up one leaf of the client's green. They weren't too happy, but then they didn't have much choice after I got through with them.

"They?"

Sure, you think some cheap floozie would have worked out that blackmailing con on her own? Naw, she had muscle. Three Brunos were waiting for me the day I showed. Only I didn't go in the front door of that crumbling wreck of a tenement. I went in the back—got the drop on them. The element of surprise; usually works like a charm, key word being usually.

"Got it . . . going in the back door when they expect you in the front. I'll have to remember that."

Great, doll, but it's too late for that now. You're already inside this musty mausoleum. How does gramps pass the time in this crypt, anyway? Watching mold grow?

"Jack, have a heart. Think how old you'd be now if you'd lived."

Baby, you ought to know me by now. I don't truck with sentiment.

"I'll alert the media."

So why not put some egg on your shoes and beat it?

"We can't leave yet. Not until our business is through."

Just then, I noticed a large, thick-legged table in the center of the mansion's library. It was stacked high with old books, some of them folio sized, all of them, I was certain, rare collector's items.

My eyes forgot to blink, and I knew how Veruca Salt felt

the moment she'd stepped into Willy Wonka's Chocolate Factory. But as I began to move toward that table, Peter Chesley put a hand on my shoulder and asked Sadie and I to take a seat by the fireplace.

I nodded politely and forced myself to turn toward the warmth and light. Unfortunately, both came from an over-sized, smoke-stained hearth carved to resemble the gaping, fanged mouth of a gigantic gargoyle. I tried to pretend my shudders were from a chill and not the creepy maw I was walking toward.

Chesley gestured for us to sit. Then, in a touching gesture of chivalry, stood patiently waiting for us to take off our coats, drape them on leather armchairs, and settle into our seats before he sank slowly into his own—a bamboo wheelchair.

On a wide mahogany coffee table sat a silver tea service. Steam rose from a pot of Earl Gray, its aroma competing with the scent of wood smoke. I wondered if Peter Chesley had any servants.

"Forgive the sparse amenities," he said. "It's Sunday, the butler's night off." Chesley laid his cane across his lap. "Shall I pour?"

Sadie leaned forward. "Allow me."

She filled one of the bone china cups and passed it to me, along with a few tiny cakes delivered that morning, according to Sadie's old beau, in honor of our visit.

I thought that was odd, considering we hadn't consented to come until late afternoon. But then Chesley had known Sadie pretty well at one time. Maybe he knew her well enough to know she'd come to him, no matter what.

"Thank you, Sadie," said Peter as she passed him his tea. "You remembered how I liked it."

Sadie smiled—a little sadly, it seemed to me. "Two sugars, no cream, no lemon."

Chesley gazed openly at my aunt. "You haven't changed, my love, not one bit."

Sadie waved her hand. "Get those eyes checked, Peter."

"Not one bit."

Sadie shook her head and turned her attention to pouring her own cup of tea, but I could tell she was pleased. And I recalled her taking extra care getting ready for our trip this evening. Over her best pleated brown slacks, she'd worn her new deep green V-neck sweater, which went beautifully with her shoulder-length red-gold hair—dyed and highlighted regularly at Colleen's Beauty Shop. And, though she wasn't a fan of makeup, she'd taken pains to put on a bit of blush, lipstick, and gloss, and fasten a cherished gold cross around her neck.

"I seldom partake of such fare these days," Chesley said with a sigh. "My condition, you see . . ."

The man's nervousness seemed to recede as the conversation continued. Sadie and Peter chatted nonstop, catching up on missed years, on the lives and fates of mutual friends, collectors, and their collections.

I only half listened, preferring to sip my tea and watch the lightning flash through the tall leaded windows. The saucer that rested on my lap was easily as old as this mansion—well over a century. It felt as though we were having a late-night tea party in a museum.

"I'll tell you frankly, Sadie, when I became the patriarch of the Chesley family, no one was more surprised than me. Given the declining fortunes of the family trust over the past few years, it has become my passion to fairly and justly discharge the family legacy—this four-story mansion, the grounds around it, the treasures in this library . . ."

Chesley paused to take in the portraits and photos on the far wall. Then he gestured to a stack of notebooks on a small desk. They were composition books, the kind college students used. There must have been at least fifty.

"Are those notebooks from your academic days?" I asked. "Research for your scholarly papers?"

"Heavens, no. My work is archived with the university

library. No, those notebooks"—he pointed a bony finger—
"are the complete catalog of this entire estate. Every painting, antique, sculpture, trophy, and piece of furniture, as
well as every book in this library has been accounted for,
its history described as best as I could research it. I thought
the process would never end, but I'm nearly through now. I
merely have the photos and portraits in this room to catalog and I'll be finished at last."

"My goodness, Peter." Sadie shook her head. "That's
what you've been up to all these years?"

"It's been quite consuming, I must admit. Some days, I'd
take down a book and then find it of interest and spend half
the day reading it!" Chesley cackled and shook his head. "In
any event, while I do not wish to part with any items in my
family's collection, I know now is the time. I set aside some
particular gems you may wish to sell. Some of these items
are treasures and should be possessed by someone who will
cherish them. I realize many of these books are quite valuable, so I am willing to offer you the lot on commission."

Sadie blinked. "That's very fair, Peter, but certainly we
can advance you a sum—"

"I am not starving," Chesley quickly interrupted. "I
shall wait for the sale to take place, and accept fifty percent
of the gross."

"Peter! That's far too generous!" Sadie cried.

"Ah, but you're forgetting, fifteen years ago you sold me
that beautifully preserved, eighteenth-century edition of
Poor Richard's Almanac for a mere two hundred dollars—"

"Did I?" Sadie replied. "I don't recall—"

"Don't say you don't remember. I know perfectly well
that physician in Boston offered you over a thousand dollars for the very same copy. You cheated yourself out of
eight hundred dollars. *That* was far too generous."

Sadie blushed. "You wanted the book much more than
Dr. Mellors, Peter. Money isn't everything."

"Exactly. Which is why this argument is over."

Chesley swung his wheelchair around and rolled across the faded Oriental rug. The wheels wobbled and squeaked. Sadie and I rose and followed the man to the goodies table. I felt like a child on Christmas morning, staring at a stack of ribbons and bows wrapped around boxes of possibilities.

But as I stood up, I could swear I heard the sound of footsteps over my head—heavy footfalls, too, as if someone were walking the corridor upstairs. I glanced at Sadie, but she seemed to have missed the sound. Telling myself I'd been mistaken, I followed the pair to the table.

Peter gestured to a large folio tied with silk ribbon.

"As you see, I have an edition of American birds by naturalist John James Audubon. I believe they were published in 1838."

I held my breath. The Audubon folios I'd seen before this were relegated to library collections or museums.

Sadie lifted a thick volume with rough-cut pages and a scuffed brown cover. "This is incredible. Is this a Caritat's edition of *Wieland*?"

Chesley nodded. "Published in 1798, I believe. The only edition that appeared in Charles Brockden Brown's lifetime. Alas, this copy is not signed. . . ."

Peter Chesley's hand rested on an odd, seemingly mismatched set of books. "Considering the theme of your newly renovated bookstore, I think you may find these volumes of particular interest."

"The Poes?" Sadie observed.

"A complete set of the Eugene Phelps editions of Edgar Allan Poe's tales and poems. Thirteen volumes edited and published between 1929 and 1931. I understand some of these books are quite rare, though most volumes garner only modest sums from collectors."

"Why is that?" I asked our host, but it was Sadie who provided the answer.

"The Phelps books were published by a rich New England eccentric on the cusp of the Great Depression," she explained. "Only the last four volumes in the set are truly valuable because they had a much smaller print run, and because they did not sell when they were first published—"

"Don't forget the most fascinating part of the story." Chesley fixed his eyes on mine and lowered his voice. "Your aunt failed to mention that over half the print run was lost when Eugene Phelps committed suicide in 1932. It seems the poor man lost his fortune on the stock market."

"That's tragic," I replied.

To my surprise, Peter Chesley threw back his head and emitted a deranged-sounding cackle.

"Dwelling on the florid, morose writings of a Gothicist like Edgar Poe, poor Phelps was probably insane. Mad as a hatter!" he crowed. "Most bluebloods are, you know. Completely useless, the lot of them."

I left Peter's remark hanging. Jack was not so diplomatic.

That's the first smart thing that dribbled through grandpa's dentures all night.

"The Phelps books will surely sell," Sadie said, changing the subject. "But to get the best price I may have to break up the set. It's a shame but—"

Chesley silenced my aunt with a raised hand. "Do what you have to. That doesn't trouble me in the least. I inherited these books when I inherited Prospero House. To be perfectly frank, I have about as much interest in Poe as I do in this nautical claptrap you see around the mansion—which is to say, not much." Chesley scowled. "Yachting was my father's obsession. Poe my grandfather's. Which explains the grotesque motif of that clock in the corner."

I'd hardly paid attention to the grandfather clock. It stood in the shadows next to that cluster of old daguerreotypes mounted in square and oval frames that I'd assumed were Chesley ancestors when I'd first entered the library.

Now I walked across the room to survey the antique. At over six feet tall, the heavy, dark wood case towered over me, its face flanked by a black cat and a stately raven, also carved in dark wood. The pendulum behind the glass was shaped like a swinging axe blade.

Cheery, ain't it?

"The images are from Poe's poetry and tales," I silently informed Jack. I hadn't read Poe since my adolescence, but I recognized some of the carvings in the clock's case—a heart, a dagger, a beautiful woman wrapped in a shroud, and a primate of some sort. I puzzled over the simian for a minute, until I remembered the identity of the killer in "The Murders in the Rue Morgue." And, of course, I understood the meaning of Prospero House now. It wasn't a reference to the magician and banished duke in Shakespeare's *Tempest*, but the prince in Poe's "The Masque of the Red Death."

Chesley spoke up. "That clock belonged to my grandfather. I imagine he had it specially made." He snorted. "Waste of good money."

Sadie cleared her throat. "Well, I shall certainly do my best to move this consignment of books in as short a time as possible,"

"Take as long as you like to sell them. And if my illness should overtake me, please consider them yours. Willed to you. A gift."

As Sadie opened her mouth to protest, a thunderous crash interrupted her, only this crash *wasn't* thunder. The noise came from over our heads, a loud bang followed by a lot of little bouncing sounds, like the sound of a heavy metal vase full of pebbles crashing to the floor.

Sadie let out a small scream of surprise.

Peter Chesley glanced up at the ceiling.

"What was that?!" I cried, quickly crossing the room to join them.

Brain it out, doll, Jack warned. *Sounds like there's more than one fruitcake in this nut house.*

CHAPTER 3

Turnaround

Listening for noises was no good. The storm was making hundreds of them.

—Dashiell Hammett, "The Gutting of Couffignal," 1925

"THAT CRASH CAME from upstairs!"

I moved toward the door. But before I took three steps, Peter Chesley rolled his chair directly into my path. His eyes were wide, and in the library's flickering firelight I swear I saw fear in them.

"Don't trouble yourself, Mrs. McClure. Such sounds are common. The house is in poor condition. Tonight's rain and the wind have not helped the situation. I wouldn't want you to get hurt . . ."

"But—"

"Please. It's nothing to be alarmed about," Peter declared. "Merely the walls settling . . ."

Pops is laying track, baby. He's taking you for a rube.

"I know, Jack," I silently replied. "I thought I heard a footstep before. What do I do?"

Don't bunch your panties up, Jack cautioned. *We're probably talking a clumsy butler here. If gramps wants to pretend we're alone, play along with his carny act, let him think we're all conned and make like the shepherd—*

"Make like *you*, Jack?"

Make like the proverbial *shepherd, sweetheart, and get the flock out.*

The grandfather clock struck nine. Peter Chesley's shoulders slumped, and his head hung low on his waddled neck. "I'm terribly sorry, but I feel suddenly tired," he moaned. "It *is* quite late . . ."

"Of course, Peter. We understand," my aunt replied. "Penelope and I should get back on the road, too. I can send someone over in our van tomorrow and pick up these books."

"No!" Peter cried, strangely reanimated. "I insist you take them now. *Tonight.* I have boxes right over there, in the corner. I'll help you pack them up."

"But, Mr. Chesley, what about the paperwork?" I reminded him. "Both parties should agree on the terms of a consignment contract, and—"

"Young woman, I've known your aunt for three decades. I can certainly trust you both to send the paperwork along at a later date. Whatever you decide is fine with me."

Ten minutes later, I was carrying a box of books out to the car while Peter helped my aunt pack up the rest of the consignment. When I came back inside, I paused at the base of the staircase, listening.

The house was alive with sounds—wind whistling through corridors, the spatter of rain on the slate roof, the rustle of the trees outside, the constant thumping of water hitting the steel pan. But I could hear no more footsteps upstairs, no human sounds up there at all. I resisted the temptation to call "Hello?" and continued on to the library to carry out the next box of books.

After the trunk was loaded up, Peter Chesley escorted us from the library to the front door. I offered to push him in his wheelchair, but, in yet another gesture of chivalry, he insisted on using his cane and seeing us out under his own power.

"It was a pleasure to meet you, my dear," he told me sweetly and shook my hand. His grip was weak and bony, but his smile was genuine.

"I'll send you a consignment contract by Express Mail first thing in the morning, Mr. Chesley," I assured him. "You should have it Tuesday, before noon."

I thanked the elderly man and discreetly moved to the car to allow Sadie a few minutes alone to say goodbye to her old friend. At the end of the adieu, I noticed Peter forcing his arthritic form to bow so he could kiss my aunt's hand.

When she finally settled into the passenger seat, I could see Sadie biting back tears. We drove away in silence. In my rearview mirror, the manor became a dark silhouette against a rolling purple sky. Roderick Road was still free of traffic, but now the rain had all but ceased. A steady wind gusting at around forty miles per hour was blow-drying the landscape.

"Oh, my, that was hard," Sadie said at last. "Seeing how much Peter aged during our years apart . . . and he's been so isolated, holing himself up in that dreadful place."

"He does live a strange existence," I said, struggling to be diplomatic. "But he spoke of finding himself the patri-arch of the family, and his responsibilities to that family. That means there are relatives out there, too. And he did mention it was the butler's night off."

"I think Peter made up that story about the butler," Sadie replied. "What butler would let his employer live in such conditions? If he's lucky, Peter has a home-care nurse who checks on him weekly."

I heard Sadie sniff, saw her brush her glove across her damp cheek. "Well, now that I know he needs me . . . that he didn't simply remarry some other woman and run off, I'm going to come visit him every weekend. I'm going to find out what's really going on in that man's life whether he likes it or not!"

I smiled, happy to hear the fight in my aunt's voice. If anyone could lift the eccentric Peter Chesley out of his gloomy, mildewed hole of an existence, it was Sadie Thornton.

"I have tissue," I offered, seeing her tears continue to flow. "In my purse in the back— Oh, no!"

"What?"

Now I knew why I hadn't heard any wisecracks from Jack since we'd left the mansion. "I was so busy loading the trunk with boxes of books that I left my purse in Mr. Chesley's library. My driver's license and credit cards are in there, everything I need . . ." (Including my connection with Jack!)

"We have to go back," Sadie declared. "Turn around."

We'd been driving for ten minutes already, but I slowed the car to a crawl, looking for a place to make a U-turn. Before long, we were rolling through the iron gates of Prospero House once again.

"I do hope Peter hasn't retired already," Sadie fretted.

I glanced at my watch. "We've only been gone about twenty minutes. I'll bet he's still awake."

"Let me go inside. I can be in and out in a moment."

I gladly agreed. Chesley's Mildewed Manor gave me the proverbial creeps, and I wasn't keen on an encore appearance. As we rolled under the stone portico, however, I noticed that both massive front doors were wide open, the wind rippling the hanging curtains in the entranceway.

Sadie stiffened. "Something's wrong."

I stopped, cut the engine, and thrust the keys into Sadie's gloved hand. "Wait here."

"What? No, Pen, wait for me—"

I was much faster than my aunt, and out of the car and up the three stone steps before she'd gotten out of the passenger seat.

"Mr. Chesley?" I called. "Can you hear me? Are you okay?"

The howling wind was my only reply.

I peered through the door and saw the motionless form on the hard stone floor. A hinge squeaked as the wind moved the door. I glanced at the locks, the doorknobs. There was no sign of forced entry.

Behind me, I heard the car door slam, and seconds later my aunt was at my side. When she saw the man on the ground, she choked back a scream, took a step forward. I grabbed her arm, stopped her.

"Just in case we're not alone, we go in together."

I was more convinced than ever that I'd heard another person in the house earlier in the evening. Now I wondered whether that person was dangerous.

Sadie understood my concern. Face pale, she nodded.

Arm in arm, we stepped over the threshold. Cautiously, we scanned the room, searching for any sign of activity. The house seemed deserted, except for the man on the floor. We hurried to Peter's side.

"Watch my back," I whispered.

I bent over the man. He lay facedown at the bottom of the stairs, one bare foot resting on the bottom step, his velvet slipper missing. I felt his flesh for signs of life, but he was already cold. Even before I searched for a pulse, I suspected there was no life left in his frail, broken form.

When I put my hand on his throat, I discovered an unnatural lump—as if he'd broken his neck—then drew my hand back so quickly I lost my balance and fell on my behind.

Sitting on the ground, I glanced around, spied the bamboo wheelchair parked in the corner of the room, far from the stairs.

There didn't appear to be any marks on Chesley, nor signs of violence beyond the broken neck. I scanned the stairs, saw his missing slipper in the middle of the staircase near the second floor.

My aunt looked away. She was distraught, sobbing. There was nothing she could do for the living Peter Chesley, not anymore, but we couldn't just leave his corpse here.

"We have to call 911," I said.

Sadie, still in shock, offered me a blank stare. "I . . . I don't know where Peter keeps his phone," she said.

"Stay here. Don't touch anything!"

My tone was brusque, almost harsh, but I needed to get through to Sadie, who was clearly shaken by her friend's sudden demise.

I strode quickly back to the library. My purse was where I'd left it—dangling by its strap from the arm of the chair. I needed the cell phone inside to call the police. But as soon as my fingers touched the purse, a familiar voice filled my head.

Miss me, baby?

"Jack, something terrible has happened—"

As I filled Jack in, I reached for the old buffalo nickel he once owned. I rubbed the coin between my fingers, like some stupid, scared kid looking for a genie in a bottle.

Call the cops, honey, but look around first, Jack advised.

"Huh?"

Wake up, doll. You and auntie were the last to see this rube alive. If he's been rubbed out, you're both in the hot seat—prime suspects.

"Jack! My God. What do you want me to look for?" I cried—out loud, as it turned out.

Can the chatter, Tinkerbell. If a square john with a badge hears you yammering, he'll get the idea you're bats.

"Sorry. I just got excited."

As I fumbled for my cell phone, a frantic cry interrupted the conversation in my head.

"Pen! Pen!" Sadie shouted. "Come here!"

Well, lamb chop, if it's at all possible, sounds like things just got a little more exciting.

CHAPTER 4

Ratiocination

While the analyst is necessarily ingenious, the ingenious man is often remarkably incapable of analysis.

—Edgar Allan Poe, "The Murders in the Rue Morgue," 1841

WHEN I RETURNED to the entranceway, rippling red lights were flickering along the wall. The glow came through the still-gaping double doors. A shiny white police car had pulled up to the manor house, emergency lights flashing.

"I'm sorry if I frightened you, Pen," Sadie said. "I saw the lights outside and didn't realize that it was the police. They certainly arrived quickly after you called them."

The cell phone was in my hand, but I hadn't yet pushed the buttons. "I didn't call them."

Two officers stepped out of the squad car, approached the open door. A second vehicle rolled up beside the first. Now four policemen were staring at my aunt and the twisted corpse on the floor.

Sadie hurried forward to meet them. "Thank goodness you've come. Something terrible has happened. My friend, I think he's dead!"

Sadie's hands were shaking, and she was tearful. I wanted to corral my aunt, calm her, but a voice in my head stopped me.

Use your noodle, baby. There's a stiff on the floor. A little opera on your aunt's part will help convince the cops that you're as innocent as a pair of Easter chicks.

"But we *are* innocent," I silently protested. "We certainly didn't do anything wrong."

Step back and look at the fishbowl you're swimming in, doll. The cops net you at the scene of a suspicious death, practically standing over the coffin stuffer. And you didn't even tip the law to the rub-out.

"But I was just about to call the police—"

Someone beat you to it. Possibly even the perp.

That got my attention.

I suddenly remembered the sounds I'd heard earlier on the second floor. Had a killer struck Peter Chesley down after we had left, never guessing we'd return so soon?

"You think Chesley was murdered," I silently said to Jack. "Did you witness anything while I was gone?"

Get a grip, honey. Outside of that fieldstone tomb of mine you call a bookshop, I've got no awareness unless you're around. But we're both on the same frequency. The old-timer couldn't walk, and he didn't fly up those stairs. Did you see an elevator?

"No. And I remember him saying the upper floors were sealed off. . . . Peter Chesley could hardly walk, yet his slipper is sitting halfway up the stairs."

It's a cinch. The perp's setting up the investigators to think gramps's big chill came from an accidental fall.

I wanted to talk more with Jack, but an officer had already moved Sadie into the library. Now his partner, a young man in his twenties, thin-lipped with a jutting chin and prominent Adam's apple, was approaching me. So I shut up. Being seen talking to myself was probably less of a red flag than talking to a ghost, but I didn't want to be caught doing either.

"Thank God you've come, Officer," I said.

Over the man's shoulder, I saw the two other uniformed officers examine Peter Chesley. One of them checked the man's vital signs and shook his head.

Meanwhile, my officer—the name on his tag read DURST—reached into his nylon jacket. He produced a pad and a pen.

"What's your name and your business here?"

"My name is Penelope Thornton-McClure. My aunt, Sadie Thornton, and I were here to visit Mr. Chesley. That's the man on the ground. Peter Chesley."

"You found him that way?" Officer Durst jerked his head to indicate the corpse.

"Well, yes . . ."

Smart cookie, said the ghost. *Tell the truth. And the more often you can keep your answers to one syllable, the better.*

"And that's when you called 911?"

I blinked in surprise. "I didn't call anyone. I was about to call emergency with my cell phone, but you and your partner showed up before I had the chance."

It was Officer Durst's turn to be surprised. "But we were responding to a 911 call at this address. A call of distress, according to dispatch."

That piece of the puzzle certainly didn't fit the scene of an accidental fatal fall. I could see the discrepancy troubled the officer, too.

Join the club, buster! I thought.

Suddenly another voice intruded.

Clam up, Penelope, Jack warned. *This badge is small fry. He's playing for time, doing the old softshoe until the big fish shows.*

I lowered my eyes, brushed my fingers against my forehead. "I'm, ah . . . feeling a little faint," I told the officer. "Can I sit down for a moment?"

"Sure," the officer replied. "I think we can wait until the detective arrives to get your statement."

Good play, baby.

I sank down on a hardwood bench, sitting against a stone wall in the foyer. The seat was cold, the walls were frigid—and since the doors were still wide open, the damp nighttime air was streaming in so the front hall was polar, too. I shivered.

Officer Durst took no notice. He was trying to raise someone on his portable radio. A moment later his partner emerged from the library. Sadie was still in there—where a warm fire crackled in the fireplace. I envied her.

Suddenly there were more lights outside, and sirens, too. I heard tires squeal on the wet pavement. Then the sound of doors opening, slamming shut again. A pair of paramedics rushed in. They were followed by an unkempt, florid-faced man with pale gray eyes and thinning brown hair edged with silver.

The man strolled into the possible crime scene with the casual attentiveness of a man looking for an empty table in a crowded diner. His beige raincoat was unbuttoned; under it, his white cotton shirt was wrinkled and untucked. His tie was too wide to be remotely fashionable, the knot askew under a gold shield that hung from his thick neck by a yellow band. The detective was large, his shoulders wide. He wasn't fat, but, over his belt, a spare tire was evident under his loose shirttails. He stifled a yawn as he approached Officer Durst.

After Durst filled him in, I watched the detective case

the foyer. He stood over Peter Chesley's corpse for a moment, then glanced into the bucket still catching water from the roof. He climbed the stairs, noting the dead man's slipper without touching it. At the top of the stairs I saw him reach into his pocket and draw out a handkerchief. He used the cloth to pick up something—Peter Chesley's cane.

"Jack . . ."

Yeah, I saw it, doll.

He leaned the cane against the tarnished gilt railing. Then the detective moved through an arched doorway on the second floor and out of sight. He was gone for a good fifteen minutes.

During that time, the paramedics had given up trying to revive Peter Chesley. A man from the medical examiner's office arrived and pronounced the man dead. Then everyone stood aside as a young woman from the crime scene unit took pictures of the area.

The detective finally came back downstairs. After another word with Officer Durst and his partner, the detective approached me. I moved to rise, but he gestured for me to remain seated.

"Please, rest. You've had a tough night. My name is Detective Douglas Kroll, Newport Police. I understand your name is Penelope McClure?"

I nodded. Douglas Kroll's voice seemed impossibly soft for a man so large and imposing—but then I thought of Mike Tyson. Pulling aside his coat, Kroll knelt down on one knee in front of me, as if he were about to propose. He pulled out a pad and rested it on his leg.

"Tell me what happened from the beginning, Mrs. McClure."

I told him everything. How we'd come and gone then returned to fetch my forgotten purse. I even mentioned the strange noise I heard while my aunt Sadie and I were visiting, suggesting that perhaps someone was lurking in the house.

To my surprise, Detective Kroll shrugged lethargically. "I was just up there. The place is falling apart. You heard the sound of the storm, the wind, and this dump falling to pieces, that's all."

"Then you think this was an accident?"

The detective looked at me strangely. "What else?"

His tone didn't imply that he was suddenly suspicious— more like I was paranoid to suggest anything else.

"Look, Mrs. McClure. It's pretty clear what happened here. Mr. Chesty there—"

"Ches*ley*," I corrected. "His name was Peter Chesley."

"The *deceased* lost his balance on the stairs."

"But—"

"His cane was at the top of the stairs. You did say that was his cane, correct?"

I nodded. "But Peter told us he hadn't gone up those stairs in a year. He said he was too weak to try."

Kroll shrugged again. "Maybe he wasn't telling you the truth."

"He said he had his bedroom moved down to the first floor," I told him. "Peter said that he was sleeping in a small room off the kitchen."

Douglas Kroll turned his head. Officer Durst was standing nearby. "You hear that, son?" Kroll asked.

"I did, Detective. I found a bedroom, right next to the kitchen."

"See!" I cried. "Why would a man as wealthy as Mr. Chesley sleep in a tiny room next to the kitchen if he could climb the stairs?"

"Why would a wealthy man live in a dump that's falling apart?" Kroll asked, then glanced at his notes. "Anyway, your statement and your aunt's match up." He turned to Durst. "You can bring Ms. Thornton back in."

"What about the 911 call?" I asked. "Officer Durst told me he was responding to a distress call. But I didn't make it. Neither did my aunt."

Detective Kroll nodded. "I already checked with dispatch. The call definitely came from this house. A male voice."

My jaw dropped. "Then the killer was in this house. We might have nearly caught him in the act—"

Detective Kroll squinted. "Now why would you assume that? Look, ma'am," Kroll continued in the most patronizing tone imaginable, "this same kind of thing happened last year to that fellow over at Bellecourt Castle. He was as old as this geezer—I mean, the unfortunate Mr. Chesley, here. The old fellow who owned Bellecourt, well he got away from his handlers and took a walk around the castle. He was suffering from Alzheimer's, experienced a bout of mental confusion—"

This guy knows all about mental confusion, griped Jack.

"—And he tripped on the rocks and broke his neck."

"But who called 911?"

"I'm going to get the transcript of the call, and maybe even a tape the first thing in the morning, but you know what I think?"

I frowned. "No. What?"

"I think the deceased made the call because he felt faint or dizzy," Kroll said with a touch of smugness. "Or maybe he was even feeling the beginning stages of a stroke or heart attack. Then maybe he went upstairs for his pills, or maybe he just got confused. The stairs are wet, the geezer looks shaky to me. Down he came."

Sounds reasonable on his end. But that doesn't make it true.

I was about to argue some more with Kroll when the library door opened. Officer Durst led my aunt out. She hurried to my side.

"Here's my card," Detective Kroll said, thrusting it into my hand. "If you have any questions, give me a call. I have your address and your statements. You can both go home. My department will contact Mr. Chesley's family and notify them of his passing . . ."

Neither of us spoke as we headed for our car. It took a few minutes for me to maneuver around all the emergency vehicles, but I managed. We were through the gate and a mile down the road before Aunt Sadie broke the silence.

"Do you think Peter's fall was an accident?"

"No," I said softly.

"What do you think happened?"

"I . . . I don't know . . . the detective's got a lot of reasonable answers for what happened to him, but I know that I heard someone upstairs. And I just can't believe your friend climbed those stairs under his own power—or called 911 himself, for that matter, unless he was afraid of being attacked and called the police for help."

The vote's unanimous, Jack said. *Gramps didn't die by accident, he was shoved into his coffin.*

"But, Pen, what can we do about it?" Sadie asked.

I squeezed the steering wheel, unhappy to face reality, but the Newport police were all over this case and, to me, Peter Chesley was a virtual stranger. In the end, I had a business to run and a little boy to raise.

"Nothing," I finally told my aunt. "There's nothing to be done."

CHAPTER 5

The Dreamer

All that we see or seem
Is but a dream within a dream.

—Edgar Allan Poe, "A Dream Within a Dream," 1827

LATER THAT NIGHT, buried under a pile of bedcovers, I tried not to lie awake, repenting my decision—and failed.

After Sadie and I had arrived home, I drove our part-time clerk Mina Griffith back to her dorm room at St. Francis College, paying her double-time for baby-sitting Spencer. Finally, well after midnight, I returned home and collapsed.

Now I lay on my mattress, eyes wide. Across the shadowy ceiling, the stripped-down limbs of our hundred-year-old oak became a bacchanal of dancing skeletons. Down the street, the long, tubular chimes, hanging from Mr.

Koh's grocery store awning became a melancholy specter, moaning on the storm's dying wind.

Need a bedtime story, baby?

"Jack?"

Well, it ain't Clark Gable.

I closed my eyes and sighed, happy to hear his voice. "Strange," I whispered.

What?

"I never would have thought there'd be so many things in life more disturbing than talking to a dead man."

Such as?

My eyes opened again. I turned onto my side, punched my pillows, then hugged one to me. "I can't get the image out of my head."

You mean, Peter Chesley's broken old body, lying at the base of the staircase he couldn't climb?

"Don't, Jack."

Don't what?

"Don't push me to pursue this."

You're the one who can't sleep, sister.

"Yes."

But it's not just because of Old Man Chesley, is it?

"No."

Reminds you of another body, doesn't it?

"Yes."

Believe me, baby, I know how it goes.

"He was right there, next to me. His head was on the pillow, sleeping but *alive* . . . and then . . . and then he was sleeping on the concrete."

There was nothing you could do.

"I got up to take care of Spencer, start the coffee . . . I came back and there he was, on the ledge. I called his name, ran to him . . ."

There was nothing you could do.

"You've said that before, Jack, but that's not how I feel."

We've been over this ground already, baby. Your husband

was sick and self-absorbed. He lied to you about seeing his doctor, taking his medication. He verbally abused you, and his family ignored the problem. Then he tried to fly. But the way he treated you, neglected his own son, fired doctors who were trying to help . . . the man wasn't even close to getting wings.

"I was right there tonight, too, Jack. And I couldn't stop it again. I was right there with Mr. Chesley, and I heard that crash upstairs. I knew something was wrong, but I left. I drove away! It was like Calvin all over again. Mr. Chesley was sick. But he was alive. He didn't deserve to die like that. Nobody does."

Baby . . . who do you think you're talking to?

I squeezed my eyes shut. "Sorry, Jack."

Forget it.

"But don't you see?" I tossed and turned again, this time landing on my back. "That's what I'm trying to do . . . forget Chesley, and Calvin . . . forget my brother, my parents. Not the good memories, but the awful pain of missing them, of seeing the life leave their eyes. I keep thinking if enough time goes by, I won't see them dead anymore . . ."

There's no forgetting, honey. Counting my war service, I've seen enough corpses to fill ten Books of the Dead, maybe a whole library, like that crumbling depository of Chesley's Molding Manor.

"Books of the Dead? . . . You know about those?"

I myself had seen one only once, in a museum collection. There were pages and pages of family corpses, dressed in their Sunday best, propped and posed for their daguerreotypes. Medicine being what it was in the nineteenth century, and disease cutting short so many young lives, there were a heartbreaking number of children in that book—babies, young people, men and women in their prime.

Old-timers still had Books of the Dead in my day, Jack said. *Passed on from their parents and grandparents. You know what some of the superstitious rubes believed, don't you?*

"You mean the thing about a photograph of a corpse preserving some part of a person's soul?"

Funny what people make up about things they don't understand.

"I don't suppose you understand why you're still around?"

The room was only slightly chilly, nothing like the refrigerator it had been last winter. Outside, the wind whipped at the sturdy window frames, as if trying to gain entry at the insulated edges. But we'd had a pretty good year financially and had splurged on new windows for the old building. All of a sudden, I felt a whispery touch on my face, as if a ribbon of air had managed to slip into my bedroom and brush my cheek.

I'm around because of you, baby . . .

"Because of me?" I repeated, the feathery touch sending prickles of electricity across my skin. "What do you mean? . . ."

It took a long minute for the ghost to answer.

I don't want to miss your latest line-up of mooks and grifters.

"Come on, Jack. Don't make me laugh."

Why the hell not? Life's short.

I refluffed my pillows. "Apparently not your afterlife."

Cheap shots now, huh?

"That's rich, coming from you."

Listen, lamb chop, you remember the last case we worked on together, that crazy debutramp with the triple-pierced ears, peddling her glorified true confession tale for the cover price of a decent day's wage in my time?

"Sure, I remember. Angel Stark and her true crime book. How could I forget?"

Remember when things were dicey, how I got your mind off your troubles?

"Yes, Jack, but I don't think—"

I got to thinking about those old photos on Chesley's wall . . . the ones next to that creep show of a grandfather clock. They reminded me of another photo . . . it was given to me during a case I worked on back in '46, a missing persons.

"A woman?"

A man. His name was Vincent Tattershawe. When I questioned his fiancée, I honestly didn't have a clue whether the guy had crawled back into a bottle, met with an unfortunate accident, or took a powder with her assets in his pocket. Didn't matter what I thought, though. I couldn't let on to the woman—Dorothy Kerns was her name. I needed as many leads as she could dole out, and I'd gotten marching orders from her brother.

"Marching orders? What kind?"

Dorothy wanted a shamus on the case, but it was her brother who'd hired me. He'd invited me up to his gentleman's club, gave me the once-over, and the okay to get started. Told me he never liked Tattershawe, and he suspected the man hadn't simply "disappeared," but instead had run off with his sister's money. That's why he wanted him found.

Seems Miss Dorothy Kerns had given Tattershawe some lettuce to invest. Now her brother wanted the money back, so he wanted Tattershawe found, but he didn't want his sister to know where the man was. I was supposed to find the guy then let Kerns deal with him.

"Okay, I follow. So what did you do?"

First thing: I interviewed the dame. Baxter Kerns warned me that his sis was this weak thing, full of dread. But, after I talked to her, I could see she was made of sterner stuff. All that anxiousness was only on the surface. Beneath it, I found some fairly solid metal . . . like you, Penelope.

My cheeks warmed. Jack had used my first name *and* bestowed a compliment—not something he did very often.

"You turning sappy on me, Jack?"

Don't get fresh, lamb chop. Leave the cracking wise to yours truly.

"Are we going to partner up again?"

Listen, Penny with the copper hair, you got lucky twice now. But you're still wetter behind the ears than a drowning flounder, so take my advice. Keep your mouth shut and your eyes open . . . after they shut for the night, that is . . . I've got some things to show you . . .

Jack's voice had gotten softer and sweeter, and soon my eyelids felt like velvet Broadway curtains slowly coming down . . .

New York City
October 18, 1946

Dorothy Kerns lived on Fifth Avenue across from Central Park. Her building had a clean granite façade and an impressive lobby with leather divans, modernistic paintings, and that peculiar scent so pervasive after the war: old and new money mixing together in presumable harmony.

Jack presented Miss Kerns's calling card to a middle-aged doorman in dark blue livery, a diminutive man with a big nose, big hands, and a big attitude. He snapped up the card, as full of himself as the people who strolled Fifth's wide, exclusive sidewalks.

Jack waited as the doorman phoned Miss Kerns. When he got the all-clear, Jack moved to the elevator. The inside aviator caged him in and took him up three flights. There were only two apartments on Miss Kerns's expansive floor—but four doors. Each flat had a front door for its residents and their guests and a service door for the help.

Jack rang at Dorothy Kerns's front door, well aware he was a hired man, no better than those going in the back.

A young maid with pinned-up raven hair and peach

cheeks received him with a shy smile. Jack tipped his brim to her, then placed his fedora in her small hands, along with his overcoat.

"Would you like anythin', sir?" Her voice was light and young with traces of an Irish brogue. "Perhaps somethin' to drink?"

"Scotch and water." He might have ordered it neat instead, but he'd had a lot to drink already. Pity, he thought, since he doubted Dorothy Kerns would be serving her guests coffin varnish. This well-heeled dame probably stocked the best tonsil paint around.

"I'm sorry, sir," the young maid said, "but Miss Kerns doesn't allow alcohol in the apartment. Would you care for a lemonade?"

Jack suppressed a shudder. "No, honey. Just bring me one on the city."

"Excuse me?"

"Water. I'll have a glass of water."

"Yes, sir. This way, please."

The maid directed him through a pair of French doors into a grand sitting room, where he was left alone for a good ten minutes. Tall casement windows along the far wall looked out on the mannerly street busy with smart-looking couples, chauffeurs in black livery, valets in overcoats walking family dogs.

It was a different world in this hemisphere—south of Harlem, north of Bowery. You had no hustlers or grifters in this pocket of wealth near the park, no beggars or booze-hounds. Off-duty cops were singing "Danny Boy" in the Irish pubs downtown, not here. And tanked-up clerks and salesmen, wailing about their war wounds, wouldn't be falling down on these sidewalks.

It was a good place for picking innocent cherries, Jack thought, if you were an operator like Vincent Tattershawe.

The maid brought him his water and Jack glanced around the large salon. If heaven had a waiting room,

he figured this would be it. The walls, furniture, and rugs
were all ivory and cream. The fireplace was white marble,
carved with tiny cherubs. Although no fire burned in its
pristine grate, he took a load off on a cloud-colored armchair nearby.

Figurines of crystal lined mirrored shelves and tasteful
paintings graced the walls. French impressionism, if Jack
was guessing right, muted, pastel views of reality.

"Mr. Shepard?"

Jack rose, and a tall woman swept toward him.

Dorothy Kerns was a blonde, but not the kind who have
more fun. She was the fragile type, like a fairy queen, delicate and untouchable, friable as a frozen bird.

From the "spinster" picture her brother had painted,
Jack practically expected a matronly dame with graying
hair and grandma shawl, a pair of knitting needles in her
arthritic hands. Dorothy wasn't even close. Yes, her lips
were too thin, her skin too pale, and her blue eyes set far-
ther apart than Great Neck and Newark; but she had high
cheekbones, intelligence in her gaze, and only the faintest
hint of wrinkles at the edges of her mouth.

No man could deny she was a striking woman—not a
raving beauty by any stretch, but nothing close to her
brother's narrow view of her. But then, Jack had noticed
how often family members viewed each other through out-
of-date glasses.

"Please excuse me for not greeting you when you arrived." Dorothy held out her hand. "To be perfectly honest,
I was in my robe and needed to change."

Jack had expected a dame like her to show up in a prim
dress or skirt. But her long legs were clad in flowing brown
slacks, a thin leather belt circling her trim waist. She wore
a white silk blouse, and a string of pearls around her slender neck, showed to advantage by upswept hair.

"Miss Kerns." He lightly took her hand, felt as if he

were trying to grasp a sparrow without crushing its delicate bones. "I appreciate your making time for me tonight."

Jack tried to release the bird, but Miss Kerns held on tight—and with surprising strength. "You must find Vincent for me, Mr. Shepard. Promise me you'll find him."

Jack could see the sincerity in her wide-set eyes. They were shining and he realized why—they were wet with unshed tears.

"I'll try to help," Jack replied and used his left hand to diplomatically pry loose his right.

Dorothy turned away, recovering herself. She dabbed at her eyes with a handkerchief she'd pulled from her pants pocket. "Won't you sit down?"

Jack took a load off again—in the same armchair by the cold fireplace. Miss Kerns sat in the chair opposite, crossed her long limbs. Her young maid brought in a tray with a tea service.

"Tell me honestly, Miss Kerns. What do you think happened to your fiancé?" Jack asked after the maid departed. "Another woman? Or maybe he was the victim of a fast money scam gone wrong? Do you think maybe he lost your investment and was ashamed to face you?"

"I would like to believe it is none of those things, but the alternative is no better. Vincent had a drinking problem, you see."

"You think he crawled into a bottle?"

"He told me he would never drink again. That was my condition for our engagement. My brother . . . he doesn't like Vincent, you know?"

"I got that impression. How did you two meet, anyway?"

"At a big New Year's Eve party last year. Vincent hadn't been Stateside long. He'd been stationed in Europe—"

"Army?"

"Yes, he'd been badly wounded after D-Day, during combat in the hedgerow country—"

Jack winced.

"You were there, Mr. Shepard?"

"Not in that action. But I knew about the losses. It was a real meat grinder. I pushed through Carentan to Cherbourg, that's where the U.S. set up her regional HQ—uh, headquarters."

Dorothy presented a weak smile. "I know what HQ means, Mr. Shepard. My late fiancé, my first one, had written me for years from the front. He'd lost his life in the same battle where Vincent lost half his left arm."

She paused and glanced at the dark window, as if looking for a memory.

"When I first met Vincent, at that New Year's Eve party, and discovered he'd been in the same action that had killed Gabriel, he and I began to talk. But not like people usually talk at social gatherings. We began early in the evening and didn't stop until after breakfast the next morning. I don't suppose you know how that can go, Mr. Shepard? Talking all night when you first fall in love?"

Jack shifted uncomfortably, thought of Sally. For a moment, in a dream, he'd seen a future with her, a home and family. But he'd slept too long. And when he finally awoke, Sally Archer was long gone.

"I know something about it, miss. Go on."

"Well, we did fall in love that first night, and it deepened as the weeks and months went by. He asked me to marry him on my birthday in June. We set a date to be married next year—June 1947—although my brother raised objections."

"So why didn't you just take off with Vincent if you loved him and your brother was so disapproving? You've got your own money, right?"

"I . . . only have a little bit left now. I gave Vincent the bulk of my inheritance to invest."

"Yeah, about that . . . I understand Vincent could earn a dollar?"

"Yes, that's right. Before the war, he made a great deal of money by investing in steel. He saw what was coming, you see? And it paid off for him. And I was sure it would again."

"So, you gave a drunk all your money . . . to invest?" Jack asked.

"He's not a drunk. Not anymore. You see, about a month ago, Vincent came upon some information about a lucrative investment in a company that manufactures air conditioners."

"Air conditioners?" Jack jotted that down. "Do you know the name?"

"Ogden Heating and Cooling Company. They're located in the South. Vincent says air-conditioning's going to transform that entire region. He got a tip that Ogden was going to be bought by a much bigger corporation. He believed he could double my money in less than a year."

"But he disappeared? With no word on your money or what he did with it?"

"I love him, Mr. Shepard. And I trust him. You wouldn't understand."

"No, I guess not."

Miss Kerns leaned forward, her eyes shining, the unshed tears threatening once again to fall. "Find him, please, Mr. Shepard. I miss him so, you see."

She was suffering so visibly that Jack wished she were right—though he believed in his heart that the woman had been taken, or her fiancé had fallen down a bottle again and something ugly had happened to him.

Jack got more information from Dorothy, standard stuff like where Tattershawe worked, where he lived, any known friends or relatives—all of whom, *no surprise*, she'd already contacted and gotten bupkus as to the man's whereabouts.

"One last thing," Jack said, glancing around the large salon. "Do you have a recent photo?"

Dorothy rose and walked out of the room. When she returned, she handed Jack a photo of Vincent in an oval frame about the size of his palm.

"Take this," she said. "It's hard for me to look at now anyway."

Jack nodded, encouraged by Dorothy's admission. Baxter Kerns had asked that Vincent's whereabouts be kept a secret from his sister. Jack wasn't all that keen on lying to the lady; but if she were angry at her fiancé, then some part of her probably knew she'd been played.

"You mean you can't stand to look at his face?" Jack pressed. "You're that steamed?"

"Not at all. I have other photos of Vincent that provide me with much happier memories. This one's the last gift he gave me. He sent it to me just before he disappeared."

Jack frowned at that response then studied the picture he'd been given. Like all black-and-white portraits, the subject was a deceptive contrast of shadows and light, a collection of shaded traits. In this incarnation, Tattershawe appeared handsome: a rectangular kisser with a long forehead, solid jawline, dark hair, and dark eyes.

Jack tucked the oval frame in his pocket, wishing someone would invent the camera that could show you whether or not a man had a dark heart.

With no more questions for Dorothy Kerns, Jack bid her goodnight, and stepped into the building's hallway. As he waited for the elevator, he heard a door opening behind him. It was the service door to Miss Kerns's luxury apartment. The young Irish maid emerged in a plain overcoat, a hand-knitted hat, and scarf. She nodded politely and waited with Jack for the elevator to arrive.

"Miss Kerns must be difficult to work for," Jack fished. "I'll bet she can be very demanding."

"Oh, no, sir. She's the sweetest woman in the world. This is the latest I've ever worked for her, and she felt so bad about asking me to stay, she gave me car fare to get home."

Jack raised an eyebrow. "You're not a live-in?"

I raised an eyebrow. "Don't worry, kiddo, I'm only going to unlock the front door for you. I'll stay out of sight."

Spencer nodded, his sense of relief visible. Together we walked down the stairs. "Do you have your Reader's Notebook?"

"Duh! I worked on that all summer, Mom. Do you think I'd actually forget it now?"

"Apparently not," I replied as we crossed the empty bookstore's main aisle.

The school encouraged reading over the summer by running a contest every year. The student who read the most books would be awarded a grand prize. Spencer had completely filled one spiral-bound notebook with titles, authors, and short descriptions of every story he'd read.

He had nothing on poor Peter Chesley with his fifty volumes, but in my view Spencer's work had been just as diligent and enthusiastic.

Of course, living above a bookstore might be seen as a blatant advantage, but I didn't allow him to read a book in our store and put it back on the shelf. I wanted Spencer to get comfortable using the local library and took him there regularly to check out new stacks of books.

When we reached the front door, I unlocked it. "Your first day for the new school year." I smiled. "Good luck."

Spencer returned my smile, then darted across the sidewalk. I heard Danny Keenan and a few of my son's other new friends excitedly shout his name when he entered the bus and I felt my own sense of relief.

My son had gone from a morose little boy who missed his father to a bright and alive young man. He no longer had nightmares about my leaving him like his daddy did. He hardly mentioned missing Calvin anymore.

The early days after his father's suicide had been awful, and for a long time, I questioned the decisions I was making. But now I was convinced that moving away from New York City and back to Quindicott had benefited Spencer's peace of mind. It had been the right thing to do—for both of us.

I now had about fifty minutes before our bookstore was scheduled to open, and I went back upstairs to check on my aunt. She was still sleeping. This was unusual for Sadie, who was always the early riser, but considering the previous night's events, it made me happy to see her get some much-needed rest.

Since I had a little time, I decided to slip on a jacket and head down the block to Cooper Family Bakery for a nosh of something special. The oatmeal was warm but hardly satisfying—and although my size fourteen jeans certainly could have been looser, I sorely needed the fresh air as much as the sugar rush. On the way, I stopped at Koh's Grocery and bought a *Providence Journal*.

It took me a few minutes before I found a small item about the accidental death of Peter Chesley. The sparse article simply stated he'd "fallen in his home" after "a long illness." There were no surprises here. It was clear to me that Detective Kroll had made up his mind before he'd even arrived at the mansion. But I took a deep breath and told myself to stop thinking about it.

"This is Kroll's case now," I muttered, "not mine."

When I got to the bakery, I saw that half the mothers in Quindicott had gotten the same idea I had—send the children off to school and head over to Cooper's. There was actually a line out the door. I waved to a few mothers who were also good Buy the Book customers.

"Penelope, did you get the new Patricia Cornwell in yet?"

It was Susan Keenan, the thirtysomething mother of Danny, one of Spencer's new friends. Danny had two siblings: seven-year-old Maura, who was in school at the moment; and two-year-old Tommy, who was sleeping in a stroller by his mother's side.

"It's in, Sue," I called to her, "stop by anytime."

"Come on, come on, move along ladies," a man's voice

boomed from the center of the perfumed mob. "Let me out of the pretty store and one of you can get in!"

Holding high his cup of steaming-hot coffee, Seymour Tarnish struggled to escape the packed bakery. As the women moved aside, I could see into the store. Behind the counter, Linda Cooper-Logan looked harried.

She wore a rainbow bandana over her short, spiky, platinum blonde hair (she'd had a thing for Annie Lennox since we were kids back in the eighties), and her husband Milner Logan (fan of noir thrillers) was nowhere in sight. My guess—the talented quarter-blood Narragansett Native American was in the back, doing his best to whip up more of those famous fresh, hot doughnuts that people drove from miles around to snag.

"Hey, Pen." Seymour looked down at me with a crooked smile on his round face. He jerked his head in the direction of the bakery. "If you're looking to buck *that* crowd, beware. Hungry housewives cruising for pastry are a dangerous breed. I almost lost my arm putting cream in my coffee."

(What Seymour actually said was *"almust lahst mah aahm"*—using the typical dropped R's and drawn out vowels of our "Roe Dyelin" patois. We might be the smallest state in the Union but, by golly, we've got a sizable accent. Sadie speaks with the accent, too, along with most of the people here in Quindicott. I lost mine somewhere between college and living in New York although the occasional slip—e.g., "You can never find pahkin' in this town!"—just can't be helped.)

Not exactly resplendent in his natty blue postman's uniform with matching coat, his hat askew, Seymour was obviously on his way to his day job.

Although thickwaisted, our big, tactless, fortysomething mailman wasn't always thickheaded. He'd won quite a bit of money on *Jeopardy!* a few years back and ever since, the town had its own local celebrity. It was the main reason the people on Seymour's mail route put up with him. Still, their descriptions of the man spanned from "irascible" to "obnoxious," depending on how diplomatic they were in choosing adjectives.

Seymour took a loud slurp from his steaming cup and smacked his lips. "Man, I needed that!"

"Late night?" I asked, enviously sniffing the aroma of his freshly brewed French roast.

"The haunted house is open right up until midnight through Halloween. I parked my ice cream truck on Green Apple Road at noon on Sunday and got home at one A.M. Cleaned up, though."

One of the things Seymour did with his *Jeopardy!* winnings was purchase an ice cream truck. It had been his lifelong dream to become Quindicott's one and only roving ice cream man (go figure), which he now was on evenings and weekends. The other thing he did with his prize money was purchase old pulps, usually collector's items, which is why Buy the Book counted him as one of its most consistent (and, yes, at times, compulsive) customers.

After another gulp of coffee, Seymour gave me the fish eye. "Man you look wasted, Pen," he observed, ever the charmer. "You got insomnia?"

"I had a late night, too. Sadie and I drove over to Newport and bought some items from a collector."

Set wide apart, Seymour's blue eyes gave his regular features an air of perpetual surprise. Now those eyes bulged like a hungry bug. "More swag! What'cha got? Anything hot and collectable?"

I mentioned the Phelps editions of Poe. Seymour shrugged.

"We also acquired an 1807 first edition of Thomas Paine's *An Examination of the Passages in the New Testament.*"

Seymour's bugging eyes quickly glazed over. "Not for me. But I'm sure your pal Brainert will wet his academic pants over them. I'm more interested in that 1931 issue of

Oriental Stories your aunt has been tracking down for me. Any sign of it?"

"Not yet. We'll keep you posted."

Seymour glanced at his watch. "Well, it's starting time for the day job. Back to the stamp mines. If I'm late again my supervisor will go postal for sure. See ya later."

With Seymour gone, I glanced at the crowd around Cooper's one last time. If anything, the line had gotten longer. Doughnutless and filled with sugary longing, I headed back to brew my own pot of coffee and open the store.

WHEN I UNLOCKED the front door at ten o'clock, there were a few more customers than I expected. They were mothers, mostly, out and about after sending their little ones off to school. They finally saw some quiet time ahead and were buying up new releases.

I rang up purchases, including Sue Keenan's new Cornwell, and sorted the mail, pointedly ignoring the three cardboard boxes of books neatly stacked behind the counter—the books we'd brought back from Peter Chesley's mansion in Newport the night before. At quarter to eleven, a local youth named Garfield Platt reported for duty.

"You're early," I noted.

Garfield shrugged and hung up his coat. "I left an hour early on Friday, remember Mrs. McClure? I have an hour to make up."

"Good. The first thing you can do is carry those boxes to the storage room. Put them next to Sadie's desk. And be careful, those volumes are quite valuable."

"Can do, Mrs. McClure."

Young Mr. Platt was our newest employee, hired because Mina could only work weekends due to her college classes. Unlike Mina, Garfield had disliked college and cut the experience short. He returned to Quindicott, and moved back in with his parents. He claimed he was making some money off a Web site he ran out of his home—doing what, I didn't ask, nor did he volunteer that information—but Garfield needed more capital to move into his own place, so he worked two part-time gigs. He spent weekday afternoons and early evenings at Buy the Book, and the rest of the night doing odd jobs at the twenty-four-hour gas station out on the highway, finishing up at two A.M. The kid was motivated, I had to give him that.

Though Quindicott was a small town, I'd never met and didn't know Garfield's parents, Mr. and Mrs. Edmund Platt. They didn't attend our church and they didn't mix socially with anyone I knew in the community, though they'd lived here for over two decades.

Garfield wasn't as reclusive as his folks; in fact, he was outgoing, well-spoken, and possessed a wry sense of humor that made him fun to have in the store. Sadie and I had figured that out the day of his impromptu job interview.

It was a breezy autumn day in early September, a little over a month ago. I'd hung a HELP WANTED sign at the same time that I placed the new Dan Brown hardcover in the "hot picks" slot in the store window display.

Garfield blew in with a gust of wind fifteen minutes later. The cool, dry air had bristled his curly brown hair and spiked his full beard. He stood an inch shorter than me—though taller than my bantamweight aunt—with a broad-shouldered build and a bright, direct gaze.

"My name is Garfield Platt. I've come to apply for the job," he announced, reaching out to shake my hand.

Garfield's voice rose a notch on the last word, so I thought he was asking a question. That miscommunication, and his lunge across the counter to shake my hand rattled me.

"Excuse me?" I replied, stepping backward.

"I think he's applying for the job," Sadie explained.

Garfield nodded, eyes unblinking. "I'd like to work here,

if you'll hire me. I have no experience and I just flunked out of college. But I read mysteries and I know authors, so I can help your customers find the titles they're looking for. And I can count and make change. Seeing this is a commercial enterprise, I'd say that's a plus."

My aunt and I exchanged glances.

"Have you ever worked retail? Do you have experience dealing with the public?" Sadie asked.

Garfield stared blankly. "None at all."

"Can you use a cash register?" I asked.

For a moment Garfield had that look of a deer before it ends up on the hood of a fast-moving car. Then he cleared his throat.

"Look," he said. "I have no useful skills—beyond computers, which are kind of like my hobby. I know my prospects don't seem bright at the moment. In fact, I probably look like a total loser to you and everybody else. Even my parents aren't proud of me, although, compared to my ex-con brother, I'm golden. But I'll learn fast, show up on time, and won't bug you for a raise once a month, so what do you think?"

Sadie and I burst out laughing—and hired the guy on the spot.

"These books smell old," Garfield observed as he lifted the final box. "Do you think they could be older than the Apple Mac I use for a doorstop?"

"Yes," I replied. "But, unlike your doorstop, I'm betting books will never become an obsolete tool; otherwise, we're both out of a job."

"Do you want me to unpack them?"

"Sure, Garfield. That would be great. Just stack them on Sadie's desk. But—"

"I know, I know. I'll be real careful."

Garfield was only gone a moment when I heard the chimes ringing over the front door. My oldest friend, J. Brainert Parker, rushed to the counter where I stood.

"Pen! I understand you've got a Phelps Poe in the store. Why didn't you inform me at once?" His voice was practically shrill with excitement.

"Ah," I said calmly, "so your mail was delivered."

J. Brainert Parker (the J. was for Jarvis, a name no one dared call him on pain of a polysyllabic tongue-lashing) was an assistant professor of English Literature at St. Francis College. Like me, he was in his early thirties. He was also exceedingly well read.

Today his slight build was clad in one of his typical preppy ensembles—a salmon-colored V-neck over a pressed white button-down, brown corduroy slacks, and polished penny loafers, with a heavily lined J. Crew windbreaker tossed on to combat the fall chill. I could see he wasn't teaching today because he was sans tie (bow or any other kind). His straight brown hair was neatly trimmed, the bangs, which he could never decide what to do with, were today slicked back off the forehead of his patrician face.

"Yes, yes, it's true," Brainert conceded. "Seymour delivered the news with the gas bill. So which volume is it? Or do you have more than one."

"I believe it's a complete set."

"Gad! Now I *must* see them. What's their condition? How much are they worth?"

"A lot, I suspect. But the problem is . . ." I sighed. "Well, I feel a little funny about the whole deal now."

Brainert blinked. "Whatever do you mean, Pen? You are *selling* them, aren't you?"

"Well—"

I was about to tell Brainert all about last night, when Garfield flew out of the storage room, interrupting us.

"Mrs. McClure! Mrs. McClure!" he cried, waving around a bundle of yellowed papers. "I found these in one of those boxes of books. Letters, or papers, or something. The stuff 's really old, too."

Brainert's eyes widened. "Is he speaking about the Phelps editions?"

I nodded, opened my mouth to speak, and the chimes rang over the front door once again.

The man who entered was such a striking figure, we all stared for a long rude moment. Tall as Lincoln and rail thin, the man's short-cropped hair was completely silver, a stark contrast against his black suit and overcoat. He strode across the store and up to the counter, carrying a shiny black attaché case in one pale, long-fingered hand.

"Madame. Are you the proprietor of this establishment?"

His French accent was somewhat pronounced, but I had no trouble understanding him.

"Yes, I am. May I help—"

"I am Rene Montour. You are certainly familiar with my name, are you not?"

"Hello, Rene. I, um . . . w-well—"

He did not smile, nor did he acknowledge my clumsy stammering. Instead, the man frowned down at me, cutting me off with his even baritone. "I believe you have some property that belongs to my client. I am here to retrieve it posthaste."

"Excuse me?" I replied.

"I am referring, of course, to a certain consignment of rare and valuable books."

CHAPTER 7

The Accidentally Purloined Letter

He was a guy who talked with commas, like a heavy
novel.

—Raymond Chandler, *The Long Goodbye,* 1953

WHILE I STOOD flabbergasted in front of the stranger,
looking less than brilliant, my aunt arrived, looking sharp
as a tack in a navy pantsuit, her reading glasses dangling
from a sterling silver chain.

"Mr. Montour! I'm so happy to meet you at last."

She crossed the selling floor with her hand extended, her
features appearing rested despite our harrowing evening.
"I'm Sadie Thornton. You and I have exchanged so many
e-mails, I feel as if I know you."

Unfortunately, my aunt's welcoming smile did little to
thaw Mr. Montour's chilly countenance. He ignored her

proffered hand, bowed stiffly instead. Unperturbed, Sadie gracefully withdrew her hand.

While Montour did cut a striking figure—from a distance—he was not particularly attractive up close, unless your taste ran toward ghouls. His flesh was pale pink against the night-black clothing, his face narrow with high cheekbones. Under a pair of circular, black-rimmed glasses his eyes were dark pits. Pencil-thin sideburns—white like his hair—reached from his ears to the hollow of his cheeks.

"I see you've met my niece, Penelope," Sadie said. "And this fellow here is J. Brainert Parker, a professor at St. Francis College."

The man jerked his head in a curt gesture I assumed to be a nod of acknowledgment.

"Mr. Montour has come from Montreal, Canada," she informed me, "to accept delivery of a set of very valuable first editions. Isn't that right?"

"Correct," he replied.

Recovering from my shock, I realized Rene Montour's arrival had absolutely nothing to do with Peter Chesley's consignment. Montour was actually expected—just early. I quickly remembered that a pickup was scheduled for later this week, but not under the name of *Rene* Montour.

Rene was obviously representing his uncle, Jacques Montour, a Quebec-based, French-Canadian investment banker and collector of twentieth-century first editions—and I mentally kicked myself for not making the connection faster. As his uncle's representative, Rene was here to take possession of a cache of Raymond Chandler rarities assembled by Sadie over the past several years.

"The arrangements were finalized months ago," Mr. Montour said. "The books were to be made ready for my arrival this week, as I understood it; and, all the details have been worked out, therefore, I, of course, trust there will be no problem."

All that yammering is giving me a headache where I don't have one—a head, that is . . .

It was Jack Shepard, intruding into my thoughts for the first time today.

"Good morning, Jack."

"Fortunately my business in New York City ended prematurely," Mr. Montour continued. "So I rented an automobile and drove to Quindicott in order to secure the consignment for my uncle, who, as you might imagine, is very eager to make the acquisition."

I'll bet this squealing rattletrap is a high-priced mouthpiece. They all get paid by the word, like some low-rent pulp writer. Either that or Bela Lugosi here is really a mortician.

Mr. Montour's eyes narrowed distrustfully. "I am, of course, well aware that my arrival was originally scheduled for Wednesday," he said. "But as I said, my work was finished in New York City, and, as an attorney, my time is quite valuable."

Didn't I call it?!

"Therefore, because the price has been agreed upon and the books in question have been paid for, I decided it was in everyone's mutual interest to make the journey to New England prematurely, in order to facilitate the transaction." One of Montour's long-fingered hands adjusted the rim of his black glasses. "I trust my early arrival has not inconvenienced you, or caused any delay in the culmination of our arrangement."

The room was silent for a moment, until Sadie realized Mr. Montour had finally stopped talking.

"No, not at all," she replied. "Your arrival does not trouble us in the least." She touched the man's arm. "If you'll come with me, I will show you the books in question. I'm sure you'll find their condition acceptable. After that, we'll pack your purchase and draw up a receipt."

As she led Mr. Montour to the storage room, Sadie called to me over her shoulder. "Could you help us, Pen?"

•

Brainert spoke up next.

"Excuse me. Since you're heading to the back room, could I tag along and check out the Phelps editions you've been hiding? I'm dying to see them."

Rene Montour's head jerked around, and he flashed Brainert an intense glare. "Do you mean the Eugene Phelps volumes of Edgar Allan Poe?"

Brainert arched an eyebrow. "Apparently they have a complete set."

Montour cleared his throat. "Do you have a buyer?" he asked, feigning only a mild interest. But the lawyer's earlier eagerness had already tipped his hand.

Sadie, bless her little entrepreneurial heart, laid it on thick. "Well, we've only *just* acquired the editions. We haven't even accessed their condition and salability. So I really can't say if we'll be offering them."

"In the meantime, it won't hurt to take a look," Brainert interjected. "Shall we go?"

Taking the lead, Brainert hustled my aunt and Mr. Montour to the storeroom. I faced Garfield. "Take over the register, please."

"But what about this stuff?" He displayed the bundle of old papers in his hand.

"Put them under the register, and keep them out of sight. I'll take a look later," I said, then hurried to catch up with the others.

The storage room was located through the store's newly established Community Events space, part of our expansion into the adjoining storefront, which actually had been part of the store's original space before the 1950s. The large room had exposed fieldstone walls, a restored parquet floor, and renovated restroom facilities. Padded folding chairs were stacked at one end beside a few floor displays and standees that we'd used to decorate the room during our last author appearance.

We moved through the empty space to a short hallway

where the restrooms were located, then through another door that led to the storage room. "Room" was a misnomer, because though the space was fairly large it was definitely *not* roomy. Much of the area was dominated by crates of inventory. We kept our own files back here, and I had boxes of Jack's old case files here, as well (the reason I had them was a story in itself, but then, I've told that tale already).

There was an old wooden desk, which Sadie used to examine the collectable books that came into the shop. On it was a laptop computer she used to hammer out descriptions for Buy the Book's online catalog.

As instructed, Garfield had unpacked Peter Chesley's consignment and laid the old volumes on the desk—except for the folios, which were too large to fit, so he'd left them in the box. The irregularly-shaped Phelps books occupied the center of the desk, next to the 1807 edition of Thomas Paine.

On a shelf against the opposite wall, the Raymond Chandler first editions awaited Rene Montour's inspection. They were arranged neatly, each volume sealed in a clear Mylar sheath. Generally the hardcovers were in good condition, with some fraying on the dust covers and, of course, some yellowing of the acid-based paper.

It took only a few minutes for Rene Montour to accept delivery of the Chandlers. He looked at each volume, took one or two of them out of the Mylar, and nodded in satisfaction.

Then, while Sadie and I spent the next fifteen minutes carefully boxing up the Chandlers and surrounding them with a protective layer of foam popcorn, Montour joined Brainert in examining the Eugene Phelps editions. The two men spoke in hushed tones about the books, as if they were discussing religious philosophy.

"Do you think Mr. Montour will make an offer for the Phelps set?" Sadie asked in a whisper.

"I don't know."

I still wasn't sure how I felt about selling any of Chesley's books. But I could tell by the way Sadie was watching Montour that she didn't share my uncertainty. Of course, she was the one who'd had the long-standing relationship with Peter Chesley.

"He's using his cell phone," Sadie whispered excitedly a few minutes later. "Maybe he's calling his uncle and he'll make an offer."

Brainert was close enough to hear Rene Montour's conversation. I tried waving him over to tell me what he was hearing, but my old friend didn't seem to notice my gestures.

Save your sign language show, baby. Your overeducated pal isn't picking up your broadcast. He's too busy jazzing over that musty pile of old kindling.

"What is the lawyer saying, Jack?" I asked.

The frog's jawing about those moldy doorstops he's been looking at. He's talking dough, too, with some high-flying top hat on the other end of that Dick Tracy wrist radio.

Rene Montour closed his cell phone. He turned his back on the Phelps books and approached Sadie.

"We're almost done here, Mr. Montour," she said.

"Excellent," he replied. Montour paused, then cleared his throat. "About those Phelps editions. My client is very interested in one of the volumes, but, unfortunately, he is not in the market for a complete set."

I stepped forward, cleared my own throat. "I'm not sure we should break up the set—"

"Oh, nonsense," Sadie interrupted. "You know very well the former owner gave us no stipulations as to how these books should be sold. What volume is your client interested in, Mr. Montour?"

"Specifically volume twelve, *The Poetic Principal*," he replied. "I have examined the volume in question and the condition is . . . acceptable—"

"It's practically mint," Sadie countered, cutting him off.

"Indeed," Montour murmured.

I could see him mentally upping his offer.

"I am prepared to advance a considerable sum for this single book," he said. "I understand that the volume in question is quite rare, but I believe that you will find my client's preemptive offer to be well above market value. As you know, my client is always generous, always fair, and—"

Sadie raised her hand. "Excuse me, Mr. Montour. But what *is* your client's offer?"

"Eight thousand U.S. dollars, and not a penny more."

Brainert's jaw dropped. Sadie blinked.

Eight thousand clams for a putrid old tome! Jack cried so forcefully in my head I felt my face twitch. *I wouldn't give you a frayed Washington for that used pile of pulp. Since when is outhouse paper worth a cool eight large?*

I was too overwhelmed by the offer to reply to Jack's less-than-tactful query. My aunt and I exchanged glances; and I realized at that moment that everyone—even me—had her price.

"Sold!" we cried in unison.

CHAPTER 8

Literary Treasure

It was a type of letter well calculated to cause uneasiness . . .

—Erle Stanley Gardner, "Hell's Kettle," 1930

SADIE LED RENE Montour to the register, where a simple credit-card transaction more than doubled Buy the Book's bank account (not counting sales tax, of course).

I stayed behind in the storage room and wrapped up the Poe volume in a sheath of protective, acid-free Mylar, then packed it in its own small box, surrounding it with a blizzard of foam peanuts, which I dumped from a fifty-gallon bag.

Sadie came back to see if I needed any help.

And that's when my conscience kicked in again.

"Aunt Sadie, are you sure we're doing the right thing, selling off Mr. Chesley's books?"

"Dear, I knew Peter very well at one time, and I remember every word he said to me last night. He called us to his place to take these books and sell them. Now that he's gone, they're ours."

My aunt wasn't wrong. The old man's last wishes had been clear enough when we'd taken possession of the lot: *"And if my illness should overtake me, please consider them yours. Willed to you. A gift."*

"He wanted us to have them," Sadie declared. "He loved this store, Pen, and these books will help to keep it financially viable. That's a wonderful legacy for Peter, and I'm committed to seeing it happen."

I sighed and nodded, promising not to fret anymore—at least, not in front of Sadie. When I carried the box to the front, everyone had gathered at the counter, including Seymour Tarnish. By now, he'd finished his mail route and had come to the store, hunting down Brainert.

I handed the box to Garfield. He laid it atop the box that held the Chandler first editions. With Rene Montour in the lead, he hauled the lot out to the man's maroon rental car parked at the curb. They returned a few minutes later.

"Well, this has been a very profitable day for us both, has it not?" Rene said, exhibiting what was, as far as I could tell, his first smile of the day. Then he addressed us all. "I wonder . . . Can anyone recommend a local hotel? Perhaps one with a decent restaurant nearby."

"The Finch Inn," Aunt Sadie replied. "It's a beautiful Victorian mansion on Quindicott Pond that's been converted into a bed and breakfast. The owner, Fiona Finch, takes great pride in her establishment, and there's a brand-new restaurant on the grounds that is absolutely fabulous."

"Fiona's place is fine if you've got money to burn," our newly arrived mailman piped up. "But there's also Comfy-Time Motel on the highway. The place is dirt-cheap and you have your choice of eats. There's a McDonald's and

Wendy's at the next rest stop. I'd avoid The House of Pizza, though. It's a pesthole."

Rene Montour grimaced in absolute horror.

So did Sadie.

"I'll call Fiona right away, Mr. Montour," she promised, pushing Seymour none too gently out of the way as she lunged for the phone behind the counter. "I'm sure she'll have a beautiful room waiting."

A few minutes later, Rene Montour left the store with directions to the Finch Inn. When he was gone, Sadie let out a long breath and collapsed against the counter. I knew how she felt. It wasn't every day our store raked in a month's grosses on one customer!

You had your chance and folded, Jack Shepard cracked. *Nanook of the North just paid eight grand for a penny's worth of scrap paper. With a brain that dusty, you could have probably peddled the sappy shill the deed to the Brooklyn Bridge!*

"Quiet, Jack!" I thought. Out loud I said, "Not a bad day's work."

"A very lucrative sale," Brainert observed. "But it was a shame you had to break up the Phelps editions. That's the first time I've seen all thirteen volumes together. Not even the university collection has a complete set."

Brainert's observation brought Sadie and I down to earth. Again I felt a little trepidation over the Chesley consignment.

"It *was* a shame to break up the set," Sadie said with a sigh. "But Mr. Montour's offer was too good to pass up. Believe me, I know the market. And that offer was thousands above the book's current value."

"Perhaps he was too eager," Brainert said.

Seymour scoffed. "If I had the dough-rey-mee, I'd pay two grand for that issue of *Oriental Stories* I've been looking for. What's money good for, except to buy the stuff you need?"

Brainert sniffed. "Who *needs* a crumbling pulp magazine?"

"You don't know collectors," Seymour shot back. "Some of them would kill for a hot collectable."

Seymour's comment gave me pause. And I began to wonder about Peter Chesley again. But not about whether we should sell his books.

Chesley hadn't seen Sadie in ten years, yet he'd urgently insisted that we make the drive to his mansion last night, despite the weather—as if the consignment were a matter of life and . . .

I frowned, not wanting to agonize about Peter Chesley's fate anymore. Last night, I had made the decision to stay out of it. But questions kept pricking my conscience; and, like the proverbial dog with a bone, I couldn't stop myself from gnawing away—

Chesley had inherited the vast old Prospero House library years ago, yet he'd suddenly decided to sell a particular part of it. Why?

The old man demanded, almost to the point of rudeness, that we take the rare books with us last night rather than send Garfield to pick them up in the morning. As frail and exhausted as he was, he even helped Sadie pack them all up. What was the urgency?

And the way he'd reacted to that crash upstairs still bothered me. Chesley seemed alarmed at first, but he'd blocked my path the moment I'd moved to investigate the sound. Now I wondered whether Chesley truly feared I would have an accident in the unstable upper floors. Or was he worried I'd run into the person that he'd known was up there already, the very person who may have murdered him?

I closed my eyes a moment, realizing how my train of thought would sound to the authorities. I had an old friend on the Quindicott police force. But as nice a guy as Officer

Eddie Franzetti was, he'd probably treat me just like Detective Kroll. He'd think I was paranoid, overly imaginative, or even a little bit crazy—

But you're not, Jack whispered.

"Excuse me, Mrs. McClure. I don't want to bother you, but what about these old papers?" Garfield asked.

"Oh, yes. I almost forgot."

Sadie turned to Garfield. "What old papers?"

Our part-time clerk reached under the register and produced the yellowing bundle. There were several identical envelopes stuffed with handwritten pages, the whole thing tied together by a strip of faded black ribbon.

"I found them with those old Poe books," Garfield explained. "They were sandwiched between two of the volumes. I figured they'd been there a long time, because the ribbon was stuck to the cover of one volume like glue."

"Yes," Brainert said, fingering the ribbon. "There's sealing wax on the knot. It must have melted and adhered to the book."

Brainert took the bundle and gently set it down on the counter. He very carefully crumbled away the rest of the wax with his fingers. Then Brainert untied the single knot and separated the bundle. There were three muslin envelopes of high-quality stock. The paper crinkled as Brainert pulled the handwritten pages out of one envelope and carefully unfolded the first page.

The papers themselves were on personal stationery, a name and address spelled out in gilded letters on top: "Miles Milton Chesley, Roderick Road, Newport." The scribbling underneath, rendered in fading black ink, appeared small and tight, and it filled both sides of each sheet of paper.

Brainert laid the letter flat and stooped over it. He squinted in concentration as he deciphered the handwriting.

"These . . . These aren't letters," he said.

"Let me guess." Seymour laughed. "It's a laundry list."

Brainert ignored the quip. "Eugene Phelps is mentioned here. He's the fellow who published the Phelps editions and— *Hello!*"

Brainert suddenly fell silent, his lips moving as he continued to read.

"Come on, Brainiac, spill!" Seymour pressed. "It's a map to a hidden treasure, right?"

Brainert straightened his posture, his expression a combination of shock, surprise, and delight. He glanced at Seymour, then the rest of us. "It seems even a broken clock is right twice a day."

Seymour squinted. "What do you mean?"

"I mean you were correct, my low-level, federal government-employee friend," Brainert replied. "This *is* a treasure map."

"What!" (We all cried that.)

"It is, yes, indeed," Brainert said. "According to these old papers, dated 1936 and written by someone named Miles Milton Chesley, the Phelps editions of Poe's works have three codes, or riddles, hidden inside of them. These riddles, when solved, will reveal the location of a secret treasure!"

"Yeah, right," Seymour said, "like where the Crusaders hid the Holy Grail? How about the Count of Monte Cristo's chest of gold coins?"

"Mr. Chesley doesn't specify what the treasure is," Brainert said. "Only that it exists."

Seymour snorted. "In your mind."

Sadie shook her head. "Oh, dear. Perhaps I sold that book to Mr. Montour too quickly—"

"Ha!" Garfield cried.

We all jumped, startled by his joyous outburst.

"Ha, ha, ha! And my mom told me I'd hate working in a bookstore because books are so deadly dull!"

"Dull indeed," Brainert sniffed, ever the scholar. "There are no greater treasures than those found in books."

Seymour poked his scrawny finger into Brainert's chest. "Whoa, there, Indiana Jones. You're not crazy enough to think this *is* a treasure map?"

"That's what it says, Tarnish. And kindly put that finger away."

Seymour folded his arms, his expression smug. "So who's to say the treasure hasn't already been found?"

"I'll, of course, have to study all of these papers to learn what Miles Milton Chesley figured out on his own," Brainert said. "But it doesn't appear he solved all the riddles."

"Or maybe he figured out it was all just a hoax," Seymour countered.

Sadie touched the other envelopes. "He certainly did a lot of work. These pages are proof of that."

Brainert scanned the pages again and frowned. "I see there *is* bad news, and it is very bad indeed."

"Spit it out, Indiana," Seymour ordered.

"It seems Mr. Miles Milton Chesley was convinced that a person had to possess all thirteen volumes to have a fighting chance of decoding the riddles."

"And volume twelve just went down Cranberry Street," Sadie said in a tone of regret.

Seymour threw up his hands. "Come on, guys! This is reality—not reality television. You can't buy into crappy crap like this. It's just . . . crap, like that wacky Leonardo code. Just a lot of hype."

"I beg to differ," Brainert replied. "Whatever is going on here, it's hardly hype. I never heard of this theory of a Poe Code before, and American literature is my field of expertise." He tapped the letter with his index finger. "For all I know, the whole thing may have been concocted by Miles Milton Chesley himself."

"So you're saying I'm right? That this *is* a lot of bunk?"

Brainert shook his head. "You don't understand. Bunk or not, from the viewpoint of literary history, the very *idea* of a Poe Code is intriguing, to say the least."

Sadie shrugged. "Mysteries always are."

"Hidden clues in unlikely places, information and mis-information, conspiracies . . ." Brainert was on a roll.

"I see your point," Seymour conceded. "Like those clues about Paul McCartney being dead."

Garfield gaped at Seymour. "No, he's not, Mr. Tarnish. Paul McCartney played Boston this summer. The old guy's career might be on the skids—I mean, I'd never heard of him until recently—but the dude's not *dead.*"

Seymour smirked. "That's not what I was talking about. Back in the sixties the Beatles were really huge. By the way, junior—the Beatles were a band. The Fab Four and all that. And I'm talking *nineteen* sixties here. You went to public school here in Quindicott, so you might not be aware that we haven't had the two thousand sixties yet."

Garfield rolled his eyes.

"Anyway, back when the Beatles were on top of the world, Paul McCartney was injured in a car wreck—"

"Oh! Yes! I remember reading about that," Brainert cut in. "A few years later some publicity mad DJ came up with the dubious notion that the *real* McCartney died in the crash and was replaced by an imposter."

"What do you mean by 'dubious notion,'" Seymour demanded.

Brainert blinked. "Seymour, don't tell me you actually believe Paul McCartney was replaced by an imposter?"

Seymour gave Brainert a look full of pity. "Hey, it took me years to accept the truth. But all you have to do is listen to the solo albums by this so-called 'Paul McCartney'"—Seymour made quote marks with his fingers—"and you know the no-talent phony from Wings just cannot hold a candle to the guy who was in the Beatles. I mean, come on! 'Band on the Run'? 'Ebony and Ivory'? Puh-leaze!"

Sadie cleared her throat, a call to get back to the subject at hand. "Maybe there is something to this Poe Code. But how can we find out what's true from wild conjecture?"

Brainert grinned, touched his head with his index finger. "We have all we need right here, Sadie. But if my skills at ratiocination are not sufficient, I do have a colleague in the literary department who knows a great deal about Edgar Poe. He's quite the expert."

"Let me guess?" Seymour scoffed. "Paige Turner, Literary Detective."

"His name is Nelson Spinner," Brainert replied with an exasperated sigh, "and he may be able to shed some light on our situation. I'm going to talk to him immediately. Meanwhile, hold on to the rest of these books. We may need to examine them further."

I swallowed hard. There was no way I would share my suspicions with Sadie—not *yet*, anyway—not until Brainert could help us confirm there really was something to this so-called Poe Code. But if there was some hidden treasure map buried inside these volumes, could that have been the reason Peter Chesley ended up dead?

Bingo, baby, Jack echoed in my head. *Bingo, jackpot, royal flush.*

CHAPTER 9

School Daze

It gives me . . . as much of pleasure as I can now in any
manner experience, to dwell upon minute recollec-
tions of the school and its concerns.

—Edgar Allan Poe, "William Wilson," 1839

BY LATE AFTERNOON, the selling day had settled back
into normalcy. I'd been checking out a customer when the
phone rang.

"Buy the Book, may I help you?"

"Hello, my name is Lars Van Riij, and I'm calling from
my office at the United Nations in New York City. A mutual acquaintance, Rene Montour, suggested I get in touch
with you in regards to the Phelps editions of Poe."

"Oh!" I looked around for Sadie, but she was still in the
storeroom, examining the Chesley lot.

"I am particularly interested in volume ten, *A Descent into the Maelstrom.* You do have it at your shop?"

"Yes, Mr. Van Riij, we have it, and I'm familiar with the volume."

That particular volume contained not only the title story but also several other examples of Poe's "nautical" works, including his rather nasty review of James Fenimore Cooper's "The Pilot."

Just then, I noticed my son walking in the store's front door. He continued right by me without a word.

"Excuse me for a moment," I told the caller.

"Hey, Spence," I said. "I didn't even see your school bus pull up. How was your first day back?"

Spencer shrugged. "Dunno," he said and kept walking.

Crap, I thought as he trudged to the back of the store, where a set of stairs would take him up to the apartment we shared with Sadie.

Looks like the kid had a bad day.

"Gee, Jack. You think?"

"I *think*, madam," said the man on the other end of the line, "that I am willing to offer five thousand American dollars up front for it."

"Uh . . ." I cleared my throat, realizing simultaneously that I'd answered Jack out loud and we'd just gotten another ridiculously high offer for, frankly, an otherwise unremarkable book.

Unremarkable? Jack piped up again. *Hold the phone. I mean it. You telling me you don't truck with your pal's treasure map theory?*

"That's just it," I silently pointed out. "It's only a theory."

Brainert had asked us to hold onto the set's remaining twelve books until he could bring his expert by to examine them. But the entrepreneur and bill-paying mother in me really wondered whether it was necessary to have all of the volumes available for examination. We'd already sold one, after all, and a part of me wanted to take this man's offer on the spot.

"I, uh . . ." (Stalling brilliantly wasn't my strong suit.) "Perhaps you should speak to my partner—"

But before I could get my aunt on the line, Mr. United Nations announced, "I shall drive up to you first thing tomorrow morning. If the condition of the volume is satisfactory, I promise you that we will work out a mutually agreeable price. Good day, Mrs. McClure."

"But, Mr. Van Riij, I don't think— Hello?"

The line went dead, and I stood there for a moment, unable to believe the man simply had hung up on me. I no sooner dropped the receiver into its cradle when it rang again, and I assumed he was calling back to tell me that we'd been disconnected accidentally.

"Mr. Van Riij?" I answered.

"No. Is this Buy the Book? Is that you, Penelope?"

It was a woman's voice, vaguely familiar, but I couldn't place it in ten words or less. "Sorry, yes, this is Penelope Thornton-McClure. Who's calling?"

"It's Susan Keenan."

"Oh! Sue! Sorry, what's up? Have you started the new Cornwell?"

"Not yet—tonight though, when the kids are in bed and my husband's doing his Internet thing—you know how it is . . ."

I *used* to . . . but one thing I did know: if I were Sue Keenan, I'd be making sure my husband's "Internet thing" was open access. When a man starts locking himself in a room with a computer, he's probably doing one of two things—neither of which were Googling for tips on home repair.

"Pen, the reason I called was because of Spencer."

I could hear a dog barking in the background and some

kids laughing and playing. Then a door shut and those noises were muted.

"What is it, Sue?" I asked. "You've got me worried."

"I met Danny and Maura's school bus. They're on the same bus as Spencer, and I saw one of the boys bullying your son—"

"Aw, no . . ."

"I had sharp words for the bus driver for not stopping it, but Syd said he can't be a nursemaid or he'll risk getting into an accident. He said the road's his priority, you know? Anyway, this Boyce Lyell, he was pushing Spencer around pretty badly. He ripped up something of Spence's too. I shouted for them to stop and they did, but I wanted you to know what was going on. I've seen at least three TV news specials on school bullies and how bad it can get if it's not nipped in the bud, and I know I'd go ballistic if my Danny was in that situation, you know?"

It took me a few seconds to digest everything Sue had just said. I closed my eyes, took a deep breath. "Thanks, Sue. I mean it."

"If you need me to talk to anyone at the school to verify what I saw, just give me a call, okay?"

"Okay . . . Thanks again."

"No problem. I'd want you to call me if you ever saw my kids in that situation, you know?"

"Of course."

After hanging up, I found Sadie in the storeroom, let her know about the call from Mr. Lars Van Hang-up, and asked her to cover the front. Then I headed upstairs.

And so, it seemed, did Jack.

You going to tell me how you're going to handle this?

"No," I silently answered.

No? Or you don't know?

"Both, but I don't want you butting in, okay? Sit this one out."

I found my son moping in front of the TV set. The Intrigue Channel was on and Spencer was already engrossed in a *Jack Shield* episode he'd probably seen three times already.

"How about a snack?" I asked.

Spencer didn't look up, just shook his head. "Not hungry."

I walked over and sat next to him on the couch. "PB&J? Or how about we take a walk to Franzetti's Pizza for a slice?"

Spencer just shook his head again.

"You've got the right idea. Don't want to ruin your dinner. I've got a delicious beef stew in the Crock-Pot and some fresh-baked bread from Cooper's Bakery."

Spencer nodded sullenly, but still refused to talk, so I leaned back and watched television with him for a few minutes.

The original *Jack Shield* TV show was one of those black-and-white mid-century *Dragnet*esque crime dramas. It followed a no-nonsense private investigator working the mean streets of New York City. The show was based on a series of blockbuster bestsellers written by the late Timothy Brennan, a former journalist who claimed he'd drawn the Shield stories from the case files of an actual deceased PI—a man he'd personally known by the name of Jack Shepard.

"Do you like this episode?" I asked my son, desperate to start a conversation—any conversation.

"It's okay."

"What's the story about?"

"This mobster guy . . ." Spencer pointed. "He's the man in the funny suit with the hat . . . he hires Jack to find his old girlfriend. Jack finds her in another city, but she's happy to be away from the mobster guy. Plus she's about to get married. And she begs Jack not to tell where she is. So Jack goes back and stands up to the mobster and tells him to leave the girl alone. The mobster gets real angry, but

Jack won't tell him where the girl is. Jack's a real tough guy . . ."

"A real tough guy. I see."

"I like that he's a tough guy, Mom. Nobody pushes Jack around."

Nuts to that!

Jack's voice exploded so loudly in my head I nearly cried out. After a few seconds and a deep breath, I calmly addressed him through my thoughts—

"Jack, I asked you to butt out."

Well, I'm butting in to set the kid straight. "Nobody pushes Jack around?" *I got pushed around plenty. This show's a load of hooey! That bloated barstool raconteur who called himself an author may have stolen my life and made a mint on it, but he got plenty wrong.*

"You're telling me that Timothy Brennan didn't base this story on your files?"

Lies about my files, sure. I wasn't hired by some goomba mobster. I was hired by an up-and-up banker. It wasn't until I tracked down the guy's honey that I found out he was laundering money for a gambling syndicate on the side. She came clean with me, and I went back to the man and you know what I told him?

"Nothing? Like in the television show I'm watching? Did you stand up to the man and demand he leave his old girlfriend alone?"

I lied, baby. I told the man that his girl was killed in an auto wreck. I even falsified some documents to cover her trail. Then I walked away. Nobody in their right mind butts head directly with a banker connected to the syndicate—not when you want to keep working in the same town. And definitely not when you can buffalo the guy and get away clean.

I thought that over for a few minutes, then I turned to my son. "You know, Spencer, Jack Shield . . . I've, uh . . . read a lot about his real life, and he's not just tough. He's also smart."

"Yeah . . . I guess."

"What I mean is . . . he doesn't always have to muscle his way out of a situation. Sometimes he outsmarts the men who want to hurt him—"

"No, Mom! You can't *outsmart* guys who are bigger than you."

"But if you—"

"When a guy's bigger than you, and he wants to push you around, you get pushed! Unless you're a tough guy like Jack Shield, you get pushed all over the place! You don't know what it's like, Mom. You don't know anything about it!"

And with that, my son stormed out of the living room and slammed shut his bedroom door.

Got to hand it to you, baby, you know how to clear a room.

I noticed Spencer had left his backpack on the floor. It was partially unzipped and I peeked inside. On top of his books was the Reader's Notebook, the one Spencer had worked so long and hard on all summer. It was completely destroyed. Every page had been shredded.

I pulled it out and pieces of parchment fluttered to the floor. As I pushed the pieces back together, I was able to make out the scripted letters—

Quindicott Elementary School
First Place Award
Reader of the Year
Spencer McClure

CHAPTER 10

Expert Opinion

The truth is, I am heartily sick of this life and of the nineteenth century in general. I am convinced that every thing is wrong. Besides, I am anxious to know who will be President in 2045. As soon, therefore, as I have a shave and a cup of coffee, I shall just step over to Ponnonner's and get embalmed for a couple of hundred years.

—Edgar Allan Poe, "Some Words with a Mummy,"
Broadway Journal, 1845

SADIE DROPPED THE receiver into its cradle, then dropped herself into a chair. "Goodness. That man nearly talked my ear off!"

"Another Poe collector?"

Sadie nodded.

I glanced at my watch. It was now just after seven P.M.

Spencer often came into the store in the evening, but tonight he remained in front of the TV, brooding.

Over dinner, I gently told my son about the call I'd received from his friend's mother. He reddened and tried to shrug off his being bullied as "no big deal," but I wasn't letting this go. Having his Reader's Notebook and first-place certificate ripped up *was* a big deal, and I was going to do the dealing.

I made a huge fuss over his winning first prize for the most books read over the summer, and told him he was getting a big reward. I would take him and a group of his friends to the haunted house on Green Apple Road and treat them to ice cream. This cheered him up considerably.

But then I told him that I'd be going to his school the next morning. He begged me to reconsider, but I was resolved. A talk with the principal was in order, whether my son liked it or not.

Meanwhile, as incredible as it seemed, Sadie had fielded five more long-distance calls inquiring about the Phelps editions. I walked over to my aunt, who'd collapsed into one of the overstuffed armchairs at the end of the aisle I was restocking.

The comfy chairs, like the antique floor and table lamps and oak bookcases, were part of the renovations I'd instigated when I first went into partnership with Sadie. Out went the ancient fluorescent ceiling fixtures and old metal shelves, in came the Shaker-style rockers, author appearances, and twenty-first-century book-selling tools.

I'd overhauled the inventory, too, adding plenty of mysteries and true crime to give us our theme, but Sadie had insisted that we keep the store's original rare book business—and, brother, was I glad she did.

"With word of mouth like this," I said, eyeballing our backlist levels on McCrumb, MacDonald, Mailer, and Marlowe, "we don't need to advertise those Poe books. The collectors are coming to us."

Sadie nodded. "News never traveled *this* fast in the book-collecting world that I can recall." With a tissue, she cleaned her glasses, which dangled from her silver chain. "Between cell phones and the Internet, things move at the speed of light! I feel like I'm suddenly in the world of high finance, the way that last caller pressured me!"

"You held out, though?" I replied.

"Yes, I certainly want to hear what Brainert's expert has to say. But he better stop by the shop soon. I've managed to fend off everyone so far, but it hasn't been easy. I'm sorry to say that last fellow actually became verbally abusive. He was convinced I was simply holding out for a better price."

Garfield, who'd finished restocking the new release table, scratched his full beard. "That's because he's probably a corporate goon. They all think you're ripping them off because *they* do it."

Junior here's a real Confucius, Jack groused. *He knows a lot, for someone who's done bupkus.*

"He's young," I silently replied. "Garfield likes to think he's sticking it to the man."

Lamb chop, I'm not reading your frequency.

"My frequency? . . . Oh! You mean my slang? Well here's a bulletin, Jack, sometimes I don't read yours either."

What's not to get? You're the one who claims to be a fan of these fantasyland detective stories you peddle, not me.

I noticed Garfield retrieving his jacket from the store closet. "Gotta go, Mrs. McClure. Time for the night shift at the gas station."

Sadie shook her head. "When do you sleep, young man?"

"Sleep! Who needs it?" Garfield smiled and waved. "I'll see you tomorrow."

"Ah, youth," she murmured as she rose and stretched. She'd already brought the store's laptop up front. While she took a seat behind the counter and read the store's e-mails, I continued checking our backlist levels. It took me about twenty minutes to finish—as well as clean up some muddy footprints tracked between Mickey Spillane and Sara Paretsky. That's when the front door chimed.

"Penelope?"

I recognized Brainert's voice. "Hey," I called, standing up and pushing the hair out of my face, now damp with perspiration. I crossed the store and rounded the corner of a bookcase to find my friend walking up to the counter. He was wearing the same salmon-colored V-neck and white button-down he'd had on this morning, save for the addition of a bow tie. He'd also exchanged the J. Crew windbreaker for a heavier J. Crew peacoat—and he'd brought another man with him.

The newcomer was tall with broad athletic shoulders. He had the sort of late-season tan you see on die-hard surfers or golfers with second homes in Palm Beach. His hair was sun-kissed golden, and he wore it in a boyish twentysomething mop, which suited him even though his attractive weathered features said, "definitely over thirty." Then his electric blue eyes focused on me, and (though I am loath to admit something like this) I actually stopped breathing for a few seconds.

Brainert stepped forward. "Penelope, I'd like to introduce you to Associate Professor Nelson Spinner, Department of English, St. Francis College."

Nelson Spinner clearly eschewed the preppy look favored by Brainert and most of the other faculty members at St. Francis. He wore a beautifully tailored charcoal suit with a crisp, blue shirt and matching Windsor-knotted tie that perfectly matched his penetrating eyes. A fine, black tailored overcoat was draped on his arm.

"Mrs. McClure, Professor Parker has told me so much about you," he said, extending his hand. His voice was pleasant, his grip firm but gentle, and I felt his hand linger in mine a beat longer than necessary.

"You're not from around here," I said, detecting no telltale signs of dropped R's and drawn-out vowels.

"Bucks County, Pennsylvania," Spinner replied with a polite smile.

"Nelson did his graduate work in Philly," Brainert noted.

"Really? You didn't have the good fortune of studying with Camille Paglia, did you?"

Spinner's smile warmed. "Actually, I attended the University of Pennsylvania and Professor Paglia is part of the faculty at the University of the Arts. But I did attend quite a few of her public lectures, and I found the experience quite edifying."

I nodded in agreement. "I saw her speak in Boston a few years ago and envied her students. I wish we could lure her here for a talk on the femme fatale in popular culture. I'm sure I could pack this place with people who'd buy up her backlist. She's a wonderful speaker, isn't she?"

"Indeed she is, Mrs. McClure."

My aunt suddenly cut in. "Let's not be so formal, Professor Spinner. Call her Penelope. And I'm Sadie."

Spinner turned to offer his hand to my aunt. "Ah, the owner of those rare volumes."

"You're talking about the Phelps books, I presume?"

"You bet," Brainert answered. "Nelson is something of an expert."

Spinner modestly waved off Brainert's compliment. "I'm no expert, truly. But I do know a bit about Eugene Phelps."

I managed to dust myself off and lose the shapeless smock I'd donned while doing the store's housekeeping. As I worried whether my powder-blue sweater and jeans were presentable, I realized Spinner had managed to come off as warm and intimidating at the same time—no easy feat . . . then again, maybe it was just me.

Stop fussing, baby, Jack commanded. *I've told you plenty of times . . . you're whistle bait. No man alive wouldn't want you heating his sheets.*

"For pity's sake, Jack . . ." I tried to will my cheeks from flaming. "Not now, please?"

Sure, honey, but why your heart's beating twice its speed for Blondie here's beyond me. The guy dresses well, but his expression's got more sap than a maple tree.

"Not everyone's as hard-boiled as you, you know."

Sweetheart, strawberry jam would be more hard-boiled than this joker.

"Stow it, Jack!"

Stow it? What are you, on a nautical frequency now? Did you join the coast guard when I wasn't looking?

"Jack . . ."

And another thing, why in hell is Bow Tie Boy wearing a peacoat? Last I checked he hadn't joined the swabbie corp— yet in he waltzes wearing navy surplus, for cripe's sake!

"Well, let's see now," Sadie said, making a show of glancing at her watch. "I'll have to close the store and shut out the register." She paused to give a theatrical sigh. "I'll be along shortly, but Penelope can certainly take you back, get you started."

"Well . . . I . . . I'm really not well-versed about the Phelps books," I said, glaring at Sadie. She winked back!

"Nonsense," she told me firmly. "Professor Spinner is the expert. That's why he's here. To tell us all about them."

"Come on, Nelson. Let's go," Brainert said, impatiently charging forward.

Spinner followed Brainert through the archway, into the Community Events space, and presumably to the storage room beyond.

As I stepped around the counter to follow, Sadie lightly squeezed my arm and whispered, "I think you should be very nice to Professor Spinner."

"I don't know what you think you're doing. For all I know, he's married."

Sadie shook her head. "There's no ring on his finger, dear. And you really should pay more attention to things like that. You won't always have me around to play matchmaker."

"You can quit anytime."

"Now, Pen, last night you were complaining that you had a better chance of being struck by lightning than meeting an available man around Quindicott. Professor Spinner looks available to me!"

"Well, the joke may be on both of us," I replied. "He's Brainert's colleague, remember? Maybe Spinner's gay, too."

Sadie grinned, patted my arm. "Have fun finding out."

I felt like a piece of undercooked meat being thrown to the lions. Clenching my fists, I walked through the archway to the events space. Only the emergency lights were glowing, so I paused (read: *stalled*) and turned on the ceiling lights.

"Come on, Pen, hurry up!" Brainert called. "The door's locked."

As the two men waited by the storeroom, I overheard Brainert reciting a blow-by-blow description of Rene Montour's purchase earlier in the day.

My keys to the storeroom were bundled with a half-dozen others on a long chain connected to my belt. It wasn't very attractive, I have to admit—looked like something a building supervisor in a New York apartment house would wear on his tool belt. But Spencer gave the chain to me last Christmas, and I found it surprisingly efficient.

While I fumbled for the right key, Brainert finished his story.

"So, Pen," he said, "any more interest in the books?"

"Six calls this afternoon."

Brainert blinked. "If they all show up in person to pick up their books, then Finch Inn is going to be booked solid. You ought to get a kickback from Fiona."

"That'll be the day."

I pushed the door open, flicked on the lights. Sadie had made the back room presentable in anticipation of Spinner's arrival. She'd briefly opened the back door to let in some fresh air and placed the Phelps editions on the desk, which had been cleared—the laptop moved up front. She'd even arranged folding chairs around the desk.

When Brainert saw the books, he smacked his lips as if he were anticipating a gourmet meal.

"May I?" Professor Spinner asked, simultaneously meeting my gaze and gesturing to the volumes.

"Of course." I settled into a folding chair and watched him pick up Volume One. He slowly ran his hand down the spine and cover. I noticed his hands were nimble, his fingers long and elegant.

Brainert cocked an eyebrow. "Interesting that these books are all bound so differently—"

Spinner nodded. He was obviously observing just that.

"—I mean, considering they're supposed to be uniform editions."

"That's because it took so long for Eugene Phelps to get the complete set out there," Spinner noted, his eyes never leaving the book in his hand. "The man was editing and publishing the volumes, one at a time, over the span of decades. Poor Phelps set an impossible task for himself—it's no wonder he failed."

"I don't understand," Brainert said, sinking into the chair next to me and crossing his legs. "There are dozens of editions of Poe. What's so challenging about putting one together?"

Spinner lifted a new book from the pile and stepped around the desk to face us, as if he were lecturing to a class. "There is, of course, no such thing as a *complete* Poe. Much of Poe's journalism—his puzzles, anecdotes, contemporary observations, things of that nature—were written anonymously and lost in the reams of yellow journalism printed in Poe's time. Phelps made a valiant effort to track down material he suspected had been written by Poe, but in the end many of the passages Phelps identified were discredited by more rigorous scholars and linguistic analysts who came later."

Spinner's pedagogical tone didn't bother me in the least. I'd heard it a hundred times—from Brainert. He went into lecture mode at nearly every meeting of the Quindicott Business Owners Association (or, as my aunt called it, the Quibble Over Anything Gang). What was fascinating to me was Brainert's reaction. It was obvious from his fidgeting that he didn't like the tables being turned. As far as my friend was concerned, *he* was the professor and everyone else was the potential student.

On the other hand, these two were in the same department at St. Francis College, and I wondered if the specter of competition was rearing its ugly head.

You talking 'bout me again, baby?

"No, Jack. Another specter. Go back to sleep. I know this isn't your thing."

Sister, you got that right. I thought those mooks you had traipsing through here, hawking their dime novels were wearing, but these chattering skulls deserve an award for most tedious discussion in half a century. I'm beginning to wish I'd caught lead poisoning in a hardware store.

I noticed Spinner was now opening Volume Eight of the Phelps editions. This one was titled *A Dream Within a Dream.*

"Unfortunately, much of Eugene Phelps's lifework was dismissed in the years after his death," Spinner continued. "One look at an index and it's easy to see why. The contents are all over the place. Several poems and even a few stories appear in more than one volume, and the way the works are assembled is utterly arbitrary." Spinner sighed and set the book down on the desk. "And of Phelps so-called commentary—well, the less said, the better."

I cleared my throat, and *almost* raised my hand. Thank goodness I squelched the impulse. "But, Professor, these volumes have always been of interest to collectors. According to my aunt, their value has skyrocketed in the last seven or eight years. Do you know why that is?"

"It's this Poe Code nonsense," Spinner declared. "It all dates back to an academic paper from a decade ago, written by Dr. Robert Conte, a professor of comparative literature at Mount Olive University in South Carolina. The good doctor stated that he'd discovered the hidden code buried in the Phelps edition, and he claimed to have deciphered it, too."

"Amazing!" Brainert leaned forward in his chair.

Spinner shrugged. "If I recall, the puzzle had something to do with the words being out of order in the text of a poem or story. I really can't recall the specific details. But Dr. Conte was only the first to make such a claim. In the years since his treatise was published, other scholars chimed in with their own pet theories, and the legend of the Poe Code was sustained."

Brainert raised a finger. "You say the legend was 'sustained.' An interesting choice of words."

"Phelps himself claimed there was a code, but he probably said that in a bid to sell more books," Spinner replied. "Of course, the idea of a secret code is certainly intriguing. Why, even I was drawn to the lure of a Poe Code, once upon a time." Spinner chuckled at the memory. "When I was a first-year graduate student, I thought about making the Phelps editions the subject of my own doctoral dissertation."

Brainert nodded. "Sounds great, why not?"

Spinner shook his head. "I realized that such a study would be a waste of my valuable time. I came to the sensible conclusion that there are more important American authors worthy of study. Literary diversions like the Poe Code are excellent fodder for less-serious academics like Dr. Conte, a scholar who prefers the works of American Gothicists like Poe, Hawthorne, and H. P. Lovecraft, over more serious, ambitious, and important American authors—novelists like Kerouac. Poets like Alan Ginsberg."

Though my friend did not react, I knew Spinner's words

had stung Brainert. Not only did he admire the works of Poe and Hawthorne, Brainert also claimed to be distantly related to H. P. Lovecraft, the New England recluse whose horror fiction has begun to rival Poe's in popularity with the public and even certain scholars. And as I recalled, Brainert was rather disdainful of Kerouac and Ginsberg.

I suspected Nelson Spinner was aware of this.

Brainert shifted in his chair. "So you don't believe there is a Poe Code? It's all a myth?"

"What's all a myth?" Sadie asked, finally showing up.

"This Poe Code nonsense," Spinner informed her.

Sadie looked to Brainert. He frowned and gestured back to Spinner.

"Eugene Phelps was a New England eccentric. That's all," Spinner said. "Follow the logic, and you'll come to the same conclusion I did. Just ask yourself these questions: If Phelps really possessed some mysterious treasure, why did he go bankrupt? And why would he blow his brains out if he wasn't flat broke?"

I nearly spoke up then. Maybe *money* wasn't the reason for Eugene Phelps's suicide, I wanted to say, recalling my own husband's descent—not into the maelstrom but into a concrete sidewalk.

Calvin and I never struggled financially. His family was so wealthy that we never wanted for money. Yet my husband chose to kill himself, right in front of me, driven by personal demons I could do nothing to stop . . . or, at the time, even really comprehend.

I wanted to say those things, but of course I kept silent. Some thoughts are too personal to share with a perfect stranger—or even a close friend like Brainert.

But not me, right, sweetheart?

"Right, Jack . . . not you."

This is a real yawnfest you've got going here, you know?

"It could have been earth-shattering," I silently pointed out, "if the Poe Code was real."

But Blondie claims it's not. Too bad, looks like he just burst Bow Tie Boy's bubble.

"What a shame," Brainert said.

He looked crestfallen. Clearly, he had hoped for better news.

Nelson Spinner glanced at his watch. "Well, this has been very pleasant. But I really do have to go. I have a long evening, papers to grade, you know." He faced Brainert. "Can I give you a lift back to the campus, Parker?"

"No thanks," Brainert replied. "I'm heading over to the theater. I'll catch a ride home from Ronny Sutter."

"Still hoping to resuscitate that old Movie Town Theater, eh?" Spinner asked.

"It's been a financial struggle, but we're almost there," Brainert replied. "And since Ronny's donating some of his time, the construction work has progressed much faster."

Brainert had obviously told Spinner about his pet project. He and three other partners (including a film studies professor at St. Francis and an elderly retired screen actress who'd moved back to New England) had purchased the broken-down movie theater in Quindicott in hopes of reopening it and showing classic old films. Brainert gave Spinner an update on the restoration work as Sadie and I escorted them to the front door.

"A shame you have to go," Sadie said. "Please feel free to come back soon, Professor Spinner. I don't know how much longer the Phelps editions will be here, but I'm sure *Penelope* would be very glad to show you the store, perhaps escort you around town."

I stiffened with embarrassment at the obvious sell job. My lord, I thought, is this how Spencer feels when I go into Mother Mode?

To Nelson Spinner's credit, he smiled warmly, took my hand, and held it. "Yes. Thank you for the invitation. . . . Do you have a card?"

"I uh . . ."

"No," said Brainert rather pointedly. "She doesn't."

Sadie glared. "Of course, she does."

My aunt came ready to play, all right. She yanked on a drawer in her old desk and handed over one of the store's new business cards.

"Thanks," Nelson said, tucking it safely into an inside jacket pocket. Then he pulled out a thin leather wallet and one of his own business cards. It was quite something, gold embossed lettering on an electric blue background—the exact shade of his dress shirt and piercing cobalt eyes.

"I'll be in touch soon then, Penelope. I know I'll enjoy talking with you again. Good night."

CHAPTER 11

The Sleeper

Oh, lady dear, hast though no fear?
Why and what art thou dreaming here?

—Edgar Allan Poe, "The Sleeper," 1831

I WOULDN'T EXPECT much from Spinner, doll.

"Excuse me?"

Alvins like him have low libidos.

"What!"

You heard me.

I'd been lying in bed, considering Nelson Spinner when Jack rudely broke into my thoughts (not exactly an uncommon occurrence).

"Well," I replied, "Sadie seems to think he's hot stuff. She's never pushed me that hard before."

She's past her prime.

"So are you, Jack. Way past."

I turned over, stared out the dark window. There was no wind tonight and the bare tree limbs looked painted on the glass, a gloomy still life.

"I can't deny Spinner is a charming professor." I murmured. "What woman wouldn't think he was attractive with that mop of golden hair and those incredible eyes . . ." That's when it hit me. "Jeez-Louise, why didn't I see it sooner?"

See what?

"Sadie described her memories of Peter Chesley in exactly the same way—when they first met, I mean—a charming professor with golden hair and spectacular blue eyes."

Sorry, doll. You're making tracks, but I'm not following.

"I don't think Sadie pushed so hard tonight just because she wants me to have a second chance."

Oh . . . I get it. You and Spinner are the sentimental stand-ins for her and Chesley.

"It's probably natural to want to replay a pattern from your past, try to make things right that went wrong before . . ."

Yeah, baby . . . I got my own version of that little notion.

"What?" I asked through a yawn. "Tell me."

No, baby . . . I'd rather show you . . . remember that missing persons case?

I yawned again. "Sure."

Well, it's time to trail a new lead . . .

New York City
October 21, 1946

Her eyes were brownish-green like a couple of olives left to drown at the bottom of a dry martini. Jack had slipped onto the barstool next to her, watched her down the dregs of gin and vermouth.

When Jack had interviewed Miss Mindy Corbett at her desk this morning, she'd been bright and chipper as the daily funnies, her short, honey-colored curls prim and neat, her features on the young side of thirty. At the end of this very long day, however, not even the dim light of the slick hotel bar could save her eyes from looking bloodshot, her skin from appearing sallow. Even her hair looked tired of curling.

She ignored him until he flagged the bartender, bought her a refill.

"I know you," she said, a little too loudly. Then she shushed herself, bringing her voice down before Jack had to advise it. "You're that gumshoe who's looking for Mr. Tattershawe."

"That's right, honey." Jack tapped a fresh deck of Luckies against two fingers, passed her one. "Remarkable memory you have."

"What are you, a comedian? You were just in the office earlier today."

Jack lit her ciggy, then his own. "How about that? Small world, seeing you again."

The bartender approached with a silver shaker. "Here you go, Miss Corbett." Into her old glass, he poured a fresh crystal stream. He put a new glass in front of Jack and filled it.

Mindy lifted her drink, admired the shimmer of alcohol in her hand like a jewel in the crown. "Oh, yeah, Bobby," she told the bartender, "that's the ticket."

Jack took a drink of the icy liquid, savored the juniper burn. He wondered how much tonsil paint it would take to pry loose Mindy Corbett's tongue.

In Jack's short time investigating Vincent Tattershawe, he found the man's friends to be supremely aloof. They knew little of Tattershawe's personal business. His family consisted of one married sister living out west who corresponded with him mainly through letters. She hadn't heard from him in over a month.

Mindy here was Jack's best lead. She worked at Carter & Thompson, an investment company on lower Broadway, near the exchanges and the docks. Before Tattershawe disappeared, she'd been assigned as his secretary.

When Jack questioned her this morning, she'd been polite but curt, claiming she worked for someone new at the firm now and didn't know anything about Mr. Tattershawe's disappearance. But—

She'd slipped up during questioning.

She'd admitted knowing Tattershawe before the war. She'd worked as his secretary for four years. And after he'd exchanged his business suit for a G.I. uniform, she'd stayed with the firm, working for another boss. Then Tattershawe returned last year from the front with half an arm missing, and she went right back to serving as his secretary again.

That kind of pattern spoke of loyalty, and Jack didn't believe Mindy had no insights into Vincent's abrupt disappearance.

"So was Tattershawe a jerk to work for?" Jack asked, hoping to provoke some more leads out of her. "Are you glad he's gone?"

Mindy put down her new drink, swiveled to face him. "You think I'm stupid?"

"No."

"I know why you're here, feeding me juice. Don't think I don't."

"It's no secret, Miss Corbett. I told you yesterday, I'm looking for Vincent Tattershawe."

"So go talk to his boss."

"I did."

Tattershawe's supervisor was Ed Thompson. Heavyset, bald, and harried, he'd claimed he knew nothing of Vincent's unscheduled three-week vacation. After trying to contact him for ten days, he'd written the man off and reassigned his clients.

The client list was private, Jack was told, and nobody else he spoke to at the company claimed they knew anything. Jack wasn't getting anywhere through the front door.

So he decided to try the back, trailing Mindy's shapely tan suit and tawny pumps to the bar after she got off work for the evening.

But the dame wasn't an easy safe to crack.

"I'm not supposed to talk about him," she insisted, then swiveled toward the bar again, showing Jack her profile as she picked up her drink.

Jack leaned close to her ear, lowered his voice for a raspy promise. "Nobody has to know, sweetheart."

"Is that right?" She fumbled with the lit cigarette, tapping too hard to get the stray ash off. "Damn. It's gone out. Heat me up again, will you?"

Jack struck another match, pulled the flame close to his body, made her lean in. She was really flying now and seemed to enjoy the little tease, following the fire wherever it went. He touched her hand to steady it as he let the blaze reignite the tobacco.

"You're an attractive woman, Mindy."

She laughed, raising an eyebrow as he held her gaze. "Don't buffalo me, shamus."

Jack let the moment hang as she surveyed his broad shoulders tapering down to lean hips; his square jaw, shaved clean; the dagger-shaped scar, promising a hint of danger.

He blew out the match. "Were you ever more than Tattershawe's secretary?"

"Yes," she said.

The unthinking admission alarmed her. She swiveled away to face the bar again, took a long quaff of martini— as if that would make it all better.

Jack leaned back, didn't press. Now that the cat was out of the bag, he knew she'd spill the rest of the litter. He could see she was dying to. All he had to do was wait.

Mindy drained her glass. He watched her fish the gin-soaked olive out, put it between her small white teeth and squeeze it slowly, savoring those last drops of alcohol.

Cripes, he thought, if Tattershawe had a drinking problem, then he wasn't drinking alone.

"I need another drink, shamus. You buying?"

"The name's Jack." He waved the bartender over and the crystal fountain flowed anew.

"You want to go somewhere more private?" Mindy asked after she'd finished another.

"Sure," Jack said. "What did you have in mind?"

"This is a hotel. We could get a room."

Jack didn't surprise easily, but Miss Corbett rendered him momentarily speechless.

"To talk privately, I mean," she added in a whisper. "See, the truth is, I care about Vincent, and I think he might be in a jam."

"WHEN VINNY CAME back from Europe, he took his old job back at the firm, and Ed Thompson let me work for him again. We all pretended like his arm didn't matter, that he wasn't a cripple, and I thought things would go back to the way they were."

Mindy was standing by the hotel room's window, looking out on the sensational view of a movie house's dingy brick wall.

Jack's view was better. Twilight had set in and Mindy Corbett's hourglass form was nicely outlined against the darkening windowpane, her snug-fitting suit an affecting distraction.

"Go back to the way they were?" Jack repeated, loosening his tie. He was sitting in the room's only chair—an upholstered number with overstuffed arms. "But not just in the office, right? Out of the office, too."

Mindy turned to face Jack, leaned her bountiful hips back against the window frame. "Sure, Vinny and me, we always used to have good times together."

"You mean you always drank together."

"That's right. It was fun."

"But the fun times stopped?"

"We tried to go back to the way it was, but Vinny couldn't. He was so unhappy after he came back from the war. It's hard to explain."

"You don't have to, honey. I follow. The war changed a lot of men."

"So Vinny met this Dorothy woman at a New Year's Eve party, and they hit it off. She's a teetotaler, but . . ." Mindy shrugged. "That's what he preferred, so what's a girl to do?"

"What *is* a girl to do? You tell me."

"What do you mean?"

"I mean, are you sure you weren't angry about Vincent getting engaged to another woman?" Jack wondered for a minute whether Mindy was truly an innocent, or had she made Vinny disappear?

"No. I swear. I wanted Vinny to be happy. And he sure wasn't happy with me. And if a guy's not happy, it doesn't take long before he makes a girl miserable."

"I get the picture."

"But Vinny and I were still good during working hours, so I stayed as his secretary. He was a real swell boss, too— polite, civil. He never ordered me around or barked like a jerk. He always asked like a gentleman. Then I came in one day, and he didn't. And the next day came and went, and the next . . ."

"And before you know it, your life's over," Jack muttered.

"Huh?"

"Sorry, sweetheart, my mind wandered. A little too much gin." It was amazing how well this tomato held her liquor. She was a real boozehound, all right. "Tell me now," Jack said. "Why do you think he left?"

"I'm sure it had to do with the way the business changed since the war."

"How do you mean?"

"I mean . . ."

Jack watched Mindy's careless expression begin to change. Her relaxed posture appeared to stiffen, and she began to chew her lower lip.

"What is it, honey? You can tell me. I'll never repeat what came from that pretty mouth of yours."

Mindy turned around, faced the window again even though there was nothing in front of her. Darkness had fully descended and the alley she overlooked was black as a coffin.

Jack sat very still. "Remember, you're helping Vincent now, sweetheart. Tell me what you know."

Jack waited for her to decide, and she slowly began to spill.

"Vinny . . . he was used to doing things on the up-and-up, square investment products for square Johns and Janes, you know? But . . . that's not how the new management operates."

She went on to explain how the firm had fallen on hard times during the war years and had been taken over by silent partners. Carter & Thompson's old, long-standing clients were still set up with good stocks and investment portfolios. It was the best front imaginable for gaining the confidence of new clients.

But for every legit client Vincent and his colleagues managed, there were two or three suckers, set up with shell investment schemes. The scheme would appear to pay off for a while, but the phony venture would soon collapse, netting the firm a hefty profit.

The swindled clients would move on, but the firm would find new rubes, usually uptown types, society ladies, and war widows, brought in through the new silent partners and reassured via the old, long-standing network of legit clients.

"And who are these silent partners?" Jack asked.

"I don't know. But I think I know where you can find at least one of them."

"Tell me."

"There's an awful lot of packages going back and forth to a place you wouldn't expect."

"What do you mean?"

"I mean, the address isn't a law office, a bank, or a residence. It's a warehouse, way over on the West Side docks, near Hell's Kitchen."

"Mindy, this is very important. Do you remember the exact address?"

Mindy laughed, her tense posture finally relaxing. "I've sent so many packages there, it's practically tattooed to my brain."

Jack wrote the address on his notepad.

Mindy's whole demeanor seemed a thousand times lighter. Sometimes, a confession will do that for a person. She strode over to the bed and flopped down on the mattress, crossed her shapely legs.

"When Vinny cut out the way he did, boy oh boy, Ed Thompson really started to panic! There were files missing, and other things, too."

"What other things?"

"Funny as it seems . . . a picture on my desk. It was a photo he'd given me before the war."

Jack rose from the armchair, dipped a hand in his pocket. "Not this one?" He brought out the small oval-framed photo, walked to the bed, sat next to her on the mattress.

"Omigosh! Where did you find that!"

"Dorothy Kerns gave it to me. Apparently, Vincent sent this to her right before he disappeared."

"But why?"

"I don't know."

Sending the photo in the first place seemed odd to Jack, but sending one that was out of date and belonged to another woman was odder still. He couldn't figure it unless Vincent Tattershawe was truly a heel, sending Dorothy a gesture of trumped-up sentiment to throw off her scent while he went on the lam with her money.

"Can I have that picture back?" Mindy asked, reaching for it.

Jack gently pulled it beyond her grasp. "Sorry, Miss Corbett. I can't."

She slumped again, letting out a sad sigh.

"Listen, Mindy, you've been a big help. But there's one more thing. Do you know anything about Ogden Heating and Cooling?"

Mindy repeated the name with a puzzled look.

"It's an air conditioner manufacturing company," Jack explained. "Do you think it could be one of your firm's phony investment schemes?"

"I've never heard of it, and believe me, I know the list of fake companies like the back of my hand."

Jack nodded. "Well, listen, baby, I guess that's about all I need from you."

He pushed off the bed, rising to his feet. "Tell you what . . . when I find Vincent Tattershawe, and I fully expect to, I'll ask him to get you another photo, maybe a more recent one."

Mindy stood too, gave Jack a sad smile. "I don't want a more recent one. I liked looking at the older picture. It reminded me of the old times, know what I mean?"

Jack nodded, slipped the photo back into his pocket. "I know."

Mindy stepped closer, gazed up at him with big olive-soaked eyes. "That's nice of you, anyway, to try replacing my photo."

Jack smelled the alcohol, but his real drink was perfume, and hers hadn't worn off yet; it was still there, light and sweet.

"You're really thoughtful, Jack. You remind me of Vinny in some ways . . . what I mean is, you seem like a really nice guy . . ."

"I'm not."

"But I bet you could be . . . for a little while, right?"

"I could be."

THE NEXT MORNING, Jack woke up in the hotel bed. Mindy was gone and he wasn't surprised. He figured she was already regretting her decision to talk, but he planned on looking her up again anyway—after this case was closed.

He showered, shaved, dressed, and headed downstairs to find two police cruisers parked on the street near the alley between the hotel and the movie house.

Jack still knew cops from his days in the department. He tossed a short nod to Jimmy Martin, a middle-aged sergeant he'd worked with as a rookie.

"Hey, Jimmy, what's the news?"

"Mugging and murder, I'm sorry to say."

"Who's the victim?"

"Young lady. Nice-lookin' one too."

Jack stiffened. "Young lady?"

"Yeah, too young to end up shot to death. Looks like they roughed her up before they killed her. Think you can identify her?"

"Don't know."

"Take a look, then."

Jack stepped into the alley, pushed through the wall of uniforms, and felt his stomach drop. Left in a heap next to the garbage cans was Mindy Corbett, shot through the heart.

CHAPTER 12

Remains of the Day

His smile was stiff as a frozen fish.

—Raymond Chandler, *Farewell, My Lovely*, 1940

JACK'S DREAM, WHICH ended more like a nightmare, should have prepared me for what was coming the next day. It didn't.

Tuesday morning began like any other, apart from my postdream disorientation. I crawled out of bed as soon as the alarm went off, not sure if I was in Jack's century or mine. But after a cup of coffee, I managed to shower, dress, dry my hair, and stop wondering what Jack was going to do next to find his missing person, and whether he felt guilty about Mindy's fate.

All the while I was thinking about this stuff, I expected Jack to break into my thoughts and answer me. But he never did.

Anticipating my meeting with Mrs. McConnell, Spencer's principal, I chose a suitably matronly, nonthreatening outfit from my closet—a long, gray wool skirt, black low-heeled boots, and an oversized black turtleneck. Vaguely aware that my outfit would have raised absolutely no eyebrows in the 1940s, as well as today, I went to wake my son.

To my surprise, Spencer's bedroom was empty, save for our snoozing marmalade-striped cat, Bookmark, which Sadie had given to Spencer as a kitten on the day we'd moved in.

The bathroom all three of us shared was also vacant, so I hunted through the apartment. The television was quiet, but I checked the living room anyway. Empty. The dining room was empty, too. I finally found Spencer in the kitchen. He was standing at the sink, washing out his cereal bowl, his back turned to me. It was more than a half hour before the school bus arrived, but he was already dressed and ready for class.

"Up early, aren't you?"

Spencer jumped, startled, then reddened with guilt. I spied his backpack on the counter, his bicycle helmet sitting next to it. I tumbled onto his scheme immediately. He'd almost made it, too. If Spencer had skipped breakfast, he would have outfoxed me.

"You are not riding your bike to school," I said.

"Why not?"

"Because avoiding the bus is not the way to solve this problem."

The bowl clattered—too loudly—in the drying tray. Spencer tossed his still-damp spoon into the silverware bin.

"Get ready to go. I'm driving you."

Spencer rolled his eyes and yanked his backpack off the counter. I could tell by his expression that he was sorry I hadn't changed my mind about seeing Mrs. McConnell to discuss what had happened on the bus the day before.

My son continued his sullen silence in the car. While I

never condoned pouting, I understood his reasons. It was bad enough that he was bullied and humiliated in front of his classmates. Now his mother was going to have a talk with the principal about the matter.

Poor Spence probably feels trapped and embarrassed, I thought, with more humiliation to come.

No, baby, more than anything, your son's pissed off.

"Back off, Jack."

Why? You can handle the truth once in a while, can't you?

"Of course Spencer is angry. You know very well a bigger boy at school gave him a hard time. But I'm going to have a talk with the principal and see that a matron is put on the bus from now on—"

A matron! Baby, your son's not going to have a matron with him every minute of every day. He's got to learn how to handle punks and Brunos.

"How?"

Jack Shepard offered a variety of tactics he himself had used in the past. I shook my head.

What's your beef?

"Things are a lot different from when you were a kid, Jack. If Spencer took your advice, I'm fairly sure he'd end up in juvenile hall or I'd end up being sued for everything—or both."

I tried to explain the wonderful world of modern middle-class public education.

What do you mean "Zero Tolerance"? Are you telling me a red-blooded American boy can't bring a switchblade or a pair of brass knuckles to school these days?

"Sorry, Jack. The future's pretty complicated."

Jack went silent.

"What?" I asked. "Don't you have any more parental advice to dispense?"

Listen up. Forget the brass knuckles. I'll make it simple because, when you're dealing with the human animal, some things will never change. Bullies look for weakness and fear. Your son has to learn how to overcome his fear

*and fight for his dignity. He has to learn how to stand up
for himself.*

I drove by the entrance to the Finch Inn, past the sign for
the restaurant, and swerved onto Crowley Road. We crested
the hill, went through the traffic light, and began rolling
down the other side when a flurry of white particles blew
across the roadway.

"Mom, look! It's snowing."

The particles swirled right into the path of my Saturn.
Then a wind funnel swept them onto the shoulder of the
road, where they collected like snowflakes. But they
weren't snowflakes.

The white torrent was formed by thousands of pellets of
foam peanuts, the finer grain we used at the store to protect
books during shipping. It was about that time that my
stomach clenched with an ominous premonition.

"An accident," Spencer said. He leaned forward and
peered through the windshield.

Crowley Road ended at the bottom of a steep hill, where
it hit Seneca. Drivers could make a right or left turn on
Seneca. Going straight wasn't an option unless you wanted
to crash through a wooden fence and slam into a tree. It
was clear from our vantage near the top of the hill that
someone in a maroon sedan had chosen the third option.

Debris from the shattered fencepost littered the grassy
field now sprinkled with foam. The sedan had left tracks in
the soft dirt, leading right to a tall oak. The vehicle's front
end was crumpled into a U around its stout trunk. The hood
was bent like an accordion and the front windshield was
shattered. The sedan's doors were open, and a thin stream
of foam continued to pour out of the vehicle. The trunk had
popped, too. On the ground next to the wreckage lay a
stretcher bearing a shrouded body.

Emergency vehicles were parked all over the place:
Quindicott Police cars, ambulances, and fire trucks. I
braked as I approached the scene.

A young officer I didn't recognize waved me around the bend, but as I swung onto Seneca and negotiated my way through the vehicle barrier, a bearlike figure stepped into the path of my Saturn. I say "bearlike" in the literal sense, for Chief Ciders of the Quindicott Police was indeed built like a bear, and not the cuddly kind. He had the disposition of a bear, too, though debate raged about whether he acted more like a hibernating bear or an angry one.

(If you want my two cents, given our little town's low crime rate, he acted like the former most of the time—until something set him off, in which case he acted more like the latter.)

The chief recognized me. I know because I saw him scowl just before he waved me into a space between two fire trucks.

"Park!" Ciders called tersely (even though, what he really cried was "Pahwk!" because his accent was particularly thick).

I had no choice but to pull over. I parked, rolled down the window, and cut the engine. The chief approached the car. Tucking his hat back on his head, he leaned his face into my window and leveled his watery gaze on me.

"Why is it, if there's trouble in this town, you and Fiona are always in it?"

I blinked innocently. "Whatever do you mean, Chief?"

"I'm talking about the dead fellow we just pulled out of this car. I just talked to Fiona and she told me he was staying at her inn last night. She claims he never checked out, never slept in his bed."

"And?"

"And apparently he got into his car at around nine o'clock last night, drove away, and never came back. Fiona said she didn't know where this guy went, but she said that you might know."

"Me?"

Ciders looked at me squarely. "Fiona said you had

business with this man. That your aunt Sadie sent him over to her inn yesterday."

You've been fingered, baby. Your pal the Bird Lady has been singing like a canary.

"Huh?"

Your friend ratted you out.

Jack was, of course, referring to Fiona Finch. He called the innkeeper the Bird Lady because, in addition to her married surname, Fiona regularly wore one of a huge collection of brooches fashioned in the images of birds.

"Was his name Montour?" I asked. "Rene Montour?"

Ciders nodded. "That's him. Canadian citizen—French-Canadian. He was a solicitor, according to his passport. He's over there on the stretcher, deader than a monger's mackerel." Suddenly the chief remembered that Spencer was in the front seat next to me. "Er . . . Sorry, Mrs. McClure."

I was too busy staring at the accident scene to voice any motherly indignation. "What did you find inside the car?" I asked.

Ciders shrugged. "A bunch of old books and a cloud of packing plastic. The box broke open from the force of the crash. There are books scattered all over."

"I need to see them," I said.

"Mom!" Spencer cried.

"Stay here, I'll be right back."

I climbed out of the car and walked toward the accident scene. I didn't get five steps before Ciders grabbed my arm.

"That's a restricted area, Mrs. McClure."

"I have to see the books," I repeated. "All of them."

Ciders cupped his beefy hands around his mouth. "Hey, Womack," he bellowed.

Near the smashed car, an officer looked up.

"Bring those books over here," Ciders commanded. "All of them."

Officer Womack picked up a large box emblazoned

with the logo for Tide laundry detergent. He carried the crate across the field, avoiding the rutted tire tracks. Finally he reached the shoulder of the road and plopped the box down on the hood of a police car.

"Go ahead, Mrs. McClure. Take a look. Then tell me what you're looking for."

I hurried over and quickly rummaged through the books. The box contained eight volumes—all Raymond Chandler first editions. All were damaged—dents and scrapes, mostly. One had a broken spine, another edition's dust cover was in tatters. All the books were damp from the morning dew, their pages curled.

"There's nothing else?" I asked. "I'm looking for a smaller box, with a single volume inside?"

Womack shrugged. "None we can find. But we ain't looking too hard."

"This box is smaller. It might not have broken open. The box might be in the trunk, or still in the back seat."

"The trunk's empty," said Officer Womack. "There was only one box in the back seat, ripped open from the crash." Womack shrugged. "I can look again, but—"

"Please," I said. "Look again. Or I will."

Officer Womack stared at me, then faced Ciders. To the man's surprise, the chief nodded and sent him on his way. The officer returned to the crash scene, grumbling. Ciders redirected his gaze toward me.

"If you just tell me what this is about, we—"

"Is this an accident or a crime-scene investigation, Chief Ciders?"

The man blinked, then his eyes narrowed. "What are you getting at, Mrs. McClure?"

"My aunt and I sold Mr. Montour a very valuable book yesterday, worth many thousands of dollars. If it's gone, then someone might have stolen it—"

"Nothing, Chief," Womack called from the crash site. "Just a lot of that packing foam."

"Thanks, Tom," Ciders replied. Then he faced me again. "What were you saying?"

"I was saying that if this book is missing, then there may have been a crime committed—"

Ciders raised his hand. "I don't know about any theft, Mrs. McClure, but it's clear what happened here. Mr. Montour went to dinner, had a few drinks. Unwisely, he chose to take a drive. On Crowley Road, at the top of the hill, he got the red light. He braked, but while he was waiting for the light to turn green, he passed out. His foot slipped off the brake and his car rolled down the hill, out of control."

"You've completely ruled out foul play?" I asked.

"This was an accident," Ciders replied, growing increasingly cranky. "You can still smell the booze in the guy's car, Mrs. McClure. This guy Montour was soused—to the gills."

"But—"

Ciders cut me off. "Look at the tire marks. The man never braked, not even when his car careened through the fence and hit the grass."

I looked at the marks—on the road and in the dirt. There were no skid marks on the pavement, no swerving curves in the grass, just a pair of straight lines right into the tree. Chief Ciders was correct: Montour never braked.

"And by the way, Mrs. McClure. I was out here last year, same place, same kind of accident. Only that time it was the high school quarterback, Tyler Scott. The kid went to an illegal drinking party, passed out at the wheel. The punk survived the crash. Can't say the same for the team. They lost the regional playoffs."

Ciders looked over his shoulder, at the shrouded form on the stretcher. "That Scott kid got away with two broken legs. Frenchy there wasn't so lucky."

CHAPTER 13

Book-marked for Murder

I want a burglar. A good, first-class burglar.

—William Brandon, "It's So Peaceful in the Country,"
Black Mask, November 1943

AFTER LEAVING THE accident scene, I drove Spencer directly to school. I was plenty agitated about Rene Montour's death, but for my son's sake I intended to follow through with seeing Principal Eleanor P. McConnell.

Tightening the grip on my handbag's strap, I entered the Quindicott Elementary School administration offices. Spencer's ripped Reader's Notebook and his torn certificate were tucked inside my bag, ready to be whipped out as incriminating evidence.

But there was no whipping to be done—not yet anyway. The school secretary informed me that Mrs. McConnell was out on maternity leave and had been temporarily replaced by a new man with "impressive" credentials.

"He got his doctorate in California and worked out there as a professor of education at a prestigious teacher's college," the secretary said. "But he's from Newport originally and even attended St. Francis College, so now he's back in the area."

"Oh," I said, recovering. "May I see him?"

"He's not in, ma'am. We don't expect him in this morning until eleven."

I automatically glanced at my watch. It was just after nine—no way I was wasting two hours waiting here. "Can I make an appointment to see him tomorrow?"

"Of course," said the secretary. She took down my name and phone number, and then I asked for the new principal's name.

"It's Chesley," the secretary said. "Claymore Chesley."

I was still reeling from that little revelation when I'd returned to the store to find my aunt wearing the doe-eyed expression of a thief caught with one hand in the till.

"I know what you're going to say, Penelope," she told me the second I'd entered. "You're going to say I was wrong to do it. But I'm glad I did."

I noticed that the Phelps editions were spread out across the counter beside the register. Sadie noticed that I noticed, and she immediately started babbling.

"Before you scold me, you have to understand that I couldn't help myself. The man was just so . . . persuasive. And his offer was generous, too generous to pass up." Her face was flushed, her hands flailing madly. "Please forgive me and try to understand," she continued, moving around the counter. "He wouldn't take no for an answer."

"*Who* wouldn't, Aunt Sadie? What's going on?" She was speaking so fast, and I was still so rattled by the morning's events, it took me a minute to catch up.

"That man who called last night," she replied. "Mr. Van

Riij from New York City. He came here about an hour ago—"

"You sold another Poe!" I shrieked.

"I know I shouldn't have done it—"

"We *have* to find this man. Right away!" I bolted for the door.

"Pen, stop!" Sadie ran after me, grabbed my arm. "It's too late. He's already on his way back to New York."

"Please, just tell me what happened," I demanded, turning to face her.

Her hands went back to fluttering like bee wings. "I sold him the book he wanted. Volume Ten, *A Descent into the Maelstrom*. He paid eight thousand dollars for it—and that's not counting sales tax!"

"Oh . . . God . . . I need to sit down." I collapsed into the nearest Shaker-style rocker.

"I know," Sadie said, grinning. "I couldn't believe the amount myself. That's nearly four times the book's market value—"

"No, you don't understand," I said, holding my head. "By selling Mr. Van Riij that book, you may have marked the poor man for murder!"

Sadie's teeth about hit the floor when I told her about Rene Montour's demise in an "accident." I recounted my confrontation with Chief Ciders, telling her how the Chandler books were scattered all over the crash scene, but the Phelps Poe was *missing*. And I was convinced it was stolen.

Despite her pragmatic nature, and her usual distaste for rationalized baloney, Sadie began equivocating.

"But, Pen, Mr. Montour's death . . . it *could* have been an accident." She began to pace the aisle. "It's possible the box containing the Phelps book was thrown clear in the crash, or it might not have been in the car. Perhaps he left the book at Fiona's inn."

I sighed and began massaging my temples.

"And, remember," she went on, "you didn't search the

scene yourself. You only have the policemen's word that the area was *thoroughly* searched. You know how unthorough the Quindicott Police have been in the past."

Instead of debating her, I met Sadie's gaze with my own. "Do you really believe Peter Chesley's death was an accident?"

For a long moment, Sadie fell silent. Then slowly, sadly, she shook her head. "No," she whispered. "I'd like to. It would be so much easier to believe it was, but . . ."

"But we both know what we saw and heard at Chesley's house, right?" I said, unwilling to look the other way any longer. "No matter what the Newport police say. We both believed that someone was in his house, and that someone instigated Peter's 'fall' down the steps. That means there's been *at least* one murder, and probably a theft."

"But what should we do about it?" Sadie asked, wringing her hands. "Should I contact Mr. Van Riij? Warn him that he's now in danger—"

"He won't believe you. Chief Ciders didn't believe me. As it stands, we have no proof of a murder plot." I shook my head. "This is one dilemma the two of us"—

The three of us, Jack Shepard cut in.

—"will have to work out ourselves. Right now secrecy is our best defense. Have you told anyone about the sale? Anyone at all?"

Sadie blinked. "Only Brainert, I guess."

"Brainert knows? Why? Was he here this morning?"

"No. He called before the store opened and asked me to scan the title page of each volume of the Poe collection, then send the digital files to him on an e-mail attachment."

"Whatever for?"

"He said he needed to examine the text on those pages in particular."

"But *why*?"

Sadie shrugged. "Something that Professor Spinner fellow mentioned apparently got him curious. Anyway, I brought all of the books to the front and made the scans. That's when Mr. Van Riij knocked on the door. I told him we weren't open yet, but he was so pushy. He barged in, saw the books near the register, and made an offer on the spot."

"So how does Brainert know about the sale?"

"He called back to let me know my e-mail came through okay. That's when I mentioned selling another volume of the set. Brainert wasn't happy, but he was relieved I'd scanned copies of the title pages before I sold any more books. Brainert claims he's on the verge of solving the Poe Code."

"What?!" I cried. "Professor Spinner already debunked the existence of the code! How could Brainert be on the verge of *solving* it?"

Sadie shrugged. "That's what he said."

TUESDAY AFTERNOON WAS Sadie's time to help out at the church with event planning. Since school for Spencer didn't end until 3:15 and Garfield wasn't on the schedule until tomorrow, I was momentarily stuck behind the counter, unable to raise Brainert by phone or leave the store to track him down.

We'd only seen a few customers all morning, which gave me far too much time to worry about Rene Montour, the Phelps editions, Brainert apparent solving of the Poe Code, and my appointment with another Chesley.

"Could the new principal really be a relative of Peter's?" I'd been muttering to myself for hours. "Maybe it's just a coincidence."

I was dying to ask my aunt what she thought, but she'd been so worked up about the second Poe sale that I thought it was best to just send her off to her church work and find another time to discuss the sudden appearance of another Chesley.

When 1:00 P.M. rolled around, I decided to close for a quiet lunch. I hung the BACK IN ONE HOUR sign and threw the bolt, then, lunch in hand, I moved to a favorite spot I'd set up in the back corner of the selling floor.

There, in an easy chair, I could eat in peace and not be visible, like some zoological specimen, to people passing on the sidewalk. Otherwise, on a slow day like this, I could almost imagine the plaque outside the window—"Female of the species *Bookstorus Independicus*, nearly extinct."

I'd just sunk into the chair when I heard a sound, like furniture bumping together. It seemed to be coming from the Community Events space.

I peeked around the archway. The room was empty and silent. Then I noticed the door to the storeroom was wide open, and strong hands seized me from behind, pinning my arms.

"Where are those books?" a male voice hissed in my ear.

"What books? This store is full of them, you know!"

The man spun me around and slammed me against the wall, bouncing my head off the Dennis Lehane co-op poster.

"The books!"

The intruder's voice was raspy, like he was trying to disguise it. I felt my blood pumping, my vision fade to red.

Calm down, doll.

Jack was here. I wasn't alone. I clung to that thought like a dinghy to an anchor in a category Four.

Trust me, sweetheart. I'll walk you through this.

"How?" I mentally demanded.

Take inventory. What's in front of you?

I blew out a held breath, tried to memorize details. The intruder was taller than me by at least a head and had broad shoulders. He wore a black denim jacket and a black woolly cap pulled down over his face like a hood.

It wasn't a tailored ski mask, I realized. This was a do-it-yourself job with just two eye slits ragged and askew. I couldn't see any other part of his face, so I tried to make out his eye color, but the man was wearing tinted glasses beneath his mask. The effect was impressively scary. He wore gloves and his grip was painfully tight.

The man shook me. "You know what I'm talking about, lady. I want the old books. The valuable ones."

I knew he meant the Phelps editions and immediately wondered if this was the same man who threw Peter Chesley down the stairs and murdered Rene Montour on a deserted stretch of road. If it was, what would he do to me?

Play Amish, Jack advised.

"What?"

Surrender. Play up the shivers. Pretend to cooperate. But be ready to clock the yancy when you glim an opening—

"Huh?"

Just do what I say.

The intruder shook me again. "Answer me. Show me the books or I'll hurt you. I mean it."

The Lone Ranger here isn't expecting you to fight. You're gonna wallop him good where and when I tell you—

"No, Jack! I can't do that! He's too big! I can't—"

You can. You're going to sock this yegg in the nose, okay? Take him to fist city then run to the front door. All you have to do is throw the bolt and you're outside. Dollars to donuts, he won't follow you.

"Okay, okay . . . I'll try."

I went limp in the man's grip, spoke in a frightened voice. "The books you want . . . They're by the register."

I felt his grip loosen. "Where?" he demanded, not nearly as stridently as before.

Use your wing, doll. Point them out.

I did as Jack commanded. To my surprise, when I moved my right arm to point, the intruder actually let go of it. I lifted my arm higher. My eyes never left the bump in the middle of his mask.

"The books are over—"

Clobber him!

I swung around with my fist and pounded the intruder right in the nose. The blow hurt *me*, so I didn't need to hear the startled howl to know it hurt the stranger.

Yelling a string of obscenities, the man stumbled backward and away from me.

Scram out, Penelope! Run!

I bolted out of the events room and through the store. I was nearly halfway to the front door before I heard his heavy footsteps coming up behind me. To slow him down, I pushed the four-foot corrugate display of P. D. James's latest title into the man's path. The display was packed with frontlist hardcovers. He crashed right into it. Books flew everywhere.

Nice move, sister!

"Thank god it wasn't her paperback edition!"

I kept on running until I slammed into the front door with enough force to ring the chime. I twisted the bolt, flung the door open, and hit the sidewalk yelling my head off for help!

I heard the squeal of tires on pavement, the sound of doors opening. Someone grabbed me, and I found myself looking into the startled face of Officer Eddie Franzetti.

I sagged with relief.

I'd known Eddie since I was a little girl. He'd been a close friend of my late brother's back in high school, before Pete had lost his life drag racing to impress a local beauty queen.

"Penelope! Calm down." He peeled off his sunglasses, pushed back his uniform hat. "What happened?"

"A burglar! In the store . . ."

"Anyone else in there?"

"No . . . just the intruder. Sadie's out."

Eddie glanced at his partner and jerked his head in the direction of Buy the Book. Bill "Bull" McCoy drew his weapon and cautiously peered through the front door.

"I need to back up my partner," Eddie gently explained. "Can you stay here?" I hugged myself and nodded.

Eddie joined his partner, and I watched them both enter the store. Feeling as if curious stares were on my back, I turned to find that a crowd had congregated around the police cruiser. Eddie appeared in the store's doorway a moment later.

"Pen," he called.

Apparently, the store was empty. No sign of the intruder.

Still nervous, I walked back in and gave Eddie and his partner the rundown on what had happened. They listened, Eddie taking notes. I showed them where I left my lunch, the knocked-over display, the scattered hardcovers. I showed them the marks on my arms, fast darkening into bruises, and told them what the man had been after. They asked to see the old books, and we double-checked the Phelps editions. None were missing.

"He must have broken in through the back door," I told them. "The one leading into the storeroom."

"We checked that out already," said Bill McCoy. "And there's a problem with that theory."

Eddie and his partner took me back to the storeroom and showed me the door. There were no signs of forced entry. Stranger still, the back door was *locked*.

"Could he have picked the lock?" I asked.

Eddie shrugged. "Anything's possible. But why lock it again when you leave?"

"You *claim* you closed for lunch," Officer McCoy said in a barely civil tone. "Did you set the burglar alarm?"

"No," I replied sheepishly.

McCoy scowled and glanced at his partner. Eddie shifted uncomfortably. "I'll put in a report," he said. "But with nothing stolen, we can only file trespassing and assault charges—and that's if we catch this guy."

I thanked the men for their trouble and promised to set the alarm next time—which I did, as soon as they both left.

I then spent the rest of my lunch hour in a daze. When Sadie returned to the store, she found the BACK IN ONE HOUR sign still hanging on the door, and me on the floor, picking up the books I'd scattered in my wild flight. I told her what had happened, from the beginning, leaving out the ghost's part in coaching my escape.

The fact that the back door was locked, and not forced open, puzzled us both.

I offered another theory. "Is it possible that an early customer came in and hid back there, lying in wait until I was alone?"

Sadie shook her head. "The only customer I had was Mr. Van Riij, and he came and went before business hours. Then you returned from the school and I headed off to church."

"And I saw only two shoppers—both of them were women."

"The only way through that storeroom door is with a key." I looked down and rattled the keys dangling from my belt. "Mine is right here."

"I have my key, too," said Sadie. "And I'm sure the store key is behind the counter."

But when we looked for that spare key ring, which we kept on a hook behind the register, it was missing. There were four keys on that ring—one each for the front door, the back door, the storage room entrance, and the cash register.

Sadie picked up the phone. "I'm calling the locksmith to have the door locks changed. After that—" She checked her watch. "I'll get a head start on setting up the events room for the Quibblers meeting tonight."

While Sadie made the call, it occurred to me that two other people had access to those keys on a regular basis— Mina Griffith and Garfield Platt.

Of course, I knew my attacker wasn't Mina for obvious reasons and also because she only worked weekends. She didn't even know about the Phelps volumes of Poe yet.

As for Garfield, he stood at about my height, but the intruder was a head taller than I. And another thing: The intruder didn't know how to locate the books he presumably wanted to steal. I'd told him the books were by the register, but he'd still needed me to point out where the register was. Both of those facts let Garfield off the hook.

I wouldn't be so sure, Jack declared. *Circumstances dictate he had access to those keys. So turn your suspect in and let the cops sort it out. If Garfield's innocent, no harm done. The coppers will cut him loose eventually.*

"No, Jack, you're wrong. There would be harm done, so I can't do that."

Why the hell not?

"Because we're not in a big city, where there are so many people that nobody pays attention to their neighbor's business. Small-town people have less people to talk about. So, of course, they talk about them more."

I'm on your frequency, honey, but I'm getting nothing but static.

"Look," I said, "when Sadie and I hired Garfield, he told us straight out about his brother being an ex-con. Do you know why?"

Because he's honest to a fault?

"No. Because Quindicott runs on gossip. Neither Sadie nor I personally know Garfield's family, but if we'd started asking around, we'd have heard the gossip about his brother. Garfield knew that. So he saved us the trouble."

Throw me a bone, baby, I'm still trying to glom your point.

"If I were to claim Garfield had something to do with a break-in and an assault on me, and he got questioned by the police, his reputation would get ruined in this town, just like his brother's. Up to now, Garfield's been a solid, reliable employee, and he obviously wasn't the man who grabbed me. I'm not going to ruin his reputation and lose his trust just because I'm desperate for a lead."

Hasn't it occurred to you that Garfield's ex-con brother might be part of the picture here? He could have been the one who broke into the place.

"But . . . that would mean Garfield would have to be involved, too, wouldn't it?"

Bingo, baby.

"Okay, all right. I'll sit Garfield down when he comes to work tomorrow and ask him some hard questions. Between you and me, we should be able to figure out whether he's on the up-and-up or pegging me for a sucker."

Now you're speaking my language!

CHAPTER 14

Quibble Me This

Once upon a midnight dreary, while I pondered, weak
and weary/Over many a quaint and curious volume of
forgotten lore—

—Edgar Allan Poe, "The Raven," 1845

"IT IS HEREBY proposed that the Quinidicott Business
Owners Association shall make a request to the Zoning
Board to extend parking hours *(pahkin' ah-wahs)* an addi-
tional hour within the city limits Monday through Thurs-
day, and an additional two hours on Friday, Saturday, and
Sunday nights."

Bud Napp, the widower who owned Cranberry Street
Hardware, paused to stifle a yawn. "We do this in anticipation of the crowds that will supposedly be drawn to the
artsy-fartsy films Brainert is going to exhibit when his theater opens next month—"

"I object to that negative remark!" Brainert exclaimed with indignation. "My theater will be a valuable addition to this community."

"If the zoning witch lets you have a permit, *maybe*," Seymour said. "Otherwise your grand movie palace is going to be one big box of empty."

Brainert scowled. "Thanks for the bulletin, Tarnish. Shouldn't you be peddling ice cream to the teeners up at the haunted house?"

"No way, Parker," Seymour replied with a grin. "Wouldn't miss this meeting for the world."

It was obvious to me that Seymour had already heard about the masked man breaking into my store and was here to learn all the juicy details.

Mailmen don't have much to live for, do they, doll?

On that, I had no comment.

"Anyone ready to second the final motion on the table?" Bud Napp bellowed impatiently.

Linda Cooper-Logan and her husband, Milner, of Cooper Family Bakery, both raised their hands. "We second it."

"Motion passed." Bud slammed the hammer down, rattling the table. He was wielding a real hammer, too—a brand-new ball peen fresh from his hardware store. Someone had absconded with the gavel after a meeting several months ago. It was one mystery the Quindicott Business Owners Association (a.k.a., the Quibble Over Anything Gang) hadn't got around to solving.

On the other hand, some of the members had helped me solve far more vexing mysteries. To wit: Bud Napp, Seymour Tarnish, J. Brainert Parker, Fiona Finch, Linda and Milner Logan, and Mr. Koh and his daughter had helped solve the murder of a visiting true crime author this past summer. Tonight, after the regular meeting adjourned, I was holding out hope they'd stay and help Sadie, Brainert, and I solve another.

Bud Napp searched me out in the crowd. "This meet's adjourned," he declared with a slam.

The room began to empty at once. Casual attendees filed out immediately—folks like Chick Pattelli, owner of the garden store; Glenn Hastings of Hastings Pharmacy; and Gerry Kovacks, owner and manager of the newly opened phone store, Cellular Planet. All were escorted through the bookstore, to the front door by Sadie. Within a few minutes, the only folks left in the meeting room were the people I'd ask to stay. Sadie locked the door and joined us.

Rather self-consciously, I stepped behind the podium set up at the front of the room. Behind me, Bud Napp sat at a table, our judge and referee in these informal gatherings as well.

For the next hour, I brought everyone up to speed—about the death of Peter Chesley in Newport, Rene Montour's fatal accident on Crowley Road, ending with the details on the attempted robbery of my store and the assault on yours truly.

Milner cleared his throat. "There's something you should know, Pen. Officer McCoy was in the bakery this afternoon. He told me what happened. And he claimed you'd made the whole thing up."

"What?!" I cried.

Linda nudged her husband with her elbow. "Tell her the rest of it," she demanded.

Milner winced. "McCoy said . . . sorry, Pen, but he made a crack about you. About how everyone around town knows all about how you became a widow, that your husband killed himself. I think he meant to suggest that maybe you were . . . you know . . . mentally unstable."

Seymour Tarnish balled a fist and banged his thigh. "That's just the kind of crap I expect to hear from Bull McCoy. What did that jerk's partner have to say?"

"Eddie wasn't there," Linda replied. "It was just Mc-

Coy, shooting off his mouth. I don't know how that moron even got on the police force."

"It's easy when you're Chief Ciders's *nephew*," Bud pointed out.

I threw up my hands. As small a town as this was, I couldn't believe no one had shared that little fact with me before tonight. "No wonder McCoy is spreading stories about me. He gets his attitude from his uncle." And everyone knew there was no love lost between Ciders and me.

"Forget it, Pen," Brainert said. "We believe you. That's what counts."

Fiona Finch rose. "Getting back on the subject at hand, Penelope, I think you should know I received a strange phone call this afternoon. . . ."

As Fiona deliberately allowed her voice to trail off, Seymour folded his arms and tapped his foot. Fiona loved drawing out the suspense when she dispensed gossip. We were all used to it by now, but it continually drove Seymour up the wall.

"Out with it!" he cried. "Who from?"

"From Rene Montour's uncle in Canada," Fiona declared.

Sadie nodded. "That's not unusual. Jacques Montour is the family patriarch and the true book collector in the family. Rene does—er, *did* bidding and buying for Jacques."

"Well," Fiona said, "Jacques Montour requested we hold Rene's luggage and personal effects until a representative of the family arrives."

"When is this representative expected?" I asked.

Fiona glanced at her watch. "He should be at the inn right now. I left my Barney at home to meet them. Whoever he is, he's going to be disappointed."

Sadie blinked. "Why?"

"Mr. Montour didn't leave much in his room," Fiona replied. "But I knew he was travelling with *something* of value because the first thing he did was ask me if the inn had a vault. I told Mr. Montour he was free to avail himself of the inn's wall safe, but after checking it out, he told Barney that the safe would not be large enough for his purposes."

"Montour obviously wanted to stash the books in a secure place," Sadie said. "He knew they were too valuable to leave in the room, so he kept them with him at all times. That's why the books were in the car when he went for a drive."

"But the question is, why did he go for a drive?" I asked. "Mr. Montour had dinner at Fiona's restaurant, he didn't know anyone in the town except perhaps Sadie. Where was the man going at nine o'clock on a Sunday night in Quindicott?"

"Mr. Montour received a phone call at around eight-thirty, if that's any help," Fiona offered. "About fifteen minutes later, he went out."

"Another *mysterious* caller," Seymour said in his woo-woo spooky voice. "Could it be the same as-yet unknown person who called 911 while you were at Chesley's mansion? Only the shadow knows . . ."

Anybody going to tell this rube he's being about as helpful as a rock in your shoe?

"Two murders and an assault over a set of books," Milner said. "What I'd like to know is why they're so special."

"Yeah, so they're old. So what?" Linda shrugged. "You can get the Poe stuff anywhere. It's not like it's out of print."

"Allow me." Brainert moved to the podium, a file folder full of papers in his hand. I returned to my seat next to Sadie.

"Eugene Phelps knew there was not much market for his Poes when he published them," Brainert explained in his professorial tone. "Phelps also knew there would be limited interest in his dubious scholarship, his rambling introductions. That's why he buried a secret code inside these books—three of them, in fact."

"Codes?" Fiona sounded almost breathless. "Like in *The Da Vinci Code*?"

Brainert appeared to have sucked on a lemon. "Kind of like that, Fiona. Only without the secret societies and that nonsense about Mary Magdalene."

"No loose women!?" Seymour cracked. "Sheesh, that's the best part."

Bud slammed his hammer. "I want to hear about those codes."

"I'm sure you do," Brainert said. "According to solicitation letters Eugene Phelps sent out to subscribers in the 1920s, there are three codes buried inside these editions. The solution to all three riddles was to reveal the existence and location of a literary and artistic treasure, or so Eugene Arthur Phelps claimed."

Bud Napp snorted. "Don't you think that the premium for that particular prize might have expired after all these years?"

"Or maybe someone already claimed this marvelous treasure," Mr. Koh said.

"Anyway it just sounds nuts," grumbled the skeptical Bud.

Brainert nodded. "Maybe. But there *is* at least one code, which was solved by a scholar named Dr. Robert Conte. Penelope, you may recall that my colleague Nelson Spinner mentioned him? Well, I looked up his research, and I have the Conte paper right here."

Seymour crossed his arms above his thick waist and stared at Brainert. "This had better be good."

"Dr. Conte did a thorough textual analysis of the Phelps books as compared to the now-standard Poe text accepted as correct by the Ford Foundation and the Library of America—"

Bud brought the hammer down. "In English, if you please, Professor. And cut to the chase."

Brainert sighed. "Dr. Conte determined that there are errant letters in the first story of each volume of the Phelps

Poe books. They look like typographical errors, but if you put them all together and reverse their order, it spells out an actual sentence—" He glanced at the papers on the podium in front of him. "Mystic Library east wall sunset reveals all."

I heard Jack Shepard groan in my head. *This is starting to sound like decoder ring hooey.*

"Is this riddle meant to reveal a hidden secret about the library in Mystic, Connecticut?" Sadie asked.

"That's what Dr. Conte believed, but he was dead wrong. According to my own research"—Brainert grinned and straightened his bow tie—"when Eugene Arthur Phelps was editing his Poes, he lived in a large mansion at the cross streets of Plum and Armstrong in Newport. In the 1940s, the house was converted into apartments and renamed The Arms, but the mansion's name when Phelps lived there was Mystic House.

"Ahhh!" said the Quibblers.

"Inside this Mystic House there was a large, well-stocked library, much of it dedicated to the study of Edgar Allan Poe."

Seymour arched his eyebrow. "Was?" he said.

Brainert nodded. "The place was destroyed by a fire in 1956."

Bud threw up his hands. "Then I was right. The treasure *is* lost."

"Frankly, I don't think this treasure ever existed." Linda Cooper-Logan waved her hand, her silver and jade bracelets janging. "Except as a figment of Eugene Phelps's imagination. But I guess anyone who becomes obsessed with Edgar Poe is a little crazy, right?"

Brainert sighed. "Eugene Phelps was a tragic figure. An eccentric, and something of a romantic, too. But I doubt he was crazy, Linda. In fact, it was easy to find parallels between Edgar Allan Poe's and Eugene Arthur Phelps's life that may have fueled the latter's obsession with the former."

"Beside the fact that both men have the same initials, what else have you got," Seymour asked. "And by the way, I have the same initials as Sharon Tate. Using your logic, I should be murdered by a crazy, Manson family–type cult."

"We should be so lucky," Fiona muttered.

"Watch it, bird lady! Mail can get lost, you know."

Brainert ignored the bickering and pressed on. "As you know, Poe was the son of a beautiful stage actress who died when he was just a child. Phelps's mother was a trained opera singer who died of tuberculosis when he was four. After his mother's demise, Poe was adopted by a wealthy family named the Allans. Frances Allan loved Poe like a son; Mr. John Allan was cold and indifferent. Mrs. Allan died when Poe was nineteen and in military service. Her death left him once again bereft and motherless, with a stepfather who neither appreciated nor wanted him. Eugene Phelps had an indifferent father as well. After the death of his wife, Eugene's father remarried, and the couple spent the next fifteen years traveling the world. Eugene remained in New England, raised by a string of nannies and servants—"

"Life in a Newport mansion," Seymour cut in. "Poor him. I could think of worse things—like the life of a mailman."

"Loneliness haunts rich and poor alike. Nobody is immune." Sadie's voice was barely above a whisper.

"No, Seymour is right," said Brainert. "At least Eugene Phelps inherited his family's money. But like Poe, he married late in life to a very young bride. Unfortunately for Phelps, she died of tuberculosis five years later and he never remarried."

"And Poe?" Linda asked.

"The pattern for Poe's life began early and never changed. He became defined by loneliness and alienation, and a hopeless quest for love and acceptance. But Poe was doomed to forever be an outcast. His poetry and prose were sometimes controversial, and in his literary criticism, Poe attacked the leading lights of his day, which didn't make him popular. In a way, Poe was his own worst enemy." Brainert shook his head. "But saddest of all, the women in Poe's life always died, leaving him alone and loveless. After losing his stepmother, Poe married a teenaged cousin when he was twenty-seven. But Virginia Clemm was weak and sickly and hovered near death for many years. Eventually she died of consumption, just like Poe's mother."

"How tragic." Linda sighed.

"Yes," Brainert said. "Though loss and mourning ultimately fueled Poe's art and led to the composition of his greatest works, eventually tragedy—and alcohol—took their toll."

During Brainert's recounting of Poe's difficult life, I saw Sadie become more and more emotional.

"How did it end?" Linda asked.

"In his final few years, Poe became a pathetic figure," Brainert continued. "Though his writings made him famous, there was little joy and less financial gain in this recognition. Poe wandered the country from Baltimore to Philadelphia and through the Antebellum South, desperately courting a number of women, simply because he could not cope with life alone."

Sadie jumped to her feet. Tears she'd been trying to hold back spilled onto her cheeks. She fled the room without a word.

For a moment, everyone sat in an uncomfortable silence. "My aunt is still getting over the loss of her friend Peter," I explained. "I'd better go see if she's okay—"

"Let me, Pen."

Before I could even rise, Bud Napp was on his feet and heading for the doorway. I wasn't surprised. Ever since he'd lost his wife to cancer, Bud had been a good customer of Buy the Book. "Turns out, good reading's good company in the lonely hours," he'd once told us.

He got started by working through his wife's old pile of

Agatha Christies. Soon, Sadie was suggesting some newer authors (although Miss Marple still remains his all-time favorite), and the two seniors had struck up a friendship. Lately, they'd been seeing each other outside the bookstore, for the occasional dinner or drive to Providence.

"So where do we go from here?" Seymour asked after Bud left. "If there was a treasure, it's gone up in smoke. And we hit a dead end, anyway."

"Not necessarily," said Brainert with the hint of a smile.

"What have you got, Brainiac?" Seymour demanded.

"Turns out there was a bundle of papers packed away with the Phelps editions—papers belonging to Miles Milton Chesley, the grandfather of Sadie's friend Peter Chesley."

I'd forgotten all about those papers, and the fact that Sadie gave them to Brainert to peruse.

"According to his letters, Miles Chesley bought each volume as they were published, mostly because he was obsessed with finding the treasure," Brainert explained.

"Did *he* solve any of the riddles?" Fiona asked.

"Only the first one, pointing to the Mystic library," Brainert replied. "The same one Dr. Conte solved." His grin reappeared. "But I solved another."

"Explain, oh great one," Seymour urged.

Brainert nodded. "Ever see those tiny numbers and letters tucked near the fold of a hardcover? Those are signature marks and they exist to tell the bookbinder in what order the leaves should be bound. Well, in the Phelps books, there is a signature mark on the title page of each volume."

"The title page?" I said. "That makes no sense."

"Exactly! The title page is page five in the front matter of each volume, far too soon for a new leaf—since leaves are typically sixteen to twenty pages. That's when I realized the marks were bogus."

"That's why you had Sadie copy the title pages for you!" I cried.

Brainert nodded. "I used a magnifying glass to examine

the tiny letters and realized they were not the initials of the book titles, as is customary. These letters appeared to be random, and one of the volumes had a tiny mark that looked like a stray period. But when I examined it closely, I found it resembled a bug! So, of course, I applied the cryptogram that Edgar Allan Poe invented for his classic detective story, "The Gold Bug," to those random letters in the title page signature marks, and I decoded the phrase 'This is indeed Life itself.'"

Seymour scowled. "And this means?"

"It's from a Poe story," Brainert said. "A very important passage found in—"

We were interrupted by a pounding noise. Someone was knocking on the store's front door. The CLOSED sign was posted and the store lights dimmed, so I wondered who it could be. The pounding began again, followed by the buzz of the night doorbell.

"I'd better get that. I don't want Sadie to be bothered." I rose and moved through the darkened bookstore to the front door. On the way, I saw flashing red lights rippling through the windows. Quindicott and Rhode Island State Police cars lined the curb. When I opened the door, a blast of frigid night air washed over me, and I shivered as three dark silhouettes stepped forward.

I saw the big, heavyset form of Chief Ciders, a scowl on his face. At his side, Eddie Franzetti shifted uncomfortably. I recognized the tallest of the three, a broad-shouldered, bull-necked man in a gray Statie uniform and Smokey the Bear hat. This time it wasn't the cold that made me shiver, but the stone cold eyes of Detective-Lieutenant Roger Marsh of the Rhode Island State Police.

"You're Mrs. McClure? Penelope Thornton-McClure?" Marsh asked, deadpan.

"You know I am," I replied.

I heard a sound behind me. Brainert and Seymour had followed me out of the meeting. Marsh saw them, too.

"Step outside, please, Mrs. McClure."

I figured he wanted to ask me questions, and wanted privacy to do it.

Suddenly Jack's shout filled my head. *Don't do it, Penelope!*

His warning came too late. I stepped across the threshold, pulling the door closed behind me. Suddenly Officer Bull McCoy stepped out of the shadows. His strong hands grabbed my arms, pulled them behind me. I heard a *click*, felt icy metal bracelets on my wrists. I tried to pull my arms free, but I'd been handcuffed before I realized it.

"Penelope Thornton-McClure, you are under arrest for grand larceny," said Detective Marsh in a voice like doom. "You have the right to remain silent. Anything you say can and will be used against you in a court of law . . ."

I hardly heard the rest of his spiel. When Marsh asked me if I understood the charges and my rights, I stared at the man in shock.

"You're charging me with grand larceny?" I repeated.

"That's right."

"What in the name of heaven was I supposed to have stolen!"

"Do you understand your rights as I've read them to you?" Marsh repeated. "Ma'am, answer yes or no."

"Yes, but—"

I heard the bookstore's door fly open and Seymour Tarnish's irate voice cry out. "Hey, you fascists, what the hell do you think you're—"

Bull McCoy stepped around me with his nightstick clutched in his fist. "Back off, mailman, if you know what's good for you or you can go to jail, too."

Behind me, I heard "Go to hell, McCoy!" a scuffle and a grunt.

"That's enough, Bull," Chief Ciders said.

Officer Tibbet of the Quindicott Police escorted me to a

squad car. Chief Ciders placed a beefy hand on my head to gently guide me into the back seat.

Still numb, I finally looked back and gasped. Seymour was crumpled on the sidewalk, clutching his stomach. Brainert, pale and in shock, stood over him. Together they helplessly watched the police cruiser carry me away.

CHAPTER 15

Headline News

A good reputation is more valuable than money.

—Publius Syrus

I WAS TAKEN directly to the Quindicott Police headquarters, a surprisingly small redbrick building on the outskirts of town.

A female officer searched me, then my personal belongings were placed in a manila envelope, including my wallet, watch, bracelet, earrings, and loose change. After that I was led into another room where I was posed against a white screen and handed a plaque with my name and date on it. A young male officer snapped my photograph with a handheld camera. Then my fingerprints were taken.

While I was wiping the ink from my hands, I heard angry voices from the next room. I recognized Chief Ciders's bellow. The other speaker was Detective Marsh, who spoke with calm authority.

I couldn't make out much, but it sounded to me like they were fighting about my arrest. Apparently Ciders wasn't happy.

A policewoman took my arm. I recognized her as a customer in my store. I'd seen her browsing with her two preteen daughters in tow. Now my face reddened with shame and I could hardly face her.

The room they placed me in was deemed a "holding cell"—a cubicle with sickly green paint on the walls, a concrete floor, fluorescent lights, and a cot, sink, and toilet. There were no bars on the doors or windows. In fact, there were no windows, except for the wire-laced pane set in the steel door so the officers could keep an eye on their prisoner. The room must have been soundproofed, because the last thing I heard was the click of the lock being thrown.

I felt like crying, but the tears wouldn't come. They'd taken everything from my pockets, including Jack's buffalo nickel. I closed my eyes, willed him to be there for me, but there was nothing. I couldn't feel him or hear him. I felt lost and completely alone.

There was no chair, so I laid down on the bunk, expecting to toss and turn all night. But I was coming down hard off an adrenaline shock, and I fell into a deep deathlike sleep. I didn't wake up until another policewoman arrived in the morning.

"Time to see the magistrate, Mrs. McClure," the woman told me.

"I need to make a phone call," I replied, wiping the sleep from my eyes. "I want to check on my son."

The woman went away, returned with a cell phone. I called my aunt and told her to stay put, to take care of Spencer and send him off to school. I also told her to call

Brainert if I wasn't back home by noon. Sadie put up a brave front, but I knew she was upset and frightened.

I was taken to Quindicott's historic, pre–Civil War era courthouse, where I waited for two hours. Finally the magistrate arrived, heard the charges, and set a trial date in early January. Since I had "ties to the community" I was not deemed "a flight risk," so I was released on my own recognizance.

Officer Franzetti drove me home after the hearing. Sensitive to my embarrassment, Eddie left the squad car with his partner and chauffeured me in his own SUV. It was nearly eleven o'clock in the morning when I got back to Buy the Book. A relieved Sadie rushed to hug me when she heard the door chime.

"Brainert called three times, frantic with worry. Seymour was here, too—"

"How is Seymour?" I asked. "It looked like Bull McCoy gave him a pretty bad time."

"He's fine," Sadie replied. "Swears he's going to make sure Bull McCoy gets the wrong mail for at least six months."

"And Spencer?"

"I just told him something came up and you had to go out. He got off to school just fine. Frankly, I think he was relieved you wouldn't be going with him today. I think he was hoping you'd miss your meeting with the new principal."

I hadn't forgotten the meeting—with yet another Chesley. More complications at a time when things were complicated enough for me already!

"Now, please, Penelope, I've been fretting all night. What in the world is going on? *Why* were you arrested? Seymour and Brainert told me the state police charged you with theft?"

"Grand larceny—a felony."

"For stealing *what*?" Sadie asked.

"Jacques Montour has charged me with stealing the Poe

book that Rene bought for him," I explained. "Apparently, his representative, a man named Gordon Hessler, showed up at Fiona's last night to collect Rene's personal belongings. After that, he went to the Quindicott Police Station to claim the effects from the accident scene.

"When Ciders turned over the Chandler first editions but no Phelps Poe, Hessler was irate. He called the state police and said that an eight-thousand-dollar book was missing and presumed stolen.

"Detective Marsh called back Chief Ciders, who'd been in charge of the accident scene. Ciders said the scene was secure. The only person who was even close to the car, besides the police and emergency workers, was me. And, of course, I had told Ciders I was looking for the exact book that was stolen. In retrospect, I guess I was pretty rude and loud about it, too."

"I see," said Sadie. "So you became the fall guy, so to speak."

"Yes, I think there was pressure on the state police to arrest me. And Officer Marsh is not exactly a fan of mine. He's marked me as a bad penny ever since the first author to appear in our store ended up as a corpse."

"But there's no *evidence* against you," Sadie cried, throwing up her hands.

"That's what Chief Ciders told Marsh. I heard them arguing while I was being booked. Eddie said Ciders was really steamed about my being arrested, but he had no choice. He actually stuck his neck out to keep me here in town instead of being booked in Providence like Marsh wanted."

Sadie snorted. "Chief Ciders doesn't stick his neck out for anyone."

"Apparently Ciders feels guilty for implicating me. Small comfort if I go to prison."

"You're not going anywhere." Sadie passed me a mug of hot coffee from the thermos we kept behind the counter.

I took my first sip, realizing only then that I'd had no

food or drink since the Quibbler's meeting. "So what do I tell Spencer?" I asked. "He's going to hear about this sooner or later."

"Then it's best he hear it from you. When he gets home from school we'll both sit him down and have a talk."

"How do I tell my son I'm innocent?"

"Don't worry, Pen. Spencer's watched enough shows on the Intrigue Channel to know people get blamed all the time for crimes they didn't commit."

I sighed, took another hit of caffeine. "How are *you* feeling?" I asked my aunt. "The meeting last night seemed to upset you."

Sadie shook her head. "It wasn't the meeting. It was all those things Parker said about Poe. I just got to thinking about Peter, how bad off he was at the end, how a stupid misunderstanding set us apart all those years . . ."

"What misunderstanding? I don't follow."

"Well, I thought I had put this behind me, but . . . remember the night Peter died, as we were leaving his mansion? You left us alone to say goodnight . . ."

"I remember."

"Peter actually asked me how 'my husband' was. The question took me by surprise. But Peter told me he'd read about my marriage in the *Providence Journal*—"

"Oh, yes! I remember that. You wrote me a letter about it while I was living in New York. The announcement said, 'Sadie Thornton married' . . . Who was it?"

"Mr. Aletti, of the Quindicott Savings and Loan," Sadie said. "The paper got the names wrong, printing my name instead of Sadie Thorners. I got ribbed about it for weeks—your friend Seymour was the worst. He'd just started his route that year. Kept saying he had a truck load of wedding gifts for the wrong bride."

"So Peter Chesley read that announcement in the paper, and he thought—"

"He thought I was married." Sadie shook her head.

"That's why he never contacted me again. Eventually I myself assumed that he was the one who'd found someone. I'd convinced myself he'd gotten remarried and simply decided to break all ties with me."

Sadie brushed her cheek of a stray tear. "But the hardest part for me is . . . when I think back, to that time when we were so close, when were a couple, I can't even recall what it was that broke us apart. Just squabbles and hurt feelings and misunderstandings . . . now it all seems so petty . . . so stupid. I can't think why we didn't try harder to work it out."

I nodded, not knowing what to say.

"You can always tell yourself that there's a chance, but when someone dies, when he leaves the earth . . . well, when that happens, it's over. A door shuts forever. What am I saying? After what you went through in your life, Penelope, I don't have to tell you that, do I, dear?"

I chewed my lip, knowing she was talking about Calvin, but wishing I could tell her about Jack.

"Well, it's all water under the bridge now," she said. "We have to focus on the here and now."

And that's what we did.

The store had only a few customers, so I pulled out a stack of trade magazines I'd let pile up and began to read through the book reviews, making notes in the margins. Sadie went upstairs to fix me a sandwich.

Good morning, baby.

"Hi, Jack. . . . I missed you."

I'll bet. . . . How was your night in stir?

"Unpleasant. And humiliating. And you were right."

Yeah?

"I shouldn't have gone outside. They didn't have a warrant to enter the premises. By exiting the store, I set myself up for an arrest."

That scam was old when I was in knee pants.

"Hard to imagine you in knee pants, Jack."

These days, it's hard for me to remember the day when I

had knees, but at least nobody's trying to bust them any-more. Jack paused. *So . . . you ready to go to the mat yet?*

"Huh?"

Are you ready to fight back?

"Against who? Against what?" I cried. Aloud, apparently.

"What did you say, dear?" Sadie asked. She'd returned with a plate in one hand and a full glass of milk in the other. She wore a puzzled expression.

"Sorry . . . nothing," I said with a sigh. "I was just think-ing out loud."

"Have something to eat. You'll feel better," my aunt commanded.

When I sat down behind the counter, I saw a white en-velope tucked next to the register. It had Brainert's name on it, written in my aunt's flowing hand.

"What's this?" I asked between bites of my Virginia ham and Swiss cheese sandwich.

Sadie picked up the envelope and opened the flap. "Brainert and Seymour helped me pack up the chairs after the meeting last night," she said. "A little while ago, when I was sweeping out the storage room, I found this . . ."

She dropped a heavy object into my palm—a quarter-inch black square of onyx with a gold crest set in the middle. I immediately recognized the coat-of-arms of St. Francis College, where Brainert was a professor.

"It must have fallen out of Brainert's ring," Sadie said. "You can give it to him when you visit him later."

"Why am I visiting Brainert later?"

"He wants you to come by, after he's had a chance to do more research on the Poe Code."

I'd had my fill of Phelps, Poe, and the ridiculous code, but I kept silent, took a gulp of milk instead. I stared out the window a moment, at the people on the sidewalk, won-dering how many of them I knew.

"I'm almost afraid to go out," I said. "I feel like the police are watching me all the time. I'm afraid I'm going to get arrested again. Most of all, I'm worried about my reputation. Word is bound to get out."

Sadie shook her head. "Don't be silly, Pen. Hardly anyone knows what happened. It will be the Quibblers' little secret."

The chimes rang when a young man stepped through the door

"Here's your *Bulletin*s, ma'am," he said, dropping a bundle of newspapers next to the door. He was delivering our store's consignment of the *Quindicott Bulletin*, the town's weekly pennysaver and local newspaper rolled into one.

"Thank you," I called.

The youth's friendly smile vanished when he saw me. He was out the door and down the street in a flash. Meanwhile Sadie pulled a copy from the stack, glanced at the front page, and exploded.

"Damn that Elmer Crabtree!"

"What's wrong?" I cried. But I knew. I knew when the delivery boy gave me that look.

The main headline dealt with the beginning of the school year, including a photo of the kids arriving on the first day. The second story involved me, under the headline LOCAL STOREOWNER IMPLICATED IN THEFT.

The story was all of three paragraphs, obviously inserted just before the paper went to press this morning. Thankfully there was no mug shot. The article was factually incorrect, describing Rene Montour as a "Frenchman" who died in a "collision." Editor Crabtree even managed to get our store's name wrong, calling it "Buy Books Here." Of course, he *did* manage to spell my name right, and give my age (not that I'm vain, but I wouldn't want my weight or bank account information in the newspaper, either).

"I'd better have that talk with Spencer real soon," I said.

Sadie folded the paper and tossed it into the wastecan. "Speaking of Spencer. Don't you have a meeting with the new principal this afternoon?"

"I should cancel. I can't leave you alone in the store—"

"Nonsense. Business is slow, Pen. And Mina is coming in an hour."

"Mina? I thought Garfield was working today."

Sadie shrugged. "He called me just after I opened the store. Said he switched days with Mina. Said it was all worked out and she would be in on time."

I had yet to have that talk with Garfield about the missing key. Now I began to wonder if Garfield was avoiding me, or if he had something to hide.

That kid's a gimp, for sure, said Jack. *I'd peg him for a grifter, but one on a leash. If someone in the Platt family is in deep, I'd pin it on Garfield's brother, the fish who's fresh out of the joint.*

"Just because someone went to prison doesn't mean they're a criminal. I was in jail last night, but I didn't do anything wrong."

Babe, stop living in Dimsville. Jail isn't the same as prison. And there are two things to remember in life: people don't change, and most of them are no damned good.

"The way I'm feeling, I won't even argue with you."

But you're still not ready to go to the mat.

"I'm going to see the principal now," I said out loud.

"That's good, Pen," my aunt replied. "And don't forget to stop by Brainert's afterwards. I can't wait to hear what he's discovered."

A visit to the Casa de Egghead? Why do you want to go there, lamb chop? You just got out of jail!

CHAPTER 16

Principally Speaking

You get a smack on the snozzle in about a minute.

—Norbert Davis, "Kansas City Flash,"
Black Mask, March 1933

"I'M SORRY, MRS. McClure, Mr. Chesley should be back any minute."

Behind the high metal counter, the school secretary, "Ms. Jane" (what Jane Wiley had been instructing kids and parents to call her since I was ten years old) checked the antique watch on a chain around her neck. She glanced out the bank of windows behind her, patted the back of her up-swept, silver-threaded brown hair, then sat down at her wooden desk and began to drum a pencil against the side of her computer.

She looked up at me again, a little nervously, then quickly shifted her attention to her computer screen. The lady seemed uncomfortable. Of course, it occurred to me Ms. Jane's real discomfort might not have been her boss's lateness but my notorious presence. After all, how many times a day did a LOCAL STOREOWNER IMPLICATED IN THEFT walk into the Quindicott Elementary School office?

Well, baby, Jack said, *if the broad introduces you as "the accused," that'll be your first clue.*

"Thank you," I simultaneously said to Jack and the secretary.

There was a line of empty chairs near the glass office door and I sat down in one. Whether it was my night in jail or the giant poster on the wall listing DO'S AND DON'TS OF SCHOOL CONDUCT, I suddenly felt like I'd been sent in here for a reprimand.

Jack laughed. *Feeling like a bad girl, are you?*

"During the six years I went to this school, I never before saw the inside of this office."

No? You mean nice-thinking, do-right, moo juice–drinking little Penelope never got into trouble? Now there's a headline.

"Stow it, Jack."

There you go with that nautical talk again, and I can't stand the navy.

I massaged my throbbing temples. "I'm charged with a felony, waiting to see the principal, and a ghost who lives in my bookstore won't stop harassing me. What happened to my life?"

Aw, baby, now don't go getting into a funk, 'cause the last time I checked, I ain't no shrink, and I got no clue where the spirit of Sigmund Freud is marking time.

"I don't need Sigmund Freud. I need a good trial lawyer. Know any?"

Sure. Abraham Lincoln. Only, like old Siggy, I don't know where he's located, either.

After fifteen minutes of verbally sparring with my ghost, watching teachers come in and out of the office (glancing curiously my way), and listening to the office phone ring nonstop ("Quindicott Elementary, May I help you?"), I began to pace.

"Excuse me, Ms. Jane?" I finally called.

"Yes, Mrs. McClure." She looked up from her computer, removed the reading glasses from the tip of her nose.

"You said Mr. Chesley was 'due back'—is he even in the building?"

Once again, Ms. Jane glanced out the window, scanned the parking lot and the long driveway leading from the road. "I'm so sorry you have to wait. He did have some personal business to take care of, but it's been over an hour now, and he really should be back soon."

This dame's a back door, you know, Jack whispered through my mind.

"A back door?" I echoed.

Sure, baby, she's a way for you to get some background on this Chesley character you're waiting for. Use your limbo to advantage. Not that I am, by the way. I can think of a lot more stimulating places to haunt than a backwoods bookstore in a town full of hicks.

Ignoring Jack's latest jibe, I chewed my lip and seriously considered his back door suggestion. I wasn't a gossip at heart. I liked my own privacy and I tried to give people theirs—"Live and let live and you'll live a lot longer," my mom used to say. But when it came to murder, Jack was right, all bets were off.

"So . . . uh, Ms. Jane, I'm curious," I said, trying to sound casual, "what can you tell me about Claymore Chesley? I mean besides what you mentioned yesterday, about his credentials."

"Well, since you asked . . ." She rose from her desk and moved across the room, placing her elbows on the high counter that separated the waiting area from the rest of the office. "He's single, never been married, and no children, as far as I know," she said, her voice low. "I've overheard him talking on the phone, and it sounds to me like he came back East to help out his parents, but he's very disappointed he couldn't find any college-level openings right away."

"Why does he have to help out his parents?"

"His father's been ill. He's in a nursing facility now, and his mother's getting on in years. So he moved back home, took a supervisory position last spring in the school district office, 'just to pay the bills,' I overhead him say. With his father's illness, they've likely mounted up."

"So he's not going to be permanently on staff here, then?"

"Oh, no! Heaven's no. This is still Mrs. McConnell's school. Mr. Chesley was sent here by the school district to cover for her temporarily. I spoke to Eleanor just this morning to keep her up to date on everything. She has every intention of returning after her baby's delivered."

Most everything else Ms. Jane knew about Clay Chesley she said she'd picked up from a memo the school district had issued to the elementary school staff, announcing his temporary appointment.

"That's really all I know," she said with a shrug. "Not much, since we've only just started working together."

Not much? Cripes, this dame would make a hell of a professional snoop. I should hire her as my secretary.

"You can't. You're dead."

Don't get touchy, honey. Jealousy'll give a girl wrinkles.

As Ms. Jane went back to her computer, I continued to look out the office's back windows. Within a few minutes, a large black SUV pulled into a reserved parking slot near the building, and I found myself holding my breath, waiting for the driver to emerge.

The door opened and a tall, well-built man stepped out. He wore a tweed blazer, white shirt, brown corduroys, and a ochre tie. I couldn't make out his facial features very well, but he had a thick head of golden hair.

Was this the principal? The man threw an overcoat over

his arm and strode toward the school entrance. Less than a minute later, I had my answer. Claymore Chesley arrived in a whirlwind, sweeping through the office door without even noticing me in the anteroom.

"Jane," the man called, snapping his fingers. "I'm back. Anything urgent?"

"Your noon appointment is here," Jane replied, rising quickly to meet the man. She gestured in my direction.

Principal Chesley half turned, finally noticing me.

"Mrs. McClure," he said, with a short nod. "I didn't see you."

That's when I realized two things—the man did vaguely resemble Peter Chesley *and* I had actually seen him before. He'd been in Buy the Book a few times. I couldn't recall waiting on him, but I was certain he'd browsed our stacks.

"Give me one more minute," he said.

Before I could respond, he spun around again, showing me his back as he spoke with the school secretary—some business about a substitute teacher's paycheck. Then he asked what afternoon appointments followed mine. She ran down the list. Finally, he took a file from Ms. Jane's hands and half turned toward me again.

"All right, Mrs. McClure, come in," he said brusquely, waving for me to follow as he swiftly strode through his open office door.

He tossed his overcoat over a cluttered corner table and sat down behind his large desk. Immediately he began tapping on his computer keyboard; his fingers, I noticed, were sans ring—wedding or any other type. Ms. Jane was right. He wasn't married.

The monitor sat at an angle and I could partially see the screen. He was scanning his e-mails, ignoring me.

The man hadn't apologized for being late. Nor had he invited me to sit, but there were two chairs across from his desk, obviously meant for visitors. Both had stacks of files, books, and reports on them.

"Excuse me? May I move these?" I asked.

"Sure, just drop them anywhere," he said waving his hand, not bothering to look up from his screen.

This Alvin's got the manners of a goat.

"Can't argue with you there, Jack."

I picked up the heavy stack of books and reports and looked for a place to put them.

How about this bozo's head?

"Easy, Jack. He looks like a very busy man. Let's give him the benefit of the doubt."

On the other hand, as I nearly wrenched my back bending to set the pile carefully on the floor, I couldn't help remembering how chivalrous Peter Chesley had been when Sadie and I had visited him.

The old man had been struggling to even walk when he'd led us to the seats next to his library's fireplace, yet he'd remained standing by his wheelchair, refusing to sit until Sadie and I had first taken our seats. And, even though it must have been a painful effort, he'd insisted on helping us pack up the books we took with us.

I spoke up as I sat down. "Mr. Chesley, are you, by any chance, related to Peter Chesley, the retired Brown University professor?"

"He's my uncle," Chesley responded tonelessly. "Or rather, he was."

It's a cinch, Jack said. *Manners skip a generation.*

"You don't seem very upset about it," I bluntly told the principal.

That got his attention. He shifted away from the screen at last and focused hard on me. His eyes were blue—big, beautiful, electric blue. Obviously, he shared that line of DNA with his uncle. But not the expression, which was frosty as it peered at me, miles away from friendly. His eyes, however, weren't what disturbed me the most; it was the body part located between them—

"Your nose is swollen," I blurted out.

Claymore frowned. His hand automatically touching the puffy, discolored skin. "Accident. Up on the highway. It was hardly more than a fender bender but the airbag deployed. That's why I'm late."

I shifted uneasily, trying not to give away how disturbed I was by this claim. Just yesterday I had clobbered a well-built masked man—

Right in his beezer! Jack finished for me.

"His what?"

His nose, his nose!

"Okay! Okay!" I silently told Jack. "But what if Claymore here is telling the truth? I can't swear the injury is fresh. What if he really was in a car accident?"

Look, baby, if this joker really was in an accident, then his boiler out there should have some sort of dent in it. A few scratches, at least. If it doesn't, you know he's playing you for a rube.

"Should I make an excuse, get up now and check?"

Don't move your keister. Check the parking lot when you leave. Right now, you've got to conduct your interview— only don't let the yegg know you're interrogating him. Facts, baby, get me some facts.

I stalled to get my thoughts in order, pretending to cough and clear my throat. Finally, striving to keep my tone conversational, I said, "I knew your uncle. Not very well or anything, but that's why I asked. And I'm very sorry about your loss."

"Thanks, but I hadn't seen the man in over twenty years."

"Really? Why is that?"

Claymore shifted in his seat; the old leather chair creaked. "Uncle Peter was part of the Newport Chesleys. My side of the family lives in Millstone. Years ago, the two sides had a falling-out. You know how it is with family feuds?"

I nodded, as if commiserating, but my mind was racing. Millstone was the next town over. Like Quindicott, it was a far cry from Newport. In fact, as property values and incomes went, Millstone was even less affluent than Quindicott.

Ms. Jane had already said Claymore needed money, that he'd come back East to help his aging parents. If that were true, then Claymore's side of the family must not have benefitted from any of the inheritance Peter's side had received. But just how cut off were they?

"So you've never been to the family's old estate near the ocean, Prospero House?" I asked.

"Not since I was very young. I remember it being fairly creepy."

"Yes, well . . . I was just there—on the night your uncle died." I eyeballed Claymore, trying to gauge his reaction, but the man just kept staring at me, stone-faced. "It looked like the mansion was falling down around his ears," I added pointedly.

"Is that so? Well . . . like I said, Mrs. McClure, all I know about my uncle's death is what I read in the papers."

"But the papers didn't say much of anything."

"I don't know what you're getting at."

"Your uncle died falling down a flight of stairs. But he had severe arthritis and he told me and my aunt that he no longer climbed the stairs. He'd even moved his bedroom to the first floor."

"That's odd, but then . . ." He shrugged. "My uncle was sort of odd, as I recall."

"So you haven't been back long?" I asked.

"What do you mean? Back from lunch?"

"No, back here in Rhode Island. When I stopped by yesterday, Ms. Jane told me about your credentials. Very impressive. You went to St. Francis College, but then you moved away, went to California to get your doctorate and you stayed out west, right? You became a professor at a teacher's college. So when exactly did you move back East? And what exactly have you been up to?"

Whoa, baby, slow down! You're moving too fast!

The second Jack said it, I knew I'd messed up.

Claymore Chesley stiffened, then adjusted his tie. "What is this? A job interview?" He laughed to undercut his discomfort, then he glanced at his watch. "Didn't you come here to discuss your son?"

"Yes, of course. I'm sorry. I don't mean to pry. I was just curious. You're one of Buy the Book's customers—I mean, I've seen you in our store—and I like to know about my customers. It helps me better serve them."

"I moved back to Millstone last February, Mrs. Mc-Clure," he said curtly. "And I browse lots of bookstores, but I *buy* them on the Internet. Now let's discuss your son. . . ." He scanned the file Ms. Jane had handed to him and leaned forward, his elbows on the desk. "Spencer, right? What's the problem?"

"Jack," I silently wailed, "what do I do?"

Talk about your son. Set the man at ease. Make him think that you're not grilling him . . . then go back to grilling him!

I dug into my handbag and laid out the reason I'd come, placing Spencer's ripped Reader's Notebook and the pieces of his first-place award certificate on the principal's desk. I explained that there'd been bullying on the bus, that a child named Boyce Lyell had been responsible and the eyewitness was Susan Keenan, the mother of one of Spencer's friends.

Claymore Chesley picked up the shredded notebook and shook his head. "This is unacceptable," he said. "We'll have to punish Boyce, of course, although . . . I *can* see how this happened."

I nodded. "Yes, I agree. No supervision on the buses is obviously a problem."

"What? . . . No, Mrs. McClure, that's not the problem. We already have supervision on the buses. They're called bus drivers."

I bristled at the man's tone, which had gone from terse to downright insufferable.

"A bus driver isn't a monitor," I replied, trying to keep my own tone reasonable and courteous. "A driver's job is to drive the bus safely, pay attention to the road, not watch the kids. That's exactly what Spencer's driver told Susan Keenan when she berated him for not stopping the bullying."

"Wait, wait! Back up. Are you telling me a parent berated one of our drivers? We can't have that sort of thing going on. That's unacceptable treatment of an employee. What did you say her name was? Susan . . ." He picked up a pen. "Can you spell her last name?"

I stared speechless for a moment. "Principal Chesley, I'm talking about a bullying incident here. I'm talking about how to fix the situation of no supervision on the buses."

"There's nothing wrong with our system, Mrs. McClure. This incident on the bus with your boy is the only one that's come up this school year."

"The school year just started yesterday!"

"Nevertheless, you see my point?"

"What point?!"

"The bus drivers are on the bus. The bus drivers are also adults. Therefore, there are adults on the buses already. You see? Follow the simple syllogism and there are no monitors needed."

We went around and around like that for five more minutes. Finally, the principal stood up. "I understand your concerns, Mrs. McClure, and I'll take it under advisement—"

"No you won't," I snapped, rising to my feet as well. "You're just patronizing me. But I'm taking this up with the school board."

"You won't get anywhere. The school budget's on a shoestring as it is. We can't afford to pay teachers to ride the buses."

"Well, the children's safety comes first. Or at least it

should. If you won't address the problem through administration, I'm sure the parents can organize volunteers to ride the buses each day and provide supervision. I'll bring it up at the next PTA meeting."

"That's very resourceful of you, but let's be frank. Your son was bullied for a reason."

"Excuse me? You don't even know my son."

"I know you own a bookstore."

"So?"

"So . . ." Claymore Chesley shrugged. "It's understandable that a bunch of angry kids were upset he won the summer reading contest. I know at least one of the evaluating teachers broached the subject of disqualifying him for having an unfair advantage."

"Unfair advantage? Let me tell you something. My boy read every single book in that notebook. And every single book he read was checked out of the public library, which every child in this school has access to."

Claymore made a scoffing face. "Oh, come on. You're telling me the kid didn't use your bookstore?"

"Yes, that's what I'm telling you. You think I'd allow him to read books then put them back on the shelf to be sold as new? You've got a pretty low view of people, don't you, Mr. Chesley?"

"People cheat all the time, Mrs. McClure." Claymore glanced at his watch. "Jane!" he called loudly and rudely through the half-open door.

"Yes, Principal Chesley," said the secretary running to see why he'd bellowed.

"Is my next appointment here?"

"Yes, sir. Mrs. Sereno wanted to discuss the decorations for the Halloween party."

"Fine. Send her in."

I couldn't believe the man's level of rudeness. I waited for him to at least extend his hand and bid me goodbye, but he simply stood there, glaring.

It took a great force of will for me to refrain from extending my own hand and offering a polite and meek, even apologetic farewell. But I'd already done that more times in my life to count—reacted to overt hostility, even blatant rudeness, with a sort of cowed politeness, pretending the insult never happened instead of facing it head-on.

I was always making excuses for people like Claymore Chesley, telling myself that they were just stressed and emotional because they had problems in their lives. But they weren't the only ones with problems! I'd had problems all my life and I never stopped striving to display manners, to treat people with respect.

That's when I realized, I'd been so desperate in the past to reestablish an atmosphere of civility (with my in-laws, my old bosses in publishing, even my own moody, verbally abusive late husband), that I'd let nasty people get a way with . . . with . . .

Bullying, baby.

Oh my God, I thought. All those years. . . . I was simply letting myself get bullied instead of standing up and saying, "Hey! Wait a second. You shouldn't treat people like that! And you're not going to treat me like that!"

Baby, why do you think I've been saying, "Take it to the mat?"

I cleared my throat, but this time it wasn't to stall. It was to make sure my voice was loud and clear. "I'm not through here, Mr. Chesley," I said, not caring that Jane Wiley and Mrs. Sereno were standing only a few feet away.

"Excuse me?"

"You said people cheat all the time. Well, some people do. And some people don't. Some people are *honest* all the time, and upstanding and trustworthy, too. Or at least they try to be. And some of us, including your uncle Peter, God rest his soul, actually have *manners.*"

"What's that supposed to mean? Are you implying I don't?"

"You didn't have the decency to apologize for being late. You never offered me a seat or your hand to shake. And you had the nerve to imply that my son, the *victim* of a crime, had it coming."

"You're overreacting—"

"I'm leaving the evidence of that little boy's destructive bullying on your desk. And by the way, it was only one boy. One bully. Not 'a bunch of angry kids.' So I expect that Boyce Lyell will be punished for his actions."

Claymore nervously glanced at the school secretary and the art teacher watching the scene with wide eyes. The man fidgeted, crossing and uncrossing his arms, clearly embarrassed he'd miscalculated. He'd called his next appointment in to embarrass me into leaving. But I wasn't leaving until I'd said my peace, audience or not.

"I also expect a letter of reprimand to go to his parents," I continued, "and I'm expecting to be copied on it, so I know I don't have to take this matter up the ladder to the school district, *over your head*, got it? Is that clear enough for you?"

"That won't be necessary," he said, my threat finally prying a civil tone out of his mouth. "I'll make sure the boy is punished and his parents notified. You'll be copied, as you asked. Anything else?"

I blinked, staring in silence for a few seconds.

"Mrs. McClure," he prompted. "Anything else?"

Yeah, pal, Jack piped up in my head. *Just one more question: Did you happen to murder your old uncle Pete? Give Rene Montour the big chill? And break into my bookstore?*

I squeezed my eyes shut. "I blew it, didn't I?" I silently asked Jack. "There's no way I'm getting anything more out of this guy about his uncle or the rest of his family."

Don't sweat it, sweetheart. You took care of things for your boy. You did good. Now scram. Blow this joint.

"There's nothing else," I finally declared. "And I'm sure you can understand why I won't be saying, it was a pleasure."

Swallowing my nerves, I reached for as much dignity as I could muster, picked up my handbag, secured the strap over my shoulder, and wheeled to face the door.

Ms. Jane and Mrs. Sereno were still standing right there in the doorway. I could tell from their expressions—a striking combination of shock and awe—that I was the last person they'd expected to read Claymore Chesley the riot act.

"Good afternoon, ladies," I said, polite as can be.

From now on, I decided, civility was going to be a *gift*. Something I'd gladly bestow on *civil* people. No more freebies for schmucks, I thought, as I pushed through the glass door and stepped into the school hall.

I heard Jack Shepard laughing and then a little boy's voice.

"Hi, Mrs. McClure."

I looked down to see Danny Keenan wiping water away from his mouth with the back of his sleeve. He was standing next to a drinking fountain.

"Were you just in the principal's office?"

"Yes, I was."

"I heard yelling. Were you yelling at the principal?"

"Yes, Danny. I was."

His freckled face broke into a grin. "I can go tell Spencer you're here, if you want. He's in the cafeteria."

"No, Danny. That's all right. But thank you for being so thoughtful."

"No problem, Mrs. McClure." He waved as he headed back down the hall. "Have a nice day."

Well, what do you know, I thought, as I struck out for the parking lot to inspect Clay Chesley's vehicle.

What?

That ten-year-old had better manners than his principal.

Yeah, honey. That's a fact.

CHAPTER 17

Assault and Battery

"If you have something to say at all, tell me where it
is."

"Where what is?"

—Mike Hammer, refusing to talk in *The Big Kill*,
by Mickey Spillane, 1951

WHEN WE WERE teenagers and still in high school, the
Parker family's rambling Victorian on Crescent Drive was
a gray monstrosity, surrounded by wild bushes and an
overgrown yard. The porch sagged and so did the gutters.
The unpruned branches of a century-old elm butted against
the three-story building's paint-chipped walls and drafty
windows.

But since inheriting the house in the early 1990s, Brainert had fully restored it to its original grandeur. Gray walls
were now sky blue, the trim around the eaves and windows

virgin white. Surrounding the house, the expansive lawn now resembled a manicured golf course; and, in the spring and summer, the path to the front door was bordered by an array of flowers.

The porch no longer sagged—because the rotting vertical banisters had been torn out and new ones put in. But the entranceway was what impressed me the most. Simple windows had been replaced with stained glass, and a carved oak door purchased from a bankrupt Victorian hotel had replaced the original flimsy plywood.

It was somewhere between 1:30 and 2:00 when I parked my Saturn at the curb and strode up the pathway to Brainert's house. I noticed his front door stood wide open—but my friend was nowhere in sight.

I began to worry. Moving closer, I spied a plant overturned on the porch, its clay pot shattered, rich, black soil everywhere. Now I was alarmed. I cautiously climbed the porch steps.

"Hello, Brainert? Are you there?" I called.

No answer.

I took a few steps through the doorway and gasped. The interior hall was a total wreck—tables overturned, a framed painting knocked askew, a floor lamp tipped over and smashed on the parquet floor.

Panic mode now. "Brainert!"

I was far enough inside the house to peer around the corner, into the living room. That's when I saw my old friend, Jarvis Brainert Parker, lying facedown on a blood-stained Persian rug.

IN MY SATURN, I hugged the bumper of the ambulance the whole way to Benevolent Heart Hospital, a stone's throw from St. Francis College. By the time I parked my car and made it to the ER's front desk, Brainert had been admitted and the doctors were working on him.

I used my cell to call Sadie, told her Brainert had been assaulted, that I was at the hospital with him. We both knew this was no random crime, no mugging or burglary, but we left that thought unspoken. My aunt promised to watch for Spencer, while I stayed to hear about Brainert's condition. It was an hour before I heard any news.

Finally the tending physician, a soft-spoken man named Dr. Rhajdiq, found me in the waiting room. I was hunched in a chair, my legs curled under me, quietly praying while I twisted and unwound the handle of my purse. Dr. Rhajdiq's darker-than-dark eyes regarded me with concern. When he addressed me, he spoke slowly and carefully and paused several times to make sure I understood what he said.

"Mr. McClure, I have moderately good news," he began. "Mr. Parker will recover. He's conscious now, but groggy—"

"Thank God," I moaned.

Dr. Rhajdiq ran a hand through his thick, curly hair. The other he kept tucked in the pocket of his OR scrubs.

"Unfortunately, the man has suffered quite a beating. He has a minor concussion and the pain and discomfort that results from it. There are also lacerations to the face and scalp caused by glass. We had to extract a few shards. Fortunately there was no damage to his eyes."

"Is he in pain?

"We're doing what we can to manage his discomfort. But a concussion is a serious matter and can be very dangerous. We are going to keep Mr. Parker here overnight, for observation."

"When can I see him?"

Dr. Rhajdiq smiled. "He's asking to see you, Mrs. McClure. Right now the staff is in the process of moving the patient to a private room. In a few minutes I will send a nurse to escort you there."

True to his word, an attractive blonde in her early twenties approached me a little while later. Slender and delicate, she looked almost ethereal in her white nurse's uniform.

"Mrs. McClure, please come with me," she said, her voice as wispy as her demeanor.

I rose and followed the nurse to a bank of elevators, trying to avoid thinking about how much I hated hospitals.

Me, I kind of like them, Jack said, his first words since I'd found Brainert. *Hospitals got great features, like this angel who's giving us the grand tour. She's got gams right up to her neck.*

"Gee, Jack, and I thought I was the only woman in your life."

You're the only one who'll talk to me, so I guess you are, baby. But I guess the scenery ain't bad here at the ol' krankhaus.

"Well, I loathe this place. The smells, the sadness, the specter of death—nothing personal."

You're disregarding the good stuff.

"Good stuff?"

Yeah, like a brace of cutie-pie angels of mercy waiting on me hand and foot.

I tried not to laugh out loud. "You better have a look around. Half the 'cutie-pie' nurses in this establishment are men."

What! I thought they were orderlies! What's this stinking world coming to when an angel of mercy has facial hair?

We exited the elevator on the third floor and passed the nurse's station. Brainert's room was all the way down the hall, in the corner.

From the doctor's cautious tone, I expected to find my friend flat on his back, swathed from head to toe in bandages, tubes running into a vein in each arm. Then I rounded the doorway to his room and heard:

"I'm quite comfortable, nurse! Please stop fussing!"

Brainert's voice was shaky, but his cranky stubbornness was undiminished, which meant he was practically back to his old self!

"Please nurse," he declared, "stop fiddling with the bed and find my friend in the waiting room. I must see her at once!"

I entered to find Brainert sitting up, a nurse gamely trying to adjust his position. He was bandaged, but thankfully no tubes were visible, though a wire ran from a dressing on the tip of his finger to a pulse and respiration monitor beeping next to the bed.

"Pen! Please come in," Brainert called when he saw me—out of one eye; the other was covered by a thick bandage. So was his nose, and both of Brainert's forearms were swathed in thick gauze.

"Your face!" I cried.

"Broken glass," muttered Brainert. "Didn't damage my eye, so it's good news. And the scars—I'm hoping—will make me look distinguished, maybe even a little dangerous. It would be a nice change for me to start looking a little dangerous, don't you think?"

Jack laughed. *Tell your bird to lose his bow tie and he might have a fighting chance.*

"I think you'll wear any scars with as much panache as you wear everything in your life, Brainert."

He smiled, then lifted his arms. "Fifteen stitches in the left, twenty-two in the right."

I raised an eyebrow. "Now you just sound like you're bragging."

Brainert and I fell silent until the nurse finished her tasks. Finally she departed along with Jack's favorite blonde angel of mercy, and we were alone.

"What happened?" I asked.

"It was around noon," Brainert began, his voice low. "I was working in the living room, papers spread out on the coffee table. I'd made several phone calls and was compiling notes, and I heard a crash on the porch."

"What did you do?"

"I went to investigate." Brainert sighed. "Like a fool I

unlocked the front door without first looking to see who was there—I might as well have invited my attacker to mug me!"

"Who was on the porch?"

"A tall man. He wore a black denim jacket and a crudely improvised mask—"

"Was the mask black?" I interrupted. "Did it have ragged eye slits like he'd cut the knitted cap himself then pulled it down over his face?"

Brainert nodded. "I remember your description from the Quibblers meeting of the man who assaulted you. I'm positive this was the same person. As soon as I saw the mask, I knew he wanted my notes—"

"Notes? What notes?"

Brainert chatted on as if he hadn't heard me. "He demanded money, of course—in that raspy whisper meant to disguise his real voice—but it was all a ruse, and a clumsy one. He was really after the solution."

"Solution?"

"He grabbed my wallet, emptied it of cash. Then he pocketed my wristwatch. As he was stuffing his ill-gotten gains into his jacket, I jumped him."

"You what!"

"I fought him, Pen. I know how to stick up for myself! I sunk my fist into his gut. I even whacked him on the snout—"

"Snout," I thought. "Oh, my God. Jack, did you hear—"
I heard.

"I was doing well," Brainert went on, "until he rammed my face into the Victorian mirror—"

"Oh, God, Brainert, you poor—"

"That mirror was a treasure. I hope it brings him seven years bad luck. *He* was the one who broke the glass, you see. My skull was merely the instrument."

Brainert was really getting worked up now. The shock obviously had worn off, anger and outrage replacing it. I saw a nurse pause at his door, curious about the commotion.

"Shush, Brainert," I said in a whisper. "Calm down."

"Yes, yes, sorry," he said, quieter now. "It's not every day a guy fights for his life."

"What happened next?"

"When I was on the ground again, and bleeding all over my beautiful custom-weave Persian rug, the intruder found the papers I was working on. He gathered all of them up, stuffed them into his jacket. I tried to stop him, but, frankly, I couldn't get up. My assailant must have seen all the blood, probably thought he'd killed me. He fled. I remember trying to stand up . . ."

Brainert touched his battered nose. "The next thing I knew I was in the hospital, doctors working on me."

"Are you sure he came for your notes?"

"I'm certain, Pen! The way he gathered up every sheet of paper, this wasn't a casual swipe. He was very careful . . . He wanted my secret!"

"The solution to the Poe Code?"

Brainert nodded.

"What is it?" I asked. "You were about to announce the solution when Detective Marsh showed up at the Quibblers meeting to arrest me. The last thing I heard you say was something about an obscure quote . . ."

Brainert smiled. " 'This is indeed Life itself.' "

"What's it from? What's it mean?"

"It's from Poe's story 'The Oval Portrait.' "

I think I gasped just then. Jack exclaimed something in my mind, but he didn't have to remind me. The case I'd been dreaming about in Jack's time involved an oval portrait. The missing man, Vincent Tattershawe, had taken it off the desk of his secretary—and old lover—and sent it to his fiancée, Dorothy Kerns, just before he disappeared with most of her inheritance.

"Is that the treasure then?" I asked Brainert. "Is it an oval portrait?"

Brainert nodded. "I believe it is, yes—although it could be just another piece of the puzzle, another part of the larger treasure hunt."

"And all of your papers, the copies of the title pages Sadie made for you, they're all gone?" I asked.

"The intruder took the papers, but I have backup files." Brainert tapped his index finger to his temple. "And I recall what I've learned."

"Then you really did solve it?"

Brainert sighed. "While I'm certain an oval portrait is involved, I'm still missing one small piece of the puzzle. There is, however, a very promising theory I have yet to put to the test . . ."

"Go on."

"You see, my attacker didn't get one vital piece of information needed to solve the mystery and obtain the treasure, because I never got a chance to write it down. . . . I was curious to find out what happened to the estate of publisher Eugene Phelps after the man committed suicide. My Providence friend examined the estate sale records and discovered that Miles Chesley—Peter's grandfather—purchased the entire contents of Eugene Phelps's library in 1935. He had it transported to his Newport mansion. This occurred years before Phelps's home burned to the ground."

I gave Brainert a blank stare.

"Don't you see, Pen? It all makes sense. Miles Chesley solved the first riddle of the Poe Code, the same one that Dr. Conte solved."

"What was it again?"

" 'Mystic Library east wall sunset reveals all.' Dr. Conte thought the reference was to the library in Mystic, Connecticut. But he was wrong. Miles Chesley, who was alive in Eugene Phelps's day, knew Mystic referred to Phelps's mansion in Newport—Mystic House. That's why he purchased the entire contents of Phelps's library after the man killed himself. And that's why the Poe Code treasure would not have been destroyed in the 1956 fire that burned down Phelps's home. Miles Chesley had already moved the library's contents to his mansion! It's probably right there in Prospero House as we speak."

I didn't buy Brainert's theory and said so. "Surely Miles Chesley discovered the secret. He *owned* the library. How could he miss it?"

"Miles Chesley died of a sudden stroke the same year he bought the library. According to tax records—which I assure you are quite thorough—the Phelps auction took place in May 1936 and Miles died in early July. There's no evidence in Miles's notes that he'd been able to locate a treasure amid the vast contents of the library or solve the riddle pointing to an oval portrait."

"But something of great value would be obvious, wouldn't it? How can you be sure some descendant of Miles Chesley didn't find it?"

"Oh, Penelope! I doubt very much that this 'treasure' is some crass piece of gold or silver, some meaningless trinket." Brainert shifted position, and a groan escaped his bruised lips. "I'm betting that only an expert on the subject of Poe would be capable of recognizing the treasure's *true* value."

"Now that you mention it . . . the men who inherited the mansion had no interest in Poe." I remembered the maritime artifacts and yachting trophies all over Prospero House. "Miles Chesley's son—Peter's father—was obsessed with all things nautical," I told Brainert. "And Peter Chesley himself was a historian focused on the Revolutionary War period. He didn't seem to care about Poe, either."

"The Phelps editions were in the mansion's library, weren't they?" Brainert asked.

"Yes."

"Well, Miles Chesley's papers survived two generations of neglect—until they were stolen today, of course. If those items remained, then the treasure might be there, too."

I was beginning to warm to Brainert's theory. I remembered the creepy Poe clock in Peter's library. I also remembered the daguerreotypes and old photos on the walls. At the time, I thought they were simply images of Peter Chesley's ancestors. Now I mentioned them to Brainert.

"This oval portrait we're looking for would likely have something to do with Poe," Brainert insisted. "Perhaps a portrait of the author, or even the wife he loved so much and who died so young, Virginia Clemm—"

Excited, Brainert tried to rise, but immediately appeared woozy and sank back into his white hospital pillows. "If only I could go there now! See for myself!"

"Where?" I cried. "To the mansion? Are you sure that blow to your head didn't do more damage than you think?"

"This is no joke," Brainert insisted. "We have to know the truth. Two men may have been murdered over this treasure. You were attacked, and so was I. When will this calamity end if we don't end it?"

I mulled this over—along with the decision of whether to share what I'd learned today about Peter's nephew, Claymore.

Might as well tell him, Jack advised. *He's in as deep as you now.*

"Of course," Brainert was saying, "there is one more piece of information I require to confirm the last part of my theory, but I can't do it from this bed. I'll have to make a phone call or two—"

"Brainert, listen to me," I said, cutting him off. "I think I know who attacked you . . . and me, for that matter."

"You do? Who, for heaven's sake?"

"When I came to see you, I had just met with the new principal at Quindicott Elementary—"

"New principal? What happened to Mrs. McConnell?"

"She's on maternity leave. The new guy's temporary. And that new guy's name is . . . are you ready for this? Claymore Chesley."

"What! Is he related to the Chesley family?"

I filled Brainert in on everything I'd learned.

He shook his head. "So Claymore badly needs money and he's obviously stung by the fact that his side of the family was cut out of the Chesley inheritance. But how would he even know about the Poe Code? He told you he hadn't been in his family's Newport mansion since he was a little boy."

"I think he was lying," I said. "I think when he moved back to Rhode Island last February, he looked up his uncle and befriended him. After all, Claymore Chesley was a professor, he'd earned a doctorate and taught, and he would have been able to establish common ground as a fellow academic with his uncle Peter."

"I suppose it's possible."

"Think about it . . . Peter was suffering from arthritis pretty badly near the end of his life. The condition he was in, he probably welcomed having a tall, strong young relative show up at his door and help him with his task of inventorying the entire mansion's contents—including the library. In fact, now that I think it through, Peter could never have inventoried that library alone. How would he have reached the higher books? No, he had help, and I'm betting that help was Claymore."

"So you think Claymore stumbled upon the code while he was helping his uncle inventory the family's library, and since he needed money, he was trying to solve it so he could steal the hidden treasure?"

"Yes, I think it was Claymore who was upstairs when Sadie and I were visiting. And I think the key is that last bit of information you told me. The treasure is in that library. It's in Prospero House. I think Peter probably suspected what Claymore was up to—that he was going to solve the code and steal the treasure right out of the mansion. And that's why he called Sadie with such an urgent offer."

"Yes, I see!"

"Peter wanted us to take those books out of the mansion right away so Claymore would no longer have access to them—or the code, or the discovery of the treasure. After we left, I'll bet Claymore came downstairs, argued with his uncle, got angry, and killed him with a blow, then tried to make it look like an accident by tossing him down the stairs."

"And the 911 call?"

"There's an explanation for that too, I think." I rose and began to pace. "After he killed his uncle, Clay Chesley could have called 911 himself and disguised his voice, making it sound like his uncle in medical distress, asking for help. That way, when the police came to the house and found Peter's body, they would assume he'd fallen as a result of medical illness or disorientation. And, in fact, that's exactly what Detective Kroll assumed." I shook my head. "That's the notorious part if you ask me. Even if Claymore killed his uncle by accident, he was completely cold-blooded in the way he covered it up."

Brainert nodded, following along. "So you think Claymore was the raspy-voiced intruder who broke into Buy the Book, too?"

"Same M.O. of disguising his voice. And he's a tall, well-built guy. But here's the fact that nails him to the wall: His SUV had no dents in it. Not one scratch."

"And that nails him because . . . ?"

"Oh, I didn't tell you! When he showed up *late* for our meeting—late enough to have accosted you, changed, and driven back to the school—he was sporting a swollen, discolored nose."

"No!"

"Yes! He told me he'd been in an accident on the highway and his airbag deployed. But if he'd been in an accident, his car would have at least had a dent or a scratch on it, and there was nothing! After our meeting in his office, I went out to the parking lot and checked out the SUV I saw him driving—there was no way that car was in an accident."

"He lied?"

"Why would anyone lie about something like that unless they had to make something up on the spur of the moment. There I was, pointing to his swollen nose and asking questions, and I think he got that swollen nose from me or you or both of us when we tried to defend ourselves."

I grabbed my coat and my purse.

"Where are you going, Pen?"

"I'm driving to Newport, right now. I'm going to stop all this for once and for all."

"How? Are you going to the Newport police?"

"Not yet. You know and I know that neither Detective Kroll, Chief Ciders, nor Detective-Lieutenant Marsh will believe some tall-sounding tale about a hidden treasure map buried in a set of books—not unless I produce the treasure to prove it's real. So that's what I'm going to do. I'm going to find the oval portrait and take it to the police with my charges against Claymore. I'm sure once Claymore realizes he can never have it, he'll confess to his crimes."

"But you don't even know what to look for!"

"It's an oval portrait, Brainert. How hard is that to find?"

"There might be a dozen or more oval portraits. Wait until tomorrow or the next day, and I'll probably be well enough to go with you. I'll recognize the treasure at once. I'm certain of it."

"No. I have a better idea."

I showed Brainert the cell phone I'd just bought from Gerry Kovacks at Cellular Planet—one of the new stores on Cranberry.

"Look," I told Brainert. "This phone captures and stores digital images. I can snap pictures of the portraits in the manor, show them to you when I get back. The display screen is right here . . ."

I could see the anticipation in my friend's one good eye.

But there was doubt, too. "There's no one at the Chesley mansion, Pen. The doors are locked up tight. How will you get in?"

Back door, Jack piped up. *One thing I've learned in the gumshoe game, baby, you can always find a back door in.*

"Well," I told Brainert as I headed out the door, "I've already been charged with grand larceny. Why not go for breaking and entering, too?"

Jack laughed in my head. *In for a penny, in for a pound, I always say.*

"No, you don't."

CHAPTER 18

Return to the Haunted House

"I think I'd better go over there and see what's broken."

—Philip Marlowe in "Finger Man,"
by Raymond Chandler, 1934

BY THE TIME I turned onto the twisting, turning, annoyingly treacherous Roderick Road, the sun was kissing the horizon. I couldn't believe it, but the sky was looking ominous and heavy clouds seemed to be threatening rain—even though there'd been only the slightest chance of precipitation in the forecast.

"All we need is a little lightning, thunder, and a big, flat-headed guy with bolts in his neck," I muttered with a shiver.

What's the matter, babe? Cold feet?

"Cold nose. It's chillier here by the ocean."

Don't you wish I could warm it, honey?

"I know what you're doing, you know?"

What?

"You're trying to make up for those comments about that nurse."

I'm a sucker for angels of mercy. Maybe someday I'll tell you that story—

"There's the gate to the Chesley house," I said, cutting Jack off. I slowed the Saturn but didn't make the turn onto the driveway. There was no point.

"Brainert was right about the place being locked up. The gate's closed—"

And padlocked.

I rolled to a halt on the shoulder of the road about a hundred yards past the gate. I parked parallel to the stone wall surrounding the manor then cut the engine and lights. Silence and darkness descended like an eerie blanket. When I opened the door, a damp chill cut through my flimsy jacket. I popped the trunk and found my big Maglite. It was just like the one my dad used to carry on the job, the one that could easily double for a nightstick. The flashlight was heavy, and the weight felt comforting.

Jack laughed.

"What's so funny?"

That's how I felt about my gat.

"Your what?"

My gun, baby. I carried a Browning .45, the same service weapon I'd used as an army officer. When I'd been a flatfoot before the war, I carried a .38. The .38 was lighter, easier to carry, but the Browning had real stopping power. Like you with your flashlight, the .45's weight was a comfort.

I moved across damp, unkempt grass to the seven-foot stone wall. As I'd hoped, it was crumbling from age and neglect. Better still, it was covered by thick, twisted ivy. Between the roots and the crumbling joints, there were plenty of places for me to grip. I shoved the flashlight into my belt and began to climb.

Good play, baby. Not too many dames from my time would pull an Edmund Hillary—

"Who?"

Who? You don't know the guy who climbed Everest?

"Don't get testy. I just forgot. This isn't *Jeopardy!*, you know."

I disagree. You could very well be in jeopardy. You know that.

"No! Not jeopardy with a small j . . . Oh, forget it," I said, continuing to climb. "Anyway, women in your day were hampered by high heels, garter belts, stockings, and skirts. I'm wearing slacks and flat shoes—though now I wish I had my sneakers. And by the way, Jack, lots of 'dames' make the trip up Everest now."

I swung over the wall and clambered down the other side. I landed on the uneven ground and steadied myself. I had a few new scrapes and bruises, but nothing to fret about.

I'm impressed, baby.

"Thanks," I said, proud as a peacock.

But I'm wondering why you went to all the trouble.

My proud expression dropped. I now saw what Jack meant. There was a hole in the shattered wall I could easily have walked through not twenty feet from the spot I'd climbed.

"Now I feel stupid."

And the night is still young . . .

Across an overgrown lawn, the manor house loomed massively. In the distance, I heard the waves crashing against the rocky shore. Through the twisted trees I could see the dull gleam of light in the gothic-style portico. But I didn't head toward the entranceway. This time I was going in through the back door, just as soon as I found one.

The rain that threatened during the drive up here now began to fall. I shivered as I followed a dark overgrown trail around the back of the estate.

"Talk to me, Jack," I begged. "I'm getting scared."

No, you're not, honey. Just keep moving. Don't lose your momentum and you won't lose your nerve.

Using my flashlight, I found a stone path and followed it up to the walls of the bleak, decaying mansion. I found a ground-floor door a moment later. It was made of wood with six small windows. I jiggled the knob. No surprise, it was locked.

"Well, what now?" I asked.

Are you talking to me?

"Jack, I have to get in. Aren't you going to show me how to pick the lock or something?"

No.

"You won't help me get in?"

Picking a lock is an art. You can't master it in a few minutes.

"So how do I get in?"

Break the window and turn the knob from the other side.

"Okay." I raised the Maglite to smash the glass.

Not like that! Jack cried. *With finesse. And real quiet like.*

"How do you break a window *quietly*?"

I heard Jack sigh. *Strip off that jacket,* he commanded.

"What?"

You heard me. Take the coat off and wrap it around the end of the flashlight. Then gently tap *the window until it breaks. There'll be some noise, but not much.*

"It's kind of funny, isn't it?"

What's funny?

"I'm breaking into a spooky house with help from one."

Real cute, baby. You're a laugh riot. Now get to work.

I did as Jack instructed. The window broke on the third tap. The glass made what seemed like a lot of noise to me, but Jack thought I did fine. I reached through the broken window frame, fumbled for the knob. I turned it and the door opened.

"This is working!"

Don't get cocky. This joint looks like there's not even an echo inside, but if someone is home, you're an intruder and if they're armed they could drill you, all nice and legal like.

That revelation sobered me in a hurry. I swung the door open and entered silently, careful not to kick around any glass. I found myself in a dark and silent kitchen and realized Peter Chesley's makeshift bedroom was just next door. I played the flashlight around until I found the exit. A minute later I was in a hallway that I recognized.

"The library is just ahead," I said.

I felt an eerie case of déjà vu as I entered Peter Chesley's library. The space looked much the same as it had the night Peter died, only darker and scarier because the lights were out and the fireplace cold. The only sound I heard was the ticking of the Poe clock, hidden in the shadows.

"I know we're looking for an oval portrait. I better get to it," I whispered.

I moved cautiously through the gloomy library, using the flashlight's powerful beam to penetrate the shadows. I brushed against a standing lamp, and it began to topple. I lunged to catch it with one hand before the lamp crashed to the floor. My body swept across a desktop in the process, scattering dozens of Peter Chesley's meticulously kept logs. I steadied the lamp, then crouched to pick up the notebooks.

In the flashlight's beam, I caught a small rectangle of cobalt blue. The unique color stopped me cold, and I settled the light on the small card. I bent down and snatched it up. It was a business card, one I recognized before I even read the inscription in gold embossed letters:

PROFESSOR NELSON SPINNER
DEPARTMENT OF ENGLISH
ST. FRANCIS COLLEGE

The card had fallen out of a notebook, which was larger than the others. When I opened it, several other business cards spilled out. One for a roofing company, another for a home-care outfit in Newport. I realized at once that this was an account ledger. Written in the same careful hand that cataloged the contents of the library were the monthly expenses paid by Peter Chesley. The electric bill, gas, food, water, nursing care, doctor's visits—it was all there, and up to date practically to the day he died.

I found a column outlining payments to one Nelson Spinner, for "archive consultation." It took only a moment to discover that Peter Chesley had written Nelson over a dozen checks—one every two weeks for the past six or seven months.

The latest entry was dated the Friday before Peter Chesley died. Apparently, Nelson had been dealing with Peter Chesley up until just two days before the man perished.

The information in this ledger book was astounding. The night Nelson Spinner had come to Buy the Book, he acted as though he'd never before seen the Phelps volumes of Poe. He picked them up and examined them and went out of his way to dissuade us from believing there was any credence to a Poe Code.

"Why would Nelson pretend that he'd never seen Peter's books before?" I whispered. "What was he trying to hide?"

I think we both suspect what he was dodging, Jack said.

"You mean you think Nelson's the killer now? But what about Claymore Chesley?"

I didn't say your sweetheart Spinner clipped anyone. I'm only saying his debunking of the code was a dog and pony show. I'll bet dollars to donuts Spinner had his peepers on the dingus—

"Huh?"

—the treasure. *Spinner's been eyeing the goods from the start. In fact, Golden Boy might have cozied up to Grandpa*

Chesley just to get close to the goods, figuring he'd put the squeeze on the geezer once he found the swag.

"Do you think Spinner might have found the treasure already?"

Nix, doll. He would have lammed it from old Chesley if he had. Why come back to this mausoleum if you don't have to?

"Speaking of the treasure, let's find it now and make like shepards, okay?"

Baby, I love it when you speak my language.

I remembered the wall of old portraits and photographs near the weird Poe clock. I ran the flashlight across the shelves of books until I located the pictures. There were over a dozen, all in frames, several oval-shaped. A closer examination revealed brass nameplates on each frame—all of the images were of the Chesley family, dating back to the Civil War and earlier.

"Dead end," I muttered.

Keep looking, cupcake. There are a lot of mug shots on these old walls.

I played the beam around the four walls, but all I found were books, thousands of them, lined up in neat rows on heavy wooden shelves. I was about to give up when the light played across something round—a large, freestanding terrestrial globe on a thick, Victorian-era wooden base. Only a portion of the globe was visible, the bulk of it tucked into a curved niche sunk into the wall between two tall shelves.

As I approached the globe, I saw a gleaming brass plaque at its base. In the flashlight's glare, I read the inscription: MADE BY NEW YORK–BASED GLOBE MAKER HERMAN SCHEDLER, CIRCA 1889. PROPERTY OF MYSTIC HOUSE.

"Mystic House, Jack! This globe belonged to Eugene Phelps, the man who hid the treasure." I played the flashlight along the curved wall behind the globe. There were four portraits hanging there, all of them in oval frames.

"Eureka!" I cried, laughing at my own unintentional Poe reference.

Close your head, doll. You're sleuthing, remember?

I should have listened to Jack, but in the excitement of discovery, I did kind of lose my head. I found the nearest lamp and turned it on. Light filled this small corner of the massive library.

Are you smoking the mud-pipe, toots? Put a sock over it!

"I need light to take these pictures. I have no choice. I'm sure there's no one here, Jack."

Your call. But me? I'm twitchy. This setup doesn't feel right.

I adjusted the lamp and removed the shade so that the bare bulb illuminated the entire niche. In order to get closer to the portraits, I pushed a thick-backed chair next to the globe and stood on it. Bending over the globe, I began to take pictures.

Two of the portraits were amateurish renderings of Poe, one in oil, the other pen and ink. They were signed EP—Eugene Phelps, I presumed—and if the artist thought these were "treasures," he surely misjudged his own skills. Below those were two images of Poe hung side by side—I recognized the high, domed forehead, the pale flesh, nearly identical. Both pictures were set in thick, heavy frames.

Poe seemed to be wearing the same clothes in both pictures, though in one he appeared disheveled, distracted.

I captured multiple images of each portrait, checking occasionally to make sure the digital reproduction was clear. When I was finished, I tucked the phone into my pocket. I was about to step off the chair when I was interrupted.

"Who are you and why are you in this house?" a raspy voice demanded. "You have no business being here."

With a startled yelp, I tumbled off the chair—and landed hard.

Flat on my back, I looked up to find a sinewy young man looming over me. He had curly dark blond hair and wide blue-green eyes. He wore jeans and a sweatshirt and his right hand clutched a long iron poker with a hooked tip.

Didn't I warn you to keep your peepers wide and your ears unplugged?

I scrambled to my feet. "What are *you* doing here?" I fired back with false bravado. "The owner of this house is dead!"

The man's eyes narrowed suspiciously. "My father died this week, it's true," he replied, his voice hoarse.

"You're Peter Chesley's son?"

"I'm Raymond Chesley. . . . Who are you?"

"Listen, I know this looks bad," I began, my words tripping over themselves. "But I can explain. My name is Penelope Thornton-McClure. I co-own a bookstore in Quindicott, and I met your father just the other night, the night he died. In fact, I was the one who found him—uh, his corpse. My aunt Sadie and I, that is. You see, it was really my aunt who—"

"Be quiet."

My mouth snapped shut.

"I don't care a whit about my father," Raymond Chesley said. "I lived most of my life in Boston, with my mother and stepfather. My father and I were estranged, so I don't want to hear your explanations. You have to leave now."

"No."

"No?"

"No."

I refused to budge. Instead, I began to tell Raymond about the Phelps Poes, the Poe Code, and the treasure hidden somewhere in this library. His reaction shocked me. He laughed, right in my face! A laugh that quickly broke into a cough. He drew a handkerchief from his pants pocket and wiped his nose.

"A treasure? You sound as insane as this despicable family—like all the Chesleys. My late mother was right to get away from them as soon as I was born."

"Listen, Raymond. We've sold two of the Phelps books. We will sell the rest. That means we owe the estate—you— some money. Thousands of dollars—"

"Keep it," he said, waving his hand. "He gave them to you, and I don't care. I'm selling everything you see as soon as possible, and giving it all to charity. An antique dealer is coming here to assess this junk and haul it away."

"What! When?"

"Tomorrow. The only reason I'm even staying in this rattrap tonight is because the man was supposed to come this afternoon and postponed at the last minute."

"But the treasure—"

"Go, Mrs. McClure. It's time for you to leave, before I call the police and have you arrested."

"Oh, for pity's sake," I muttered. "Not again."

CHAPTER 19

Dream in a Ditch

Maybe I did have a taste for death. Maybe I liked it too much to taste anything else.

—Mike Hammer in *One Lonely Night*,
by Mickey Spillane, 1951

"DAMN THOSE WEATHERMEN! Slight chance of rain, my rear!"

The precipitation had been light when I left Prospero House, a pacific patter on the roof. I'd slid behind the wheel of my Saturn, started the engine, and once again negotiated the twisting turns of Roderick Road.

By the time I reached the highway, however, the skies opened up. Sheets of rain transformed my windshield into a mini Niagra. The road was awash in water, and I half expected to see men with beards and yellow slickers trolling for cod.

Don't get excited, baby. Eyes on the road.

"No jokes?" I thought. "No jibes?"

That's when I realized Jack was as worried for me as I was. I tried to calm down and concentrate on the driving, but it wasn't easy. My mind was still racing with the revelation that Nelson Spinner had been working with Peter Chesley and he hadn't bothered to mention it. In fact, it seemed to me, he'd gone out of his way to hide it.

And then there was Raymond Chesley. So hostile to his biological father that it made me want to cry. The guy looked pretty hardy. Was he capable of murder and assault?

What's wrong, baby? I know it's not the weather.

I shook my head. "Peter Chesley must have been a real bastard at one time. Certainly, his own son seems to think so. I found him sweet and eccentric . . . but then, I only spent an hour or so with him."

What's your auntie's take?

"She's struggling with a lot of regrets about what happened between them. She says their squabbles all seem petty in retrospect, but I know my aunt. She's made of pretty stern stuff and she's got a lot of fight. The man must have been a real jerk for her to have wanted the relationship to end."

I had a dame tell me something one time. It seems to apply.

"What's that?"

If a guy's not happy, it doesn't take long before he makes a girl miserable.

"Sounds like my marriage."

Well, we know your husband wasn't happy, that's for sure.

"What gave you your first clue? The swan dive?"

And how about your old friend Claymore?

"What do you mean?"

I mean the apple doesn't fall far from the tree.

"There's a thought. If Peter was anything like Claymore

at the same age, then I can see why his relationships went south."

Maybe that's why the yegg left his sweet gig in sunny California. In the end, Claymore may not be such a great son, running home to help out Ma and Pa Chesley. Maybe he'd already burned his bridges and was looking to start over anyway.

The highway was slick, and there were very few cars behind me. When the single car ahead of me turned onto an exit, I flipped on my high beams for better visibility. A minute later, I saw the illuminated road sign for the Comfy-Time Motel rest stop, and I exhaled with relief. Quindicott was just around the next dark corner.

"Jack, that 'dame' you quoted a minute ago, why do those words sound so familiar to me?"

You tell me, baby.

"Wait! That was Mindy Corbett who said that. I dreamed she said it to you the night before she was murdered—"

I was slowing the car down, anticipating my exit's tricky off-ramp when I felt a violent bump.

"Whoa! What the heck?!"

I checked the rearview and saw bright headlights bearing down from behind. The car was big and black—an SUV, for sure—but I couldn't see anything more than the dark silhouette of a man in the driver's seat.

"What the hell does this jerk think he's doing?!"

I never got an answer.

The impact came just as I'd turned onto the exit ramp. The SUV slammed me from behind but not full on. He hit me at an angle, driving me off the road and into a shallow ditch. The front end bounced down then up, and smashed into the massive trunk of a very old tree.

Like a ragdoll, my body had been thrown forward, then back, then forward again. With an exploding hiss, my airbag deployed, and I felt the painful impact of the bag's cold inflated material smacking my face.

Dazed, close to passing out, I heard the sound of a car door slamming somewhere nearby. The jerk, I realized. The jerk is coming to pull me out.

But he didn't.

I heard a car door opening and realized the man had entered my car through the back door. He was searching the back seat for something. Then he opened my door and felt around the floorboard for the trunk release. I was strapped in and nearly unconscious, but I willed my head to turn out of the bag. The night was so dark, the rain still falling. All I could see was the silhouette of a man in black, a ball cap shoved low on his head, a dark scarf tied around his face.

"Who are you?" I murmured, the words jumbled gibberish to my own ears.

The sound of the trunk popping open was the only reply. Then the man's dark image was gone; the cold rain continued to pelt the windshield, and my eyes fell heavily closed.

New York City
October 22, 1946

My eyes opened.

I stood in a dim alley between two run-down tenements. Dingy brick walls rose five stories on either side of me; rusted black fire escapes clung like dead vines to their dirty sides. Laundry hung from frayed ropes between the buildings. The faded clothes fluttered over my head like dejected flags—patched and repatched, the sort of threadbare garments I'd seen people wearing in histories of the Great Depression.

I heard shouts and followed the sound out of the dim tunnel until I reached the sidewalk. Like a period movie, I watched the street action play out in the day's waning light.

Kids with grimy faces in dirty pants, fraying sweaters, and flat newsboy caps were playing some sort of dice game on a stone stoop, next to a passed-out man clutching a bottle in a brown paper bag. A taxicab driver and a bicycle messenger were shouting their heads off at each other. And impossibly huge cars, not boxy like SUVs, but antique Packards and DeSotos, long and wide and heavy, rumbled down the one-way street.

The smell in the air was a combination of putrid garbage overflowing from cans lined up at the curb and a strong, stinging smell that I guessed was unleaded gasoline.

I started down the block and noticed the cross-street signs. "Tenth Avenue and Forty-Fourth Street?" I recognized the address, but nothing else.

In my time, this Hell's Kitchen neighborhood wasn't notorious or scary—just an extension of Times Square's flashy theater and restaurant district. The residential housing consisted of a mix of renovated brownstones and yuppie high-rises, the occasional quaint little bistro tucked just below street level.

But this wasn't my time.

And these, I realized, weren't my clothes. A pencil-thin wool skirt clung to my hips and tight-fitting sweater hugged my padded bra. The nylons on my legs felt scratchy and uncomfortable. I felt my thigh and realized I was wearing a garter belt.

"Hey, there, girly, you lost?" A pasty-faced man approached in a soiled suit and battered fedora. He reeked of cheap alcohol. "Or maybe you're lookin' for a date?"

"No," I said, stepping backward. "Not interested."

"How do you know, if you don't try a sample?" He moved quickly, backing me against the dirty wall before I knew what was happening.

"Back off or I'll scream!" I warned.

"Scream away. Nobody's gonna care about our little business."

"I will."

The voice was deep and clipped and familiar. I looked up to find Jack Shepard in fedora and slate gray suit, looming behind the man who'd accosted me.

"Feel that, shitbird?" he growled. "It's the business end of my .45, jammed between your third and fourth rib. You still interested in doing business here?"

"No, mister. I don't want no trouble. Pretty girl here smiled at me and I guess I misunderstood—"

When the drunk was gone, stumbling quickly up the sidewalk, I straightened my sweater. "Yuck. I did not smile at him."

"I know."

"So why are you scowling at me then?"

"Because"—Jack flicked the safety on his weapon, then slipped it back into the shoulder holster hidden beneath his double-breasted suit jacket—"you shouldn't have left the alley, that's why. I put you there for safekeeping until I came back."

"Back? Where did you go?"

"Come on."

As Jack took my elbow and hustled me down the sidewalk, I realized why I was here. It was Jack's ongoing missing persons case. He was close to solving it now, and he wanted me with him—presumably to clue me in on something important in my current case. What, I had no clue.

"I hate this neighborhood," Jack groused as we strode swiftly along. "One of the worst slums in the city and the Men's Night Court ten blocks away."

"Men's Night Court?"

"Eight in the evening till one in the morning, the Seventh-District Magistrate sees an unending column of drunks, panhandlers, pickpockets, wife beaters, and brawlers. Every petty offender arrested in Manhattan and the Bronx is brought to this neighborhood for a hearing—but, of course, you know all about hearings, don't you, sister?"

"What's that supposed to imply? You know I wasn't guilty."

Jack's gunmetal gray eyes flashed with amusement. "Just trying to keep your fight up, baby. You're going to need it tonight, remember that."

"Fine. Now how about enlightening me where we're going and why?"

"Just follow my lead."

We dodged traffic on Tenth and continued heading west, toward the freight yards, garages, and docks. At the very end of the street, the island of Manhattan dropped off into the Hudson River—and I was hoping Jack would slow his bullet pace before we hit water. The sun was sinking just below the horizon line now. It looked like a big orange ball, threatening to smash New Jersey under its fiery weight.

Jack pulled me up short between two buildings and silently pointed into the shadowy tunnel between them.

"Not another alley!"

"Let's go."

In the dim light, I heard a noise like a man whispering, "Pssst."

Jack grabbed my arm and pulled me behind him. He moved carefully forward, dipping his hand into his double-breasted jacket and once again drawing his .45.

"Put your gat away, it's just me," rasped a young man. He was skinny with short raven hair, dark eyes, and a prominent nose.

Jack holstered his gun again and made a quick deal with the young man he called "Beak," handing him a five-dollar bill and receiving two folded brown garments and matching hats.

"It's grand theft what you're charging me," Jack complained.

"So call the cops," said the young man with a high-pitched cackle. Then he disappeared, seemingly melting back into the alleyway's shadows.

"Here," Jack said, handing me one of the folded garments.

I unfurled it. "Overalls?" I saw a logo on the pocket. "SWIFTY DELIVERY."

"Put them on."

Jack gave me his back as he walked to a fire escape's ladder, peeled off his jacket, and hung it over a low rung. His muscled shoulders and chest were nicely outlined by the tight-fitting leather holster. He slipped it off and began to strip down to his undershirt. When he went for his belt, I protested.

"You're changing? Right in front of me?"

Jack glanced around, raised an eyebrow. "You're the one looking. And didn't I tell you to change, too?"

"Right here? In the alley?"

"Stop bucking for the Miss Priss award, will you? It's dark enough back here to develop crime-scene photos." He turned around and continued disrobing. "Now move. We don't have much time."

I frantically searched for some sort of private Idaho, found a discarded fridge, and put it between me and Jack. Then I unzipped the skirt, pulled off the sweater, stepped into the overalls, and zipped them up. They were too big so I folded the cuffs at the bottom of the legs and the edges of the sleeves.

When I stepped out, I found Jack waiting, arms crossed, his back to me to make sure I got my privacy, his front to the alley entrance to make sure no one surprised us.

"Okay," I said.

He turned and took me in, couldn't stop a small smile from lightening his usual granite profile. "You look cute as a button. Here."

I stuffed my hair into the hat and followed him out of the alley.

"Jack?" I asked nervously. "Do you still have your gat—er, uh, gun?"

"Baby, I don't take a piss—excuse me, *visit the facility*,

without my rod. I transferred everything I had in my pockets to the pockets of these overalls. If a hobo finds my clothes they can have them, but not the stuff inside. You follow?"

We reached a warehouse and Jack pulled me into yet another alley.

"This alley thing of yours is becoming a real obsession."

"Quiet, baby. We're going in."

"Don't you want to brief me?" I whispered.

He glanced at his watch. "It's time for the shift change. Follow my lead."

Again with the lead! I thought, but kept my lips zipped. Jack never looked more serious. He'd unzipped the top half of his overalls, and I knew why. He wanted easy access to the gun strapped under his arm. This, of course, meant that we were heading into life-threatening danger.

"Put your hands in your pockets and keep your head down."

I looked down at my hands and realized someone had given me a manicure with bright-red nail enamel. I shoved my painted fingers into the overall's pockets.

"Keep your mouth shut and your ears open. Got it?"

"Gee, Jack," I couldn't resist whispering, "you really know how to show a girl a good time."

"You want a good time, baby, my offer's a standing one. Let me take you on the town, get us a room at a nice hotel."

"I told you before, Jack. I'm a married woman."

"In your dreams, baby."

The back door stood open and Jack sauntered in as if he owned the place. Some men stood around a desk, smoking and talking. They all wore the same Swifty Delivery overalls that we were wearing.

Jack partially averted his face, tipped his hat, and grunted at one of the men who glanced his way. The man returned Jack's gesture with a short nod. I kept my head down and followed Jack like a loyal puppy, happy to stay cowed because these men looked like pretty rough trade—tattoos and scars, faces lined with the track marks of hard living.

Jack led me through a door and into a deserted stairwell. He bent down to tie his shoe, pulled me close, whispered hot and low against my ear. "I've cased the place and paid off a pigeon. The records are on the third floor. Let's go."

We minded our business and the few people we passed— more rough-looking men—minded theirs. Unfortunately, the records room was locked. Jack pulled a small kit out of his deep overalls pocket, opened it to reveal a set of thin silver instruments.

Jack looked tense. I thought a joke might help.

"What's this," I whispered, "you have a sudden urge to practice dentistry?"

Jack scowled. "Go to the end of the hall and light up a cig. Act like you're on a break. See someone coming, cough loudly."

"But I don't smoke. So I don't have any cigarettes."

"Cripes." Jack fished for a pack of cigarettes and lit me up.

I coughed. He grimaced.

"Uh-oh," I said, coughing again, "the signal might not work."

"Don't smoke it then, just look like you're smoking it."

"Oh, right."

Feeling like one of Jack's "rubes," I did as he asked. No one came, thank heavens. Jack picked the records room door, and I quickly stamped out the foul, unfiltered cancer stick.

We closed the door behind us and relocked it. The room was dark but Jack didn't turn on the lights. He went to the single small window and cursed. "No shade, no curtains, nothing."

"What's the matter?"

"We turn on the lights, someone might notice from outside."

"But how are we going to read the files otherwise? We don't have flashlights."

"We'll have to chance it."

Jack flipped a switch and two bare bulbs came to life, bathing the room in cheap yellowish glow. A gray row of battered metal file cabinets lined one wall. A wooden desk and chair sat against the other.

"Let's get to it," he whispered, quickly scanning the labeling system on the drawers. It wasn't alphabetical—but rather, set up by calendar. Each cabinet was a year, each drawer a few months of the year.

"What are we looking for?"

"Any files you can find under the names Dorothy Kerns, Vincent Tattershawe, Ogden Heating and Cooling, or even . . . Mindy . . . Mindy Corbett."

Jack had a little trouble saying her name. I knew why.

We searched for ten minutes and found nothing. Then, finally, I hit pay dirt. "Tattershawe. I've got one."

"Pull it."

We took it to the desk and examined the contents. There were carbons of forms he'd made outlining deals. "No Dorothy Kerns," muttered Jack. "No Ogden Heating and Cooling. But what's this?"

Jack's finger stopped on a name: Grant Barneby. A short typewritten note scrawled next to it read, *Contact through the Madeleine.*

Jack rubbed his lantern jaw, rough with the beginnings of a five o'clock shadow. Without a word, he went to a cabinet at random and pulled out a stack of files. He rifled through them. Every few pages or so, he'd find a client with the words: *Contact through the Madeleine* scrawled beside the name.

"Well, I'll be damned."

"What is it?"

"Mindy said her investment firm was setting up legit clients, but suckers, too. They were being brought in by silent partners. She said Tattershawe didn't like it much. I think Vincent Tattershawe realized how dangerous these scum are and skipped town to get out of the business without losing his life—and it's looking like he used Dorothy Kerns's inheritance to fund his getaway. Dorothy, being a sucker for romance, still thinks Tattershawe's her knight in shining armor, so she insisted a PI be hired to track him down. She had no idea he was tangled up in some dark deals. I think that's why her brother stepped in to hire me. He needed to be in control of any investigation. He has too much to lose if Dorothy or the police find Vincent before he does."

"But I thought he was trying to recover his sister's money?"

"I don't think Baxter Kerns cares a fig about his sister's money. He probably never expected her to fall for a guy working at the very firm he's using to scam cliff-dwellers and war widows. Now he's just trying to protect his nut."

"Wait, back up. You're saying you think Baxter Kerns is involved with this corrupt investment company? Why?"

"The Madeleine. It's one of those private clubs on Forty-fourth. Baxter's a member. Had me meet him there. And that's obviously where he's pulling in some of his suckers, probably highly recommending Carter & Thompson as 'smart bets' for investing—you know how it goes. Seems to me the only reason he wants me to find Tattershawe is to give him lead poisoning before he can spill to his sister or anybody else."

"But, Jack, a lot of men belong to that club. Why do you think Baxter is one of the silent partners?"

"My gut, baby. This stack of coincidences is just too high to be random. Think it through. If Baxter were as innocent as a spring lamb, and he suspected Tattershawe of taking a powder with his sister's money, then why didn't he go to police with his tale? Why wasn't he looking for an all-out investigation of Carter & Thompson? Why did he hire me to find Tattershawe but reveal his whereabouts to no one but Baxter himself? I'll tell you why—because Baxter Kerns is dirty too."

"But there still might be other explanations. To accuse him, you'll need proof—"

Just then, we heard voices in the hall.

"Hey, what is that?" (A smooth male voice.)

"What's what?" (A much gruffer male voice.)

"There's a light under the records room door."

Jack didn't say a thing; in about two seconds, he stacked up the files on the desk, picked them up, and grabbed my arm. Before I could utter a word, he pulled me into the far corner and shoved me down.

We were tucked between the outside wall and the file cabinets—well hidden unless anyone walked all the way to the end of the room; then they'd see us crouched here, for sure. Jack maneuvered me behind him and pulled his weapon. He didn't have to tell me not to make a sound.

The knob rattled as the men unlocked then opened the door.

Smooth voice said, "Who left these lights on?"

"Dunno." (Gruff was a real genius.)

"Well, we're going to find out."

"Whatsa matter, you worried 'bout the electric bill?"

"I'm worried about a fire, you idiot. This place is a fleapit and the last thing we need is an electrical fire." We heard the men come into the room. A file drawer opened and shut, then another, then a third.

"Turn the lights off and let's go," said the smooth voice. "I've got a meeting with Baxter Kerns across town in less than an hour."

Before the door shut, Jack carefully peeked around the file cabinet—to get a good look at the men talking, I assumed. When they shut and relocked the door, I heard him exhale a long, furious breath. His left hand was balled into an angry fist, and his right was clutching the gun so tightly, his knuckles had turned white.

"For what they did to Mindy," he bit out low, "this whole operation is going down. And if I get my hands on Baxter Kerns, even his sister's not going to recognize him when I'm through."

Jack put the gun back in his holster, then we carefully left the room. I thought we were in the clear; the hallway looked empty, but the two men who'd just left were doubling back, complaining about grabbing the wrong file.

"Hey! You there!" The smooth guy, in a dapper suit, two-toned shoes, and sharp fedora turned to the swarthy giant by his side. "Get them!"

Jack went for his gun again, but by the time he cleared it out of his overalls, the gruff thug lunged at him. Jack wasn't a small man and when the two crashed together, it was like a pair of freight trains colliding.

The two men grappled then went down hard. I heard Jack cry out on the floor. The gun had flown down the hall and I ran off to get it, but I didn't know how to remove the safety or properly aim and fire it. I held it, feeling helpless, trying at least to keep the gun ready for Jack when he could get clear of the big man.

The giant tried to kick Jack, but he rolled and got back on his feet. The big man rose too. Fists flew and blows were exchanged. Finally, Jack got the upper hand. He used some evasive maneuvers that looked like rudimentary martial arts. He'd said something about learning jujitsu in the service, and it sure looked effective to me. The guy was bigger and he'd gotten the drop on Jack, but now he couldn't touch the PI.

In a few swift moves, the giant was down, holding his head and moaning. The smooth, dapper gent had disappeared, and I assumed he'd run off to sound the alarm and get more help.

"Let's go," Jack barked, taking my arm.

"How do we get out? Back stairs again?"

"No, honey. When you break in the back, and they catch you, you might as well go out the front."

And that's exactly what we did.

We ran all the way back to our alleyway. Amazingly, no one had disturbed our clothes, although a few fat rats were sniffing around the old fridge where I'd left mine.

"Shoo!" I cried. They weren't impressed. So I changed with an audience.

"What the hell . . ." Jack muttered.

I looked up, as I zipped my skirt. "Jack, what is it? Are you okay?"

He was still half undressed, standing in his undershirt and boxers, but the blood made me forget all modesty. I rushed over to find him bleeding from the thigh. The cut wasn't too bad, but I was puzzled how it happened.

"The oval frame broke," he informed me. "I transferred everything I was carrying into the overalls, including that picture of Vincent Tattershawe. So when the big guy sent me down, the glass must have broken and cut me."

I lifted my wool skirt and pulled down my slip, used it to clean the wound, then pressed it to see that it properly clotted.

"Thanks, baby. You make a pretty good nurse, you know?"

"What is it with this nurse obsession?" I smiled. He smiled back. Then he finished dressing and transferred his personal items from the overalls back into his suit pockets. He tossed the broken glass and the oval frame into a nearby trash can, keeping only the photo.

"What's this?" he murmured, removing the photo from the frame backing.

"What's what?"

He showed me a small key. It had been taped to the backing of the frame, hidden between the photo and the glass.

There was a tiny slip of paper wrapped around the key—like the ticker tape used to update stockbrokers on the market. My hands were smaller so I unrolled it.

"It's a Sixth Avenue address in midtown," I said.

"Looks like we got ourselves another clue."

"What do you think this key will open?"

Jack examined it. Three very tiny letters were engraved on the side. "SDB," he murmured, puzzled for a moment, then lifted an eyebrow. "Safety-deposit box."

CHAPTER 20

Out of Order

It was a wild explanation, for a dozen reasons it wouldn't hold water. Yet I couldn't think of anything better.

—Francis James, "Dance of the Bloodless Ones,"
Terror Tales, July–August 1937

I OPENED MY eyes to the sound of an emergency siren. I soon realized that I was flat on my back, strapped to a rigid pallet, staring at the interior of a speeding ambulance.

In another case of stone-cold irony, the wailing vehicle brought me directly to Benevolent Heart Hospital. Only now, instead of marking time in the dreary old waiting room, I was treated like royalty.

While a helpful administrator processed my medical insurance information, I was whisked by stretcher into the triage center where my cuts and scrapes were cleaned and bandaged, injections were offered and accepted, and X-rays were taken. At last, I was placed on a gurney and wheeled into a white, featureless room.

Through an interior window, I watched the medical staff scurry around. A nurse arrived after fifteen minutes or so and took my blood pressure and temperature—for about the hundredth time.

Finally, a young intern arrived to pronounce sentence. His shaved head and the barbed-wire tattoo encircling his muscular biceps threw me for a moment, but I soon figured out he was a doctor because he wore green OR scrubs and had a stethoscope draped around his neck.

Cripes, Jack said, *this guy looks like a Merchant Marine. With male nurses and docs as tough as this palooka, the medical profession must be hell these days.*

I wasn't sure what threw me more, my woozy head or being back in the present again. I was about to speak to Jack about the dream when the doctor spoke up first—

"Mrs. McClure? I'm Dr. Fortino, a physician on staff here at Benevolent Heart Hospital."

I figured he was giving me his job description because I was eyeing him kind of funny, like I thought he should be out drinking with his fraternity buddies instead of staffing an emergency room.

"Uh-huh," I said eloquently.

"Fortunately there's no sign of a concussion that we can find, but by your own admission you lost consciousness for a period of time right after the accident, and that's never a good thing. So I've scheduled you for a more thorough evaluation in the morning. We'll take another look at that bump on your head, and I'd like a specialist to check out the hairline fracture on your left forearm."

The arm in question was black and blue, and every beat of my heart caused it to throb with a pain that radiated from my wrist to the tips of my fingers. I was actually surprised the damage was not much worse.

"You could get out of here tonight, but I recommend you remain here for observation, until the tests are conducted in the morning. If all goes well, you'll be out of here by noon."

I agreed to stay for a lot of reasons. I was tired and a bed sounded nice, and I didn't relish the look on the face of my son when he got his first peep at his mommy the mummy. But mostly I agreed to stay overnight because it fit in with my plan.

Dr. Fortino said goodnight, and I was wheeled by a pair of nurses—both young and attractive women, to Jack's delight—into an elevator and transported to the fourth floor, where I was placed in a bed. It wasn't a private room, but the other bed was empty. The room was an antiseptic-white space with a single window overlooking the parking lot.

Outside, the sky was purple and the rain fell much lighter now, dewing the window with tiny drops that twinkled in the glow of the halogen street lights.

I waited until the nurses tucked me in and left me alone, then I grabbed my scuffed purse and fumbled for my cell. I checked that the digital pictures had survived the crash. Of course, before I'd left Chesley's mansion I'd dispatched a copy of the files to my aunt's cell, just in case. But I was relieved to find my own digital files inside the phone's memory.

Next, I called my aunt. She hadn't heard from me since I phoned that afternoon, and she was worried sick. It didn't help her state of mind that Brainert had phoned her requesting information, and mentioned that I was headed for the Chesley mansion.

I told Sadie that I'd made it in and out of the mansion in one piece, and had an encounter with Peter's son, Raymond. I left out that nasty part about being run off the road, and being admitted to the hospital. No need to trouble my aunt now, she'd only make herself sick with worry.

"Garfield Platt came by the store this afternoon," Sadie

said. "He gave me the keys from behind the register. Found them in his jacket this morning, he said. He figured he must have walked out with them on Monday when he left work."

"You buy his explanation?" I asked, still wondering if those keys were used by my attacker to get through the back door.

"I believe him, Pen. I believe him because today Garfield gave me his two weeks' notice—"

"What?"

"He's leaving. The reason Garfield missed work was because he was busy selling his Web site."

"You're kidding."

"No, it's wonderful for him. Apparently Garfield developed a unique type of software program. It allowed his Web site customers to download novelty ring tones into their phones. He said a young marketing executive at a major Hollywood studio contacted him. They want to use his software exclusively. They've hired him to head the ring tone unit, or whatever they call it. I'm so proud of that boy! He'll be leaving for Los Angeles in three weeks."

"Well, that's great," I said with mixed feelings. I was happy for him, of course, but sorry we were losing a reliable employee. "His parents must be proud. Now he'll have a chance to explore the world beyond Quindicott while he's still young."

"When you come home, I'll tell you more about it," Sadie said. "You *are* coming home soon, aren't you, Pen?"

"I . . . I have to do something first."

"Where are you?" My aunt's voice was suddenly filled with concern—and suspicion.

"I'm at the hospital, Aunt Sadie." (No lie there.) "I'm going to visit Brainert, show him the photos I took." (True again.)

"But how will you get inside, Pen? Visiting hours ended a long time ago."

"You'd . . . uh, be surprised," I replied. "And don't wait up for me, I may be here all night." (Again, a statement as true as George Washington could have given.)

"But—" I could hear the concern in my aunt's voice.

"Gotta go. Give Spencer my love. I'll see you soon. Bye."

I climbed out of my bed. The hospital didn't provide much in the way of clothing—I wasn't walking the halls in that opened-back nightshirt they gave me—but fortunately I found a terrycloth robe in a plastic bag hanging in the tiny cubicle that passed for a bathroom. I donned that and a pair of blue, rubber-soled socks I found (also swathed in vinyl) in the dressing table.

I retrieved my purse. Then I crept out of my hospital room, into the dimly lit corridor. I didn't risk taking the elevator, for fear of being spotted. Instead I found the stairwell and went down one flight. The corridors on the third floor were as quiet as the fourth, and I made my way to Brainert's room without being seen by any staff or patients.

I found my friend sitting up in bed, illuminated by a pool of light, papers scattered across his silver meal table. He squinted through his unbandaged eye at the pages he'd been writing. I had no doubt Brainert was attempting to re-create the research that was stolen from him during the assault.

"I didn't appreciate your calling my aunt," I announced. "If I'd wanted to worry her, I would have phoned her myself."

"Pen, you're back—" He looked up at the sound of my voice, and the color drained from his face. "My God! What happened?"

I slid a padded fiberglass chair next to Brainert's bed and told him about my evening, in reverse order.

"You're sure you were run off the road deliberately? It wasn't just an accident?" Brainert asked when I was through telling him about my Allstate moment.

"Trust me, this was no accident. The driver rammed my

bumper at an angle, just enough to push my Saturn off the ramp and into a tree. I didn't get a look at the driver, but I know before I passed out that he got out of his vehicle and searched my car. He was looking for the treasure, Brainert. I'm sure he thought I'd retrieved it at the mansion."

"Did you?" Brainert asked excitedly.

"We'll get to that later."

Brainert nodded. "It sounds as if your attacker was lying in wait for you."

"Apparently. Unless it was Raymond Chesley, in which case he followed me. He did have a motive to kill his father, and he pretty much fits the description of our mutual assailant, down to a raspy voice caused by a bad case of the sniffles."

"What about Claymore Chesley? Could he have been stalking your movements?"

"That seems really unlikely. What is possible, however, is that he had your code-breaking papers and figured out what the treasure was. He could have arrived at the mansion to steal it, but saw me leaving and assumed I'd gotten it first."

"Yes, Pen, yes. That's very possible."

"I have one more theory," I said. "Did you know that Nelson Spinner was working for Peter Chesley, helping the old man archive his extensive library?"

Braniert blinked. "I had no idea."

"So Spinner never indicated to you that he may have had direct contact with the Phelps editions, or that he knew the books were in the Chesley mansion?"

"Never," Brainert replied.

"Now tell me one more thing. This is very important. Did you contact Nelson Spinner tonight?"

"Yes, I did. I called him and asked him to research a piece of information for me. He refused. Said he had papers to grade—"

"What time was this?"

"Right after you left for Newport. When he turned

down my request, I immediately called Sadie and she helped me out."

"Did you tell Spinner that I was going to Newport?"

Brainert paled. "I . . . mentioned it to him . . . in passing . . . oh, my God, Penelope, you don't think my colleague . . ."

"Yes, I do, Brainert. And I'm sure you boasted that you were on the verge of solving the Poe Code mystery—"

"Not on the verge. I *solved* the mystery, Pen. Or my end of it. It all depends on what you found at the mansion. So what did you find?"

I drew the cell phone out of my purse, called up the images on the tiny screen. "There were four portraits on the wall, hanging above a Victorian-era globe that was definitely a part of the Mystic House collection. Look at the images and tell me what you see."

I handed Brainert the phone. He studied the artistic renderings, first. "Nothing here," he said with undisguised disappointment.

Then he shifted to the first photographic image.

I rose to look over his shoulder. "I think I've seen this photo before," I said.

"It's not a photo, Pen. It's a daguerreotype—silver etched on glass," Brainert clarified. "And this"—he tapped the cell phone screen—"has to be a copy, made of paper. This image is not new. It's well known, taken in the final year of Poe's life. The original is in the Brown University Library collection."

"He looks a mess," I said. "Bags under his eyes. Hair uncombed. His vest is unbuttoned."

"The image was taken locally. Poe was visiting Providence to woo a woman named Sarah Helen Whitman. He wanted to present her with a photo. Sadly, their affair ended tragically; and, before another year passed, Poe was dead—he died raving in a Baltimore hospital, probably suffering from acute alcohol poisoning and the throes of withdrawal. Kept screaming for someone named Reynolds. 'Reynolds, Reynolds,' over and over again until he fell into a final coma."

"Who's Reynolds?"

Brainert shrugged. "It's a mystery still."

Brainert's attention shifted back to the cell phone images. He flipped to the digital picture of the final portrait. He squinted as he stared at it. Then he blinked. "What in the—"

To get a better look, Brainert lifted the bandage that covered his other eye. I winced at the sight of the ragged black cut held together by stitches.

Brainert made sputtering sounds of excitement, then he looked at me, breathless.

"What is it? Tell me!"

"You've found it, Pen. The treasure. This is it—or part of it."

"This picture?"

"This picture," Brainert affirmed. "In the past few days, I've immersed myself in Poe's life, his works, in the images of him taken while he was alive." He tapped the phone screen again. "This is a previously unknown picture of Poe."

"How do you know for sure?"

Toggling the button, Brainert jumped back to the previous image. "If you look closely you can see that Poe is wearing the same suit of clothing in both daguerreotypes. But in the known image, his hair is uncombed, the lower buttons of his jacket are undone, his shirt ruffled and unkempt—"

Brainert called up the image of the second daguerreotype. "Same suit, same overcoat—but the jacket is no longer undone, his hair is combed. My guess is that Poe was unsatisfied with the first image, so he commissioned a second."

"I didn't know old Edgar was so image conscious."

"Oh, but he *was* Pen. Like many orphans, Poe suffered from an inferiority complex, a constant craving for love, attention, and self-esteem. He once wrote a short biographical sketch of himself that was, shall we say, wildly exaggerated."

"You mean he made it up?"

"Indeed he did." Brainert raised an eyebrow. "What? You thought only certain modern writers did that?"

To that, I had no comment and Brainert went back to ogling the cell phone image. "You see how thick the frame is? This is not a paper copy. It's likely the original daguerreotype. A veritable *treasure*!"

Suddenly Brainert's mouth widened into a toothy grin. "And there's more . . . Much more."

"Oh my God," I said. "I know what you're going to tell me!"

"You do?"

I thought of Jack's dream—and knew at once why he'd shown me that case from his past. "There's something else, something of equal or even greater value behind that photo! Hidden in the frame!"

Brainert stared at me speechless. "How? How did you figure it out?"

It's a cinch, Jack whispered through my mind with a laugh. *She had out-of-this-world advice.*

I stammered. "I really can't tell you," I said. "It just came to me."

Jack laughed again.

Not to be outdone, Brainert sniffed, "Well, I'll be happy to explain why you're right." He pulled out a sheet of paper from the pages scattered across his meal table. I reached for it, but Brainert held it out of my reach. "Not so fast," he said. "We must start at the beginning."

I sat back down and crossed my arms like an obedient student. Like it or not, I was in for the long haul.

"Poe was fond of riddles, and he was a romantic man who thirsted after love. He married Virginia Clemm when she was only in her early teens. Knowing his fondness for riddles, and his literary talent, in her girlish way she wanted to impress him. So one day Virginia wrote a poem to her husband. The poem was also a riddle, but a simple one. The feat delighted Poe as she hoped it would, and he always cherished that moment, even long after her death."

Brainert sighed. "Now, I don't have that poem in front of me, but the riddle is easily explained. Virginia wrote the poem so the first letter in each of the thirteen stanzas spelled out Poe's name. Thirteen stanzas, EDGAR AL-LAN POE."

"Seems simple enough," I replied.

"So simple that both Miles Chesley and Dr. Conte tried that solution with the Phelps volumes—that is, taking the first letter of each of the thirteen volume titles to see if a cryptogram existed."

"And?"

Brainert displayed the paper in his hand. "It spells this," he said. "FRMEWIHDOAPTE, which is—"

"Gibberish."

"Right."

"Exactly the conclusion both Miles Chesley and Dr. Conte came to," said Brainert. "But you recall that much has been made of the unscholarly nature of the Phelps books. How he chose the names from sometimes-insignificant works as titles to his volumes. I mean, who ever heard of Poe's essay 'Music'? Hardly anyone beyond scholars, yet he chose to give that title to Volume Three."

"Okay, but where are you going with this?"

Brainert slipped me another page. "Here are the titles and volume numbers of the Phelps editions. The first letter of each title is highlighted."

For Annie, Volume 1

Romance, Volume 2

Music, Volume 3

Eleonora, Volume 4

William Wilson, Volume 5

Israfel, Volume 6

Hop-Frog, Volume 7

Dream Within a Dream, Volume 8

On Imagination, Volume 9

A Descent into the Maelstrom, Volume 10

Pit and the Pendulum, Volume 11

The Poetic Principal, Volume 12

Eureka, Volume 13

"I still don't get it."

Brainert sighed as if he were dealing with a particularly thickheaded pupil.

"It's simple, Pen. The Virginia Clemm riddle solution doesn't work because the Phelps books weren't published from volume one to thirteen, in that order. They were actually published out of order."

"Huh?"

"His contemporaries thought Phelps was again being slipshod. Those who purchased his volumes assumed as the operator of an amateur press, he didn't do things in the proper order because of production delays and whatnot. But they were wrong."

Brainert waved another piece of paper under my nose. "Eugene Phelps was very careful and deliberate in the order he published the books, and in the controversial titles he chose. When taken together, these elements combine to break the code and solve the mystery!"

Brainert shoved another page into my hand. "It was your aunt Sadie who researched the actual order of publication.

She called me with the results of her labors. She'd been on the Internet all evening, checking collector sites. And it paid off. The Poe Code is broken."

I scanned the paper in my hand and found the order of publication was off drastically. Volume One published first, Volume Thirteen last, but everything in between was a mess:

For Annie, Volume 1

Romance, Volume 2

A Descent into the
    Maelstrom, Volume 10

Music, Volume 3

Eleonora, Volume 4

Dream Within
    a Dream, Volume 8

William Wilson, Volume 5

Israfel, Volume 6

The Poetic Principal, Volume 12

Hop-Frog, Volume 7

Pit and the Pendulum, Volume 11

On Imagination, 9

Eureka, Volume 13

"And the secret message reads . . ."

"FRAMED WITH POE," Brainert declared.

I smiled smugly. "Just like I already figured out."

Jack grunted in my head.

"Okay," I silently conceded to the ghost. "Like *we* already figured out."

Brainert nodded and grinned, gesturing to the image on the cell phone. I leaned in for a better look at the tiny screen. The portrait glowed like an unearthed jewel.

CHAPTER 21

Fingered

Kidding around about women is all right . . . But let me tell you something, I've been a mailman for nine years, and I can say that we have a respectable bunch of women around here.

—Bruno Fischer, "Five O'Clock Menace,"
Black Mask, March 1949

BRAINERT STARED AT me with his one good eye.

"Not only have we found a new, previously unknown image of one of America's greatest writers," he declared, "we have also discovered another, as-yet-to-be-determined treasure, hidden behind the image, inside that thick wooden frame."

"Yeah, okay," I said, "but what do we *do* about it?"

That's my baby. Without action, words are only good for heating up the air.

Brainert thought it over for a minute. "After the doctors spring us tomorrow, the first thing we should do is drive back up to that mansion. We have to retrieve the treasure before it gets lost again—perhaps forever."

"It's going to be tough getting past Raymond Chesley," I warned him. "He's got big muscles and he's fond of waving a poker around."

"I'll knock him down myself, if I have to!" Brainert declared. "No one will stop me from solving a mystery for the ages."

What do you know, Bow Tie Boy's turned into Action Man.

Using my cell, Brainert called Seymour Tarnish, who had just returned home after a slow night of trying to sell ice cream.

"Stinking rain," I heard Seymour complain. "The haunted house was a complete washout. Not a rugrat in sight."

Brainert told Seymour to come pick us up at the hospital first thing in the morning and drive us to Newport. He also issued strict instructions that Seymour was to tell no one where we were, what we were looking for, or where we were going—not even Sadie.

"You got it, Brainiac. I could use a sick day. The mail can deliver itself. I'll see you at sunup."

"Ugh. Nine o'clock will be sufficient," Brainert replied.

"I'm up at the crack of dawn every morning," said Seymour. "You should try it."

"Yes. Whatever. Good night."

He handed me the cell phone. When I opened my purse I saw the envelope Sadie had given me earlier in the day. I'd forgotten all about it.

"Oh, here! This belongs to you."

Brainert took the envelope, shook the stone into his palm, and examined it under the bedside light. "This isn't mine," he declared.

"But . . . it's got the St. Francis emblem, doesn't it?"

"Indeed it does. It's similar to mine." To illustrate the point, he showed me the ring on his finger. The stone was still in place. He handed the envelope back to me.

"Anyway, black onyx isn't for the teaching faculty. It's for the sports teams, the coaches, and trainers."

I thought that over, remembered the store burglary. "Any chance this could be Nelson Spinner's?" I asked. "Is he involved in any of the college athletic teams?"

Brainert snorted. "Spinner's sport is women. Preferably co-eds; the younger the better, which is why I tried to discourage your aunt from playing matchmaker with you two. He's got a harem of admirers. It's a wonder he gets any work done. I suspect he doesn't. His tenure is hanging by a thread—"

"Oh, really? What more do you know?"

Brainert shifted uncomfortably. "I didn't mention it before because I don't like to cast aspersions on fellow academics, but—"

"Spit it out, Brainert!"

"A few years ago Spinner was denied tenure," Brainert explained. "A scandal about a plagiarized paper. There were other issues. He was using paid teacher's assistants to paint his house instead of doing scholarly work, that kind of thing."

"What happened?"

"What usually happens," Brainert replied. "The college gave him a lecture and a second chance, but I don't believe he's published yet, and in my field it's publish or perish. I believe Spinner will be out of a job in a year or so, when his contract runs out."

"Solving the Poe Code would go a long way toward securing his position, wouldn't it? Which is a pretty good motive for murder."

"Indeed," said Brainert. "Although I hate to think that a colleague of mine could be capable of such brutality."

I waved the envelope in my hand, thrust it into my

purse. "You know, Spinner could have hired, or even black-mailed, some poor dumb student to do his bidding. And it was that student who attacked me—and lost the stone from his ring. Or . . . it could be from Claymore Chesley's ring, if he has one. He did go to St. Francis as an undergrad. I didn't notice a school ring on his finger, but that could be the reason he wasn't wearing it the day I saw him—he could have lost the stone in my bookstore. He does look the type to be involved in athletics."

Brainert nodded. "Sure, but the stone might have nothing to do with the burglary."

I sighed. "We're going to have to investigate both Nelson Spinner and Claymore Chesley," I concluded, then yawned and stood up. "In the morning."

I PUT MY head on the crisp, white hospital pillow and what seemed like a minute later, someone was shaking me out of a deep, dreamless slumber.

"Jack?" I muttered.

"Ho, ho," someone whispered. "Our sweet little Penelope has a secret lover."

I opened my eyes—and yelped.

"Seymour? What are you doing here?" I cried, yanking up the sheets to cover my flimsy hospital gown.

Brainert appeared at Seymour's side. He was dressed and ready to go. "Hurry, Penelope. We have to get out of here."

"Oh . . . Okay." Still groggy, I noticed the light coming through the hospital window was a pale pink. "What time is it?"

"Quarter to seven," said Seymour. "And you better hurry."

I sat up, finally awake. "What's wrong?"

Seymour frowned. "I got up this morning, called in sick. Then I headed down to Cooper's looking to beat the mommy set to the croissants. I ran into Eddie Franzetti, QPD. He warned me to warn you: The autopsy on Rene

Montour came in late last night. His wounds were not consistent with a car crash. He was probably dead before the wreck—beaten about the head with a blunt instrument."

"Oh, God," I murmured.

"That isn't the bad news," Seymour continued. "Detective Marsh is on his way to town. He's looking to talk to you."

I threw my legs over the side of the bed. "Turn your backs, both of you," I ordered. "I'll be dressed in a minute."

"Make it snappy." Seymour snapped his fingers to punctuate his command. "We have to move. Five gallons of ice cream only buys so much time."

"Huh?"

"I know the security guard downstairs. I deliver his mail. And he's a customer—you'd know it, too, if you saw him. A real porker. I bribed my way in here with a tub of rocky road. Unfortunately his shift ends in ten minutes."

I pulled on my slacks. "Seymour, I need your help to clear my name."

"You got it, Pen. I'm not going to let some CSI-type railroad a friend of *mine*."

I chewed my lip, trying to think of something clever fast, not easy on a sleep-deprived, caffeine-starved brain. The only thing I could come up with was Jack Shepard's backdoor philosophy. Darn, I thought, that character "Beak" and his stolen Swifty Delivery uniforms would come in handy about now—

You don't need my street rat, Jack cracked in my head. *You've got one of your own.*

Of course! I finally realized what was standing right in front of me. Or rather *who*.

"I'll need to borrow a few things, Seymour," I said at last.

"Sure. Like what?"

"For starters? Your postman's uniform and mail bag."

CHAPTER 22

Male Drop

"There's probably a smart way to do this, but I can't think of it at the moment."

—Philip Marlowe in "Trouble Is My Business,"
by Raymond Chandler, 1934

"I COULD GO to a federal penitentiary for aiding and abetting a suspected felon, you know," Seymour groused.

"And *you* know Pen didn't murder anyone," Brainert replied. "Pen and I both suspect two people. One of them is Nelson Spinner and he's closer to the hospital, so we're starting with him."

"But I'm a bona fide agent of the U.S. government," Seymour complained. "I have responsibilities."

Brainert rolled his eyes—I mean *eye*, the other one was still swathed in bandages. "You're a postal worker, Tarnish, not Elliott Ness. Get over yourself!"

Seymour Tarnish was behind the wheel of his ice cream truck. Brainert was seated next to him. I was in the back compartment, surrounded by freezers, trays of plastic plates and spoons, and containers of sundae-making fixings. This was the spot where Seymour stood while he sold his cones and banana splits and nutty bars. I was stripped down to my underwear, trying to keep a low profile so no one would see me through the big side windows while I attempted to adjust one of Seymour's tent-sized uniforms so it would fit me— an impossible task with a mere box of safety pins.

"Couldn't you get a mail truck, Seymour?" I asked. "An ice cream wagon is going to attract attention."

"Yeah, I can get a mail truck," Seymour replied. "And I can guarantee a bevy of postal inspectors to go with it, ready to arrest us!"

From my vantage point in the rear of the ice cream truck, I could see the gates to St. Francis College looming ahead. I'd managed to fix the dark blue uniform shirt by bunching it up in the back and pinning it, then pinning the sleeves up at the shoulders. The effect was somewhat ridiculous.

Meanwhile, Brainert continued to curse our bad luck. "I can't believe we've solved the mystery of the Poe Code, and were just about to secure the treasure. And now we have to deal with this! This . . . distraction!"

"Hey!" I cried. "Perspective, please! I'm being framed for murder. That's a little more than a distraction!"

Brainert reddened, apparently getting a hold of himself. "You're right, Pen. I'm sorry."

The ice cream truck hit a speed bump and bounced, throwing me against the counter just as I was trying to get my little leg into Seymour's big pants. I looked up and saw that we'd passed through the college gates.

"Bear right, Seymour," Brainert directed. "This road will take you to the center campus."

St. Francis was a crescent-shaped campus built around

Merrick Pond, a small body of water that was there when the institution was founded by Franciscan monks in 1836. Most of the halls and dormitories were built on the rolling hills that circled the pond. The oldest structure on campus, a massive stone monastery now transformed into the main administrative building, occupied the highest point on the property.

We were on Lowry Road, which curved around the entire campus. Just past the 1960s-style circular dome called Kepler Auditorium, was Fenimore Hall, a massive four-story brick building where Brainert and Nelson Spinner taught classes and had their offices.

"Park over there," Brainert said, pointing to a spot against the wall, right next to a bright orange Dumpster. Meanwhile, I called Brainert to the back compartment to help me adjust the pants. Even Seymour's belt was too big!

"Here, use mine," said Brainert, slipping it off. "I still have my thirty-six waist from college."

"Braggart," Seymour muttered.

"How do I look?" I asked, turning around like a cream pie on a pastry display.

"Absurd, but this shapeless coat should hide a multitude of sins." Brainert tossed me the garment and I slipped it on, folded up the sleeves. He peered through the service window, at Fenimore Hall's front entrance. "The guard is on duty. That means no one gets into the building without a valid student or faculty ID. Nobody, that is, except the mailman. Pen's plan is wise, I have to admit. No one pays attention to the mailman. He's invisible."

"I resent that," Seymour snapped.

Brainert Parker arched his visible eyebrow. "Tarnish, hasn't it ever occurred to you that your extroverted behavior, your constant craving for attention, your anger and negativity, and that acerbic wit of yours, are merely desperate means of overcompensating for your meager station in life?"

"I'm not angry," Seymour replied. "And I don't have an acerbic wit. That's all you, Parker—"

Their argument was interrupted by a student in a varsity jacket. He stood outside the truck, tapping on the service window with a coin. Seymour slid the pane open, glared at the shaggy-haired youth.

"What d'ya want?" Seymour demanded.

"I want some ice cream."

"Ice cream!" Seymour cried. "What's wrong with you, Joe College. It's nine o'clock in the morning. You can't have dessert until you've cleaned your plate, so scurry off and find a traditional breakfast. You don't want to grow up looking like Oprah before the diet."

Seymour slammed the window. "Stupid hair-head," he muttered.

"Okaaay," said Brainert, "here's the plan. I'll go up to my office on the fourth floor and wait for Pen. She will follow in two minutes. The mail drop is on the first floor, but Pen will tell the guard that she has a package for me that I need to sign for personally, and he'll send you up."

"But I don't have a package," I pointed out.

"Take this." Seymour shoved a small box in my hand. The words FLAVO-RITE PLASTIC SPOONS were emblazoned on the side.

I stared at him. "I'm going into an institute for higher learning, not a food court."

He rolled his eye. "Just cover the label with your arm."

"When you get upstairs, a grad student may or may not be watching the door," Brainert continued. "If one is on duty, give them the same story you gave the guard—that you have a package for me. Meanwhile, I shall determine if Spinner is in his office. It's only two doors down the hall from mine so that will be easy."

"What next?" Seymour asked.

"I'm going to keep watch while Pen breaks into Spinner's office and searches for incriminating evidence. If she fails to find any, we're going to break into his apartment next. Then we'll move on to searching Claymore Chesley's personal space."

Brainert paused to catch our eye. "Before noon today, however, I insist we proceed to Newport, no matter how far along we are with the snooping—"

"Yeah, yeah," Seymour interrupted, "so we can pick up this supposed 'treasure.'"

Three minutes later I climbed the short flight of stairs to Fenimore Hall. The security guard faced me with a bored expression. "The mail drop's just inside the door, to your left," he said.

"I have a package for J. Brainert Parker. He has to sign for it."

"Fourth floor. Elevator's straight ahead," the guard replied. He turned away to check a student's ID and I was forgotten, just as Brainert predicted.

The hall was long and dark and smelled vaguely of floor polish. I went directly into the elevator, pressed four. At the third floor, a distinguished-looking man with curly gray hair and a tweed suit stepped into the car. He casually nodded to me as the elevator arrived on the top floor.

The security desk was deserted. Brainert was actually waiting for me in the corridor as the doors opened. His expression suddenly changed when he saw the other passenger.

"Dean Halsey! How nice to see you," Brainert said, grinning broadly.

"Heavens, Parker. What happened to you?"

Brainert touched his face. "Had an accident . . . Antique hunting. A run-in with a Victorian mirror."

I stepped out of the elevator, around the men.

"You're just the fellow I was looking for, Parker," said Dean Halsey. He put his arm on Brainert's shoulder and steered him to the waiting elevator. "I hope you're up for a walk across campus. We'll have coffee in my office—"

"But I—"

"No excuses. This is an emergency. I need someone who can organize next year's faculty luncheon—"

Just before the elevator doors closed, Brainert shot me a helpless look that told me I was on my own.

No you're not, babe. You've got me.

"Oh, Jack, thank goodness you're here. I have to find Nelson Spinner's office—and I'm really hoping he's not in it."

I needn't have worried on that score. The fourth floor was completely deserted, the long corridor lined with locked doors. Clipboards hung on each, displaying the professor's name and office hours. From the schedules I saw, no one showed up at this place before noon.

I found Brainert's office—the door was ajar—and then I found Spinner's. He had no office hours scheduled for today, and I breathed a sigh of relief.

Spinner's door was locked, of course. The lock itself was pretty flimsy, not like the one on Prospero House's back door. This one was identical to the one on my bathroom door back home. I'd already figured out how to trigger a lock like that.

Back when Spencer was still inclined to dark moods, after his father's suicide and our move to New England, he sometimes locked himself in the bathroom. He gave up when he figured out his mom wasn't letting him get away with hiding in there.

Need advice on the lock, babe? You could maybe use that fire extinguisher on the wall over there to smash the knob. It will make a lot of noise but—

"That won't be necessary," I said with a bit of pride.

I didn't have a credit card, but Seymour's plastic Post Office ID badge served my purposes. I shoved the card between the door and the jam and wiggled the knob a few times. The lock sprang with a satisfying click, and I slipped inside the room.

Nice, baby. Quiet, too.

"Thanks."

The office was stuffy, the morning sun streaming through the wood-framed window, heating the room unbearably, so I left the door slightly ajar. There was a pair of filing cabinets, a desk with a computer on it, books and papers piled up everywhere. There were no personal touches I could see, beyond diplomas hanging on the wall.

I noticed a lot of personal correspondence, all of it indiscreetly scattered about the desk. Letters and postcards from at least three women—or should I say girls. From the sorry tone of each missive, the women were lovesick and devastated, and likely spurned by Spinner.

I went through each drawer, came up with nothing. The bottom drawer was locked, however, and I immediately focused on it. I began working the old lock with a letter opener. It took only a minute to splinter the wood enough to yank the drawer open.

A student folder lay on top of a pile of stuff inside the drawer. Something about the name on that file—Tyler Scott—triggered my memory. When I saw that his home address was in Quindicott, I remembered when I'd heard the name. Tyler Scott was a quarterback on the Quindicott high school team. He was the boy who Chief Ciders told me had wrecked his car in the same manner and at the same spot where Rene Montour died.

I cracked the file and saw the papers Scott had written for Spinner's class. All of them had failing grades, except the last. On that paper, Spinner had scrawled the word *Plagiarism* across the title page. A note attached read: SEE ME AFTER CLASS TODAY, MR. SCOTT. YOUR ATHLETIC SCHOLARSHIP AND YOUR FUTURE AT THIS SCHOOL ARE IN JEOPARDY. It was signed "DR. SPINNER."

The note was dated Monday, and I found the timing interesting. It was the day after Peter Chesley died, the day before Rene Montour was killed, and two days before I was attacked.

"He could have blackmailed this boy into attacking me and stealing the Phelps editions from my store," I said to Jack. "Possible?"

Possible. But like you told me in your dream, honey, you need proof. Keep looking.

I'd been digging down through the papers in the locked drawer, and the very next file made my heart stop—

"Oh, my God."

The file contained the photocopies that my aunt had made for Brainert, and pages upon pages of notes that belonged to him—I knew because there were *bloodstained* fingerprints on several sheets of paper!

Baby, you struck the mother lode!

I continued rummaging through the pile—only to freeze when my fingers closed on a book. I pushed the pages aside and pulled out *The Poetic Principle*, volume twelve of the Eugene Phelps editions of Edgar Allan Poe. The book Sadie had sold to Rene Montour the day he was killed.

"Eureka," I whispered. "It *was* Spinner who murdered Montour."

"Well, aren't you a resourceful woman?"

It wasn't Jack's voice. And it wasn't in my head. Nelson Spinner was standing in his office doorway. He stepped inside, then closed the door behind him. Without wasting a second, he drew a handgun out of his charcoal-gray suit jacket and pointed it at my heart.

"Seems the state troopers are suspicious about Montour's car accident. They questioned my landlady, but I slipped out the back, came here to destroy the evidence. It's a good thing I did, wouldn't you agree, Mrs. McClure?"

Steady, baby. He's a paper pusher. I doubt he spends much time on the firing range, and I'm betting his aim ain't true.

"Jack? What do I do?"

Guns recoil, he's going to brace before he fires. Watch for it. Then take the chance you have to take.

"Why are the police looking for you?" I asked, stalling for time and praying Brainert would make it back to rescue me.

Spinner shrugged. "I suspect the state troopers traced the call I made to Mr. Montour at the inn on the night he died— an invitation to see a collection of rare books soon to be auctioned. He fell for it, naturally, and I laid my trap—"

"With the help of Tyler Scott, right? A poor kid you blackmailed to help you." I waved his file.

"Yes, Tyler did prove helpful. Not with you, of course. I provided him with a universal key to break into your storeroom, but thanks to your theatrics, the dolt almost got caught. It made him all the more ruthless with Brainert, however, which did prove fruitful. As for Montour . . . after Tyler told me about his own mishap on Crowley Road, I simply helped re-create it."

I was horrified and sickened, furious and scared, but I had to keep my head, I had to keep stalling.

Questions, baby. More questions. The man likes to brag, let him.

"You were working for Peter Chesley," I told Spinner. "That's how you found the volumes. But why did you have to kill him? Why?"

Nelson Spinner offered me that super-slick smile of his. I could see why teenaged girls melted—and why Sadie and I had too. We were all too dazzled by the bright surface to see the darkness underneath.

Don't beat yourself up, honey. Jack whispered in my head. *You were the one who never bought it completely. You were the one who kept digging until you unearthed the truth.*

"I did *try* to convince the stubborn old compulsive to sell the books to me," Spinner said. "Or at the very least let me investigate the riddle. But the fool rebuffed my offer— insisted any treasure would be found by his family, not me. Then he had the audacity to fire me. That's when I made the decision to take it to the next level."

"Mr. Chesley sensed you were coming for those books. I knew he was afraid. He even suspected you were lurking in the house the night he died."

"Yes, when I came to take possession of those volumes, I found Chesley had company—you and your aunt. He never had guests before, so I was surprised. The old man never saw anyone but me. He was still marginally rich, but the fool didn't even employ a butler. Claimed he was saving all the money for the next generation of Chesleys—to reunite the two long-estranged branches of the family, or so he said."

Spinner shook his head. "I confronted Chesley after you left. He told me that he'd given the books to you to sell, that you'd be getting bids too high for me to ever come close to matching. He'd trumped me and he was smug about it, too. Made sure I could never solve the code and track down the treasure. I was so angry, that . . . well, you know what happened, unfortunate as it was."

"What *happened*, Spinner, was murder."

"Not according to the Newport police. They received a 911 call, if you remember. Old Chesley telling them he was in much distress. Fortunately for me, I worked with the man long enough to imitate his voice."

"Nobody will believe you if you shoot me. Someone will hear the shot, for one thing."

"Who, Mrs. McClure? This floor is empty. I'll kill you now, dump your corpse in Quindicott Pond tonight—*after* I plant evidence to prove it was you who killed Montour and stole the book."

He smiled. The man's smugness was off the charts.

"You're a genuine sociopath, aren't you?"

"Diagnosed in my teens." He smiled. "Doesn't bother me."

Then I saw it, the thing Jack said to watch for—

He's bracing baby, he's going to fire.

Suddenly, the entire building was rocked by a horrible,

howling din. The fire alarm had gone off! The noise so startled Spinner that he looked away—

Now, baby! Take your chance!

That's when I jumped him. My right hand managed to knock the gun aside just as he pulled the trigger. The bullet slammed into a diploma, shattering the frame. I hung on to his wrist like a bull terrier, knowing if I let go he could aim and fire again.

But Spinner was much stronger than I was, and I was still hurting from the accident. He soon had me at a disadvantage.

"I should have killed you on the road last night!"

Kick him, Penelope. Right in the—

I did. Spinner wheezed and stumbled backward. Unfortunately I lost my grip on his arm. He staggered against a filing cabinet and raised the gun. I tensed, poised to attack again, determined to go down fighting.

But just then the office door flew open. Seymour was standing there, legs braced, face flushed, his shirt torn. He saw me, saw Spinner, he even saw the gun as the man tried to shift his aim to the newcomer.

With a roar, Seymour slammed into Spinner like a fullback. The gun flew out of Spinner's hand as he reeled backward—crashing right through the window.

I heard shattering glass, a horrified scream. Spinner took the plunge amid a shower of splinters and shards. Seymour rushed to the broken window, peered down.

"What a lucky bastard," he said. "The trash broke his fall."

I went to the window to see what he meant. Nelson Spinner had fallen four floors, but he'd landed in a Dumpster, which seemed a fitting place for the likes of him.

"Hey, Pen, you think this is what my teachers meant when they told me, 'garbage in, garbage out'?"

Just then, a security guard burst into the office with two campus policemen as backup.

"See," Seymour cried to the uniformed men. He pointed

to me then the gun on the floor. "I told you she was in danger. But, no, you wouldn't believe me!" As the guards wrestled Seymour to the ground, he continued to rant.

"I knew I had to do something, Pen," he cried. "I saw that geezer lead Brainert out the door. Then I saw Spinner coming in and knew you were in trouble. I tried to explain to these jokers, but they refused to believe me. So I tripped the fire alarm and ran for the stairwell. These goons tried to stop me, but I broke loose—"

"Don't worry, Seymour," I quickly assured him. "We have all the evidence we need right here in this office. I'll get you out of this mess, I promise. I'll tell everyone what really happened."

"Tell them, Pen. Tell the world!" Seymour bellowed as the police dragged him down the empty college corridor. "The truth will set me free!"

EPILOGUE

Poe had tried to imagine how death might not exist, although it certainly did, and not only existed, but also made possible his art.

—Kenneth Silverman, *Edgar A. Poe: Mournful and Never-ending Rememberance,* 1991

"HERE YOU GO, Pen. One chocolate sprinkle."

I took the ice cream cone from Seymour and passed it to the next child in line, a freckle-faced little Keenan.

"Here you go, Danny."

"Thanks, Mrs. McClure."

It was one week after the St. Francis male drop, and things were getting back to normal. Sunset had barely descended and already a line had formed on Green Apple Road to get into the haunted house. Spiderweb-covered speakers were blaring spooky music and ghostly sounds, interspersed with seasonal classics like "The Monster Mash" and "Purple People Eater." Dozens of flickering jack-o'-lanterns were scattered across a lawn decorated with scarecrows and ghosts made from old sheets, no doubt donated by mothers all over Quindicott.

Seymour was back to his old self, doing the job that made him the happiest. As it turned out, campus security didn't hold him long. After the staties arrived, I showed Detective Marsh the evidence I'd found in Nelson Spinner's office, and all charges against Seymour were dropped.

Spinner was fished out of the Dumpster and put in traction, where, thanks to a combination of his own smugness and the pain-killing drugs, he'd confessed everything to Marsh. Of course, he claimed he'd never "meant" to kill Peter Chesley, said it had been "an unfortunate accident" during a struggle. As for Rene Montour's death, that again, he claimed was "unintentional."

According to Spinner, Tyler Scott had flagged Montour down on the crest of Crowley Hill, pretending he'd just been in an accident and needed help. When Montour stepped out of his vehicle, Spinner emerged from behind a bush and struck him from behind with a flashlight. They put Montour back at the wheel of his car, took the Phelps volume, and sent the car down the hill and into a tree. Montour wasn't supposed to die from the blow. Spinner claimed this was "simply an unfortunate result."

Tyler Scott was arrested after Spinner's confession, and I understand both of their lawyers are working out a plea agreement with the authorities. Whatever the authorities agree to, however, I doubt Tyler will be seeing freedom anytime soon. And Spinner will have all the time to work out any code he can dream up—behind bars.

"Next up, two butterscotch swirls." Seymour gave me another cone. I handed the treats to two more friends of Spencer's—Danny's little sister, Maura, and a shy boy named Keith Parsons.

"Thank you, Mrs. McClure!"

"Yeah, thanks."

"The rocky road," Seymour declared. I gave the cone to the next boy. "Here you go, Boyce. Enjoy."

"Thanks, Mrs. M," Boyce Lyell said, running off to join Spencer's invited group.

"And, finally, the guest of honor, the old half-chocolate, half-vanilla, doubled-dipped in strawberry coating." Seymour winked at Spencer. "That was always my favorite, too."

"Thanks, Mr. Tarnish," Spencer said. He took a bite, then faced me. "I'm getting on line with my friends, okay, Mom?"

"Save a place for me."

"Hey, Pen." Seymour motioned me closer. "Isn't that kid Boyce Lyell the snot you said was bullying Spencer?"

"It is. But, as you can see, things worked out."

"I'm all ears." Seymour leaned out the window of his truck, and I stepped closer.

"Well," I said, lowering my voice, "the day I went to see Principal Chesley, his face was bruised and swollen from a car accident. He wrecked his Toyota sedan while running errands at lunch—running them at very high speeds, it turns out. Anyway, I got confused when I saw him drive an SUV into the school parking lot. I thought he was lying to me about the wreck when I saw there were no dents on his vehicle. Turns out it wasn't his vehicle. He'd borrowed the SUV from the garage that had towed his sedan away from the accident, which was also why he'd been so late for our meeting."

"Wait a second there. What the heck does the principal's car wreck have to do with Spencer being bullied?"

"Everything. One of the kids overheard me arguing with their principal in his office, and the next time they saw the man, his nose looked like a swollen sausage." I shrugged. "It seems kids can jump to the wrong conclusion as easily as adults."

Seymour's eyebrows arched in disbelief. "You mean?"

"The rumor got spread that I smacked around the new principal. The way I heard it, that story scared Boyce Lyell so badly he was shaking in his sneakers. I mean, you've got to figure, if Spencer's mom can beat up their new strapping jock of a principal, what would she do to the kid who bullied her baby boy?"

Seymour laughed. "That's hilarious, Pen. But it still doesn't explain who invited the kid here."

"Spencer did."

"Spencer?"

"Yeah. Like a little lawyer, he approached Boyce all by himself to work things out. Instead of twisting the knife and scaring the kid with his mom's new rep, he invited Boyce to join us."

"That's pretty evolved for a ten-year-old. Me? I would have tortured the snot."

"Yeah, I know. I can't tell you how proud I am. You know what he told me? He said he'd seen an old *Shield of Justice* episode where Jack said, 'In the P.I. game, it's always better to make a friend than burn an enemy.' How about that?"

Seymour scratched his head. "You know, I love that show, and I swear I've seen every episode three times, but I don't remember that quote."

"You don't?"

"No."

"Then where did he? . . ." I tapped my chin.

"Kid probably just dreamed it up," Seymour said with a shrug. "You watch enough of that stuff it gets in your blood."

I tried mentally asking Jack for an explanation, but all I could hear in my mind was a low, teasing chuckle.

A new group of customers stepped up just then, ready to place orders for ice cream, so Seymour handed me my cone—vanilla dipped in chocolate and rolled in peanuts—and went back to work. I was about to join my son in line when someone called my name.

"Pen! Great news!" Brainert cried, getting out of his car. "I've just returned from Providence."

"What's the word?"

After everything had been settled with Spinner, Brainert and I had driven back to Newport. In the light of day, (thanks to Brainert's breathless persuasion) Raymond Chesley had agreed to allow Brainert to examine Poe's oval portrait hanging in the mansion's library. Just as both of us had suspected, there was something preserved inside that portrait—a literary treasure. A handwritten poem, one never before discovered, signed by Edgar Allan Poe.

Brainert grinned as he walked up to me. "Three handwriting experts and two document analysts have concluded that that the poem we found inside the picture frame was, in fact, written by the hand of Poe."

"Did you ever doubt?" I asked between bites of melting ice cream.

"Not after an examination of the paper and the ink showed them to be authentic. And of course no one doubts the authenticity of the Reynolds daguerreotype itself."

I noticed the gash under Brainert's eye was almost healed. He'd turned out to be right about that, too. The scar *did* make him look more dangerous.

"I still can't believe you got Raymond Chesley to cooperate," I said. "He was so nasty to me the night I met him."

"Never try to reason with a man after you've broken into his house, Pen." Brainert shook his head. "In the light of day, one always sees the light."

If that were only true, I thought. It certainly wasn't for Nelson Spinner. The truth might have set Seymour free, but it would put Nelson behind bars for a long, long time.

That's the thing about the PI game, baby. Digging for the truth can be a dirty business.

So can eating ice cream, I thought, as I stepped over to Seymour's truck to retrieve some paper napkins.

"That's another mystery solved," Brainert crowed, following me over. "Who could have imagined that Eugene Phelps was the great-grandson of the daguerreotype-maker who captured that image of Poe? Or that Poe would have paid for his daguerreotype by writing an original poem?"

"Or that the man's name was Jericho Reynolds," I noted, wiping some sticky drippings off my hands.

Reynolds, of course, was the name Poe had called in his dying hours. For over a century, many scholars had speculated about the man's identity. Brainert was now preparing to write a bevy of academic papers on the subject, offering his theory on that mystery as well.

"So what's going to happen to the poem and the daguerreotype?" I asked.

Brainert rubbed his chin. "The two sides of the family share Peter Chesley's estate evenly and they don't agree on much, but they did decide to place the daguerreotype in the St. Francis College Library—"

"I'm glad to hear it won't stay private. Something like that should be available for study and appreciation."

"The Chesley family will continue to own the likeness, of course, and each time the image is reprinted, the family stands to gain. The same is true of the poem. I've dealt with both sides of the family—even that favorite principal of yours, Claymore Chesley—and they are close to resolving their differences."

"It seems Peter's last wish is finally coming true."

"Yes. The feuding branches of his family are going to be reunited at last."

I gave Brainert a sad smile. "I'm just so sorry it took his death to accomplish it."

Why, baby? Jack piped up. *You of all people ought to know. Dead guys can accomplish an awful lot.*

I DIDN'T HEAR from Jack again until hours later. I was tucked under the covers, reading the Penguin edition of Poe's *Selected Writings*. When I finally shut off the light, I felt the room's drop in temperature, the soft kiss of wind brushing my cheek, that frisson of electricity tickling my skin.

You ready for that night on the town yet, baby?

I smiled, settled into the pillows. "You'll never give up, will you?"

A guy can dream.

"So, apparently, can a girl."

You did good. You should be proud.

"I didn't do it alone."

Yeah, that geek show you parade around with helped a little.

"I meant you, Jack. Thanks."

Don't thank me. Without the trouble you get into, I'd be bored out of my skull in this hick town.

"Did you just give me another compliment? You're spoiling me."

Yeah, well, don't let it go to your head. You've still got a lot to learn. Back in my time, when your gumshoeing wasn't hinky it was lousy.

"I'll keep that in mind."

So what were you reading tonight, lamb chop?

"Poe's short story 'The Oval Portrait.' I'd never read it before, and I decided it was about time."

Give me the highlights.

"It's about an artist who's so obsessed with his work, he neglects his young bride. So she agrees to sit meekly as his subject. The artist spends weeks painting her. He's so enamored of the image on the canvas, he never notices how the cold, shadowy turret of his studio is withering the health of his bride. Day after day, she grows weaker and sicker. Finally, he finishes the oval portrait. Gazing on it, he cries out, 'This is indeed Life itself!' Then he turns to regard his wife: she's dead."

Sounds like a happy-go-lucky yarn.

"Well, Poe was a gothicist. He had reason to be, of course, since he'd lost a young wife whom he'd loved dearly. That's where the story comes from—he drew imagery and emotion for his writing watching his bride suffer and die slowly from tuberculosis. Her death fueled his art. Morbid and sad, but true."

You know, that old Chesley geezer sounds like the painter in the story, holing up for years, obsessing over the cataloging of that moldy mausoleum.

"Yeah, I'd hate to think of Aunt Sadie trapped in a place like that. I think, in the end, she did okay without him."

And you did okay, too, baby.

"What do you mean me?"

I been around guys like that rummy late husband of yours. Alkies, wife-beaters, it don't matter. They're all the same. They drain the life out of the ones who love them.

I lay quietly, considering what Jack had said. He wasn't wrong. I'd been obedient and meek in my marriage, just like the bride in "The Oval Portrait." I wondered what would have happened if Calvin hadn't bailed. Would I have wised up on my own? Or, little by little, over time, would he have crushed my spirit? Drained the life out of me?

Not for nothing, sweetheart, but there are some questions you'll never get answered.

"Well, how about your life then? Now that it's over, maybe you can give me a few . . . answers, I mean."

What do you want me to spill?

"First of all: what ever happened in that Vincent Tattershawe case? You never showed me."

Not much to show. The address on the ticker tape wrapped around the key led to a bank. The key opened a safety deposit box. Inside was a pile of stock certificates for Ogden Heating and Cooling. Turns out it was a legit business. Some big conglomerate bought it, and the stock paid off ten to one. Dorothy Kerns was a multimillionaire before the year was out.

"You mean Vincent Tattershawe was on the up-and-up all along?"

Yeah, baby, Dorothy Kerns's picture of Tattershawe turned out to be the one that rated after all. He left a short note in that bank box, told Dorothy it was better for her if they never saw each other again. Seems he'd been building a case against the firm. Was going to take it to the authorities. But his boss caught on, tried to have him clipped. Vincent escaped the lead poisoning and took a powder.

Grabbing the photo off Mindy's desk was a last-minute idea. He figured no one would suspect a photo having incriminating info. A straight letter could have been intercepted and he was pretty paranoid. Judging from what happened to Mindy, turned out he was right.

"And what happened to Baxter Kerns and the corrupt investment company?"

I dropped a dime on both of them, honey. Went to the feds with the address of the warehouse, info on the records room. Caught up with old Baxter nice and private like before the badges took him away.

"What did you do?"

Let's just say I introduced him to a new gourmet dish: brass knuckles.

"Is that what went wrong that you set right again?"

Excuse me?

"Last week, you said there was something that went wrong in your life that you wanted to see go right in someone else's."

Dorothy Kerns and Vincent Tattershawe. That's what went right. I helped Dorothy find him.

"How?"

Tattershawe didn't leave any contact info, but I noodled out where he'd gone just the same—back to Cherbourg. That's where I would have gone. After serving over there, he knew the old HQ like the back of his hand. So I took Dorothy to France, and we tracked him down. They got hitched over there and stayed. Started a family right away, too. Adopted two little orphan girls.

"Jack, that's amazing . . . but if that's what went right, what was it that went wrong? For you, I mean?"

It's not a happy story, baby.

"Tell me anyway."

Back in the '30s, before I did my bit for the war in Europe, I'd been seeing a woman—

"Wait, did you actually say a *woman*? Not a dame? Not a broad?"

Her name was Sally Archer. She was a nurse. She had a russet pageboy and a pert little nose. She was small and practical, full of sunbeams and fresh air but strong enough to kick a stevedore into holding the door for her.

"Sounds like she was right up your dark alley. What happened to her?"

Well, she wanted to get hitched, but I was a pretty angry, unhappy bird back then, and I was fairly sure I'd make any dame miserable, so I walked away. I joined the army, spent four years over there, you know, like the song . . .

"And?"

And . . . they say one bad night in a foxhole can change any man. I had hundreds of them. But by the time I got back stateside, Sally was married. A doctor she worked with had snatched her up, and she was living in the suburbs, had a kid already and another on the way.

"Jack, that's so sad . . . but couldn't you find another woman to settle down with?"

No, sweetheart. Went through plenty. But none were Sally. There's only been one other woman who's reminded me of her since . . .

"Who was she?"

I waited for an answer.

"Jack?" I called. "Jack?"

But all the ghost said was—

I'll see you in your dreams, baby.

Then his whispering presence temporarily receded, back into the fieldstone walls that had become his tomb.

REMEMBERED
(FOR REYNOLDS)

A moment gone, a moment captured
In this countenance displayed—
An image, bloodless, everlasting
An instant Death cannot dissuade.

Herein the goodly spirit,
Herein the sorrows woe,
Herein both truth and falsehood—
What will this likeness sow?

A thousand thoughts on paper
Captured by this hand
Inscribed for time eternal,
An amaranthine land.

Like stars hung in the Heavens,
Like books shelved on a wall,
Now you have made this monument
Even Death cannot befall!

'Tis true the image cannot tell
what secrets lie within—
If the heart of one is troubled
If the mind of one has sinned.

But perhaps the greater purpose
Of this new and valiant art
Is to keep the memory sweet
When another loses heart.

For a man who's well remembered
In mind, in thought, in tale,
For him, life is eternal
And Death shall finally fail!

Don't Miss the Next

Haunted Bookshop Mystery

The Ghost and the
Femme Fatale

After nearly a decade, Cranberry Street's old Movie Town Theater is finally restored to its former glory. The grand opening "Noir Week" is the biggest event Quindicott, Rhode Island, has seen in years. Dozens of old films are scheduled for screening, along with a roster of special guests and lectures.

No sooner do the festivities begin, however, than special guests start dropping—from decidedly unnatural causes—and Penelope Thornton-McClure wants to know why "Noir Week" has taken a genuinely dark turn.

Penelope sets her sleuthing sights on eighty-something Hedda Geist. The ghost of PI Jack Shepard well remembers the dame (albeit a much younger version of her) from her years burning up the silver screen as a sultry, seductive femme fatale in 1940s crime dramas. Jack also remembers that Hedda abruptly left Hollywood at the height of her career, for some mysterious reason, retreating from the public eye until now.

Are the murders related to Hedda's past? Or could the

killer have a more modern motive? Perhaps the culprit is Quindicott's own, local femme fatale? Or is Hedda herself really as deadly as her film persona?

Pen knows she's over her head with this one. Good thing she can turn to her spectral gumshoe for help—even if he and his license did expire more than fifty years ago.